CORINNE,

THANK YOU FOR
READING MY BOOK

THE GAMERS SAGA
BOOK I of II

Penned by
Donald O. Semora

OMNI
Book Publishing

The Gamers Saga Book I, The Alterverse Chronicles #1
Copyright © 2009 by Donald O. Semora

Cover design by   Village Graphics
                   PO Box 171, Homer MI 49245
                   www.800graphics.com

Author photo by: Donald O. Semora

The opinions expressed in this manuscript are solely the opinions of the author and do not represent the opinions or thoughts of the publisher. The author represents and warrants that s/he either owns or has the legal right to publish all material in this book.

ISBN-13: 978-0-9822364-9-9
ISBN-10: 0982236499

First published in 2010

10 9 8 7 6 5 4 3 2 1

Published by   OMNI Book Publishing,
                    134 S. Bostwick Place. Charlotte Michigan.48813

PRINTED IN THE UNITED STATES OF AMERICA

DEDICATION

I would like to dedicate this book to my Mother
Always an encouraging word
Always a well placed critique
Always there for me
There for 33

SPECIAL THANKS

To Tina who listened to my endless droning about the story,
and who helped me in so many ways.

And to Melissa's way out in the boondocks... you know who
you are. Thank you for your encouraging critiques, and also
your enthusiasm that helped fuel my desire to finish the books,
Good gamers all think alike.

And thanks to my Brother Mike who so long ago one day in
the car told me that I should write a book and started the bug
in my ear for this story. Thanks Brother.

Also to another artist who drew the guard of Dark Home and
also the Samfors Living Room. I appreciate you donating these
two pieces.

Tena of the Alterverse

<u>Also by Donald Semora</u>

Gamers Trilogy Book I

Gamers Trilogy Book II (coming January 2010)

Alterverse Anthology (Spring 2010)

E.R.D (2010)

Authors Advertising Ideas Made Easy (Spring 2010)

Modeling the German Tiger I Early Version
(coming in Summer 2010)

End of Days (Coming March 2010)

Authors Note

This book is going to be the first book that will chronicle many adventures in the Alterverse. I have made a serious attempt to make this book something that I will be able to later build on. My plan to you the reader is to make this a foundation by which I write other books and stories based on this world. There are several really interesting characters in this book, ones that in my test manuscripts many people were excited about.

I assure you that most likely your favorite character in this two book series will appear once again in other books and an Anthology I am also writing. These characters will appear sometimes as a continuance of their adventures, and sometimes it may be a story of "how" they came to be where they are in this book.

You will also maybe have a question of "how" something came to be, or maybe "what" happened to make a certain event happen. Or even possibly I may reference a historical event, one that is not fully explained in the book as it only has a bearing on the story as a reference. Please keep an eye out as I am sure the whats, hows, and whens will be fully detailed in later adventures of characters yet unknown, and adventures that have yet to be taken up.

I ask you to read my humble words with an open mind, and think what it would be like to one day read a book and actually become a part of the adventure.

If you have a good imagination I think you better sharpen your sword, strap on your back pack, fill your water skins, and stock up on torches and rations. As you my reader are about to enter the Alterverse.

Donald Semora
November 4th, 2009

INTRODUCTION

The old man in the white robe sat in the tall oaken chair. His long robe, worn and travel stained, was gathered at his sandaled feet. As he looked over the table he saw that there were ten men and women sitting. Their robes were varying shades of color, some white, some red some gray and some of the strange multi-colored combinations. The old man gazed at the gathered group, his thick eyebrows shading his dark eyes, and he pondered the argument at hand.

There was a debate going on for this eve they had to address the evil vile magic known in the Realms as Dark Magic. The two powerful Arcane guilds in the Realms represented drastically different thoughts on what magic was and how it should be used. On one hand, there was the Guild of light who in fact were having this debate. These mages felt that magic was there to help and heal and to be used to do positive good things in the world. On the opposite end of the philosophy of Arcana was the Shadow Guild: these wizards followed and studied Dark Magic, a vile and twisted magic that was designed to be used for revenge, spite and control. Its members lived in secret and those that knew of them feared them.

One never knew who they were, for that sweet old man who lived in that farm may indeed be a practitioner of the vile art, or maybe that nice lady down the road who gave free butter away was indeed one of them. No one knew, for those of their order were experts at disguise and guile. It was a late summer's eve and the Guild of Light were in a fierce debate as to what course of action they should take.

"It must be forever destroyed, there is no other way for if we allow it to exist its followers will eventually plan against us and destroy us. It is only a matter of time!" said a woman in a dark maroon robe, her dark eyes looking at the other men and women sitting at the long oaken table, her fists clenched before her.

"Crysta, you speak heresy; magic is not meant to be destroyed. We must negotiate with them, it is the only way," said an obese wizard in gray robes with silver piping on his hood, his chin wobbling as he spoke.

A fist was pounded on the table turning over a wine filled goblet by a wizard in light green robes. "Zarkam, destroy them, we must!, there is no other way. Every day they gain power and every day they attract more converts and followers. Their plans lay within plans, and they do not make deals, it is not their way!" The wizards in light green robes screamed half standing up, the veins in his neck distending with anger.

"What right do we have to say what magic has a right to prosper? We are powerful, let them come." A small wizard in red robes said quietly neither rising, nor raising his voice. And to that tone the debate raged on. Some felt one way and some other ways. The debate raged for hours until the old wizards in the white robes had enough, he stood up breaking his many hour's long silence. As he stood everyone stopped talking looking to him as he walked over to the large cavernous fireplace on the wall, he stood there for a few minutes his head bowed in thought his hand folded into his robes.

The old wizard turned to the others and spoke, his voice was soft but everyone heard him clearly, as the leader of their order, he was the most powerful and also the most respected, his words were to be listened to. "We have come to a crossroad here. It is a time for decision, not debate. We have talked of this, and it is time to vote on a course." And to that they settled down and voted for a definitive course of action. The voting went on in the large room for one hour, small slips of paper were handed out to each wizard making his or her mark for or against on its yellowed face; of the ten wizards that sat at the table eight voted yes for a course of action to be taken. However, two voted no. What the others did not know what that the two who voted no were indeed not what they appeared for they were followers of the Dark, they were spies to report back to their order. They were Dark wizards.

"It is decided." The old wizard said sitting back down in his chair looking over the other wizards, his eyes sad for he truly wished that there was another way, but deep down, he knew there was not. For the next several days the assembled wizards developed a plan, they would hunt down the Dark wizards and one by one destroy them; they would enlist the help of the local regents and fiefdoms, it was time for meetings with Kings and Queens to call back the many favors that were done by their order. They would go to the Dark wizards' towers bringing them to rubble, they would burn every dark book, and they would melt down every cursed weapon. What could not be destroyed would be locked away forever never to see light again. It was time to destroy once and for all the very vestiges of the Dark Arcane Arts. Once the great meeting concluded the various mages that were assembled went back to their own castles and keeps and towers and put into motion the plans that there order had decided to act on.

The two wizards that voted no traveled in secret for several weeks and took an indirect route to their master, for they knew that the words that were on their tongues could save their order and stop the guild of light from dealing a death blow to their order. They approached the Horn Peaks with dread as the trek to their guild was dangerous, as their master tended to let loose all manners of vile creatures to stop those that were curious, or more accurately foolish, from approaching. They made their way up to the steep slopes and rocky crags, the snow started to fall as this high up to Winter was upon them. The snow was heavy and thick on the wind and finally after several days made it to the dark Blood Oak door amazed that they did not run into any of their masters' wandering wards and guards.

"Zarkam, you knock." The older wizard said with a sneer in his voice. The younger obese wizards looked nervously as it was known that many traps guarded the door. The young wizard reached out a trembling hand and rapped once on the door. There was no sound, they stood there for a few moments in the wafting snow, then the door opened, a warm wind emanating from the opening doorway with the smell of death and decay coming from it.

Malphit Doom stood in the door shocking both wizards, they immediately bowed to their dreaded master; he looked at them, his eyes scanning them. "Come in my friends, I sense you have news I have been waiting for," Malphit Doom said in a dry dusty voice. His voice held no warmth, no glee, all traces of humanity were stripped from his words. The two wizards groveled their appreciation and entered, dread in their heart for they entered where most never left.

The tower was built into the side of the dark Stone Mountain, its dark rock face covered in frost and packed snow. They entered the tower and saw they were in a room, the room's black granite walls were shiny as if wet and there were several huge iron lanterns the size of barrels hanging from the ceiling, raging fires were in these lighting the room, on the floor was a large symbol etched in the dark wet granite. The symbol was a circular with many faceted edges that were covered in strange glyphs and symbols. This was the symbol of their order.

Standing in this room were five others; they stood there quiet their black robes lined with golden sigils and runes, fear emanated from them like a thick warm wet blanket, the rustling of their robes sounding like snakes crawling on the floor. Malphit Doom walked slowly over to a golden throne and turned, then slowly sat on its cold surface. He spoke in a deadly quiet voice.

"You have much news for us, speak now, and I shall tell you what you will then do." The older wizards stepped forward and knelt down, he spoke carefully choosing his words as he spoke, his seeming arrogance amused Malphit Doom but infuriated the others that were gathered there for he merely had silver on his robes.

"Master, the Guild of Light acts against us as even now their members plot our destruction." He looked up with one eye afraid to look at Malphit Doom in the eyes. There was a gasp in the room from the other wizards, a buzz of surprise. Looking over, the older wizards saw the other five wizards, their hoods bent to each other, their voices hushed.

"Silence." Malphit Doom said and the other wizards ceased there talking. Tapping one long nailed finger on the arm rest of the throne he spoke carefully. "Blazak, you bring good news for you have warned us of pending doom to our order, if this was not brought to us, we would have been caught by surprise." The older wizard smiled, his heart leaped in joy, smiling, he looked at Malphit Doom. "However, why did you not send word via a messenger such as a Crow or a Bee, is it possible you look to have me destroyed thus your long trip and long delay of this information?"

The older wizard who was knelt to his master looked with consternation to Malphit Doom then over to the other wizards who mumbled in agreement. In a trembling voice filled with fear he pleaded. "Master, please believe me... honestly I am loyal, I brought this to you for I wanted to..."

Malphit Doom then raised a hand cutting his words off. "Silence Blazak!, you are a fool, you wished to impress me, to bring gold to your robes, instead your selfish delay may have caused us much harm, and your greed cannot be allowed to go unpunished."

Blazak pleaded with his Dread Master, his face and eyes pleading. "Please Master!, I only serve you and the art, please... I honestly am loyal!" The other mages in the room whispered amongst themselves, their hoods close to each other there words agreeing with their Master. Malphit Doom looked at the groveling old man, his black eyes cold narrowing slightly, he spoke, "Serack unter Painceal" a dark red light flashed striking Blazak in the face. Screaming Blazak grabbed his face standing up, staggering backwards, the other wizards moved out of his way, the younger wizard who came in with him leaped back with a start fear in his face. Blazak staggered for a few feet then slowly collapsed his body melting into a pile of flesh on the floor, from an iron grate on a wall came several three headed dogs that dragged the warm bloody mass into their den, their growls only interrupted by their feeding on the pile of melted flesh. Blazak was dead.

Malphit Doom looked to the other obese Dark wizard who knelt before him groveling now on the floor in fear, his eyes wide with terror, his heart pounding so hard one could almost hear it through his robes, his mouth opened to plead, but nothing came from his mouth. Malphit Doom sat there for a moment looking at him, his dark eyes hard and unforgiving, he shifted in his seat causing the obese wizards to jump. "Zarkam, so tell me whom do you serve, or should I ask to what ends do you serve?"

The wizard shaking and terrified looked over to the grate in the wall where Blazak was just dragged, then he looked to his Master with a pleading look, wringing his hands he spoke, his voice trembling. "Master, please, I serve you and only you and your ends. No one else do I serve. I only acted under orders and instruction by my mentor, I told him we should warn you by messenger, he refused, I tried to convince him but he..." Malphit Doom waved a hand at him in contempt his eyes boring into the trembling wizard's eyes.

"Silence, your groveling irritates me, if you serve only me and our order then serve you will, I have a plan that will destroy not only the guild of light but the very threads of light magic." To this there was a gasp from the other wizards, their shock at the gravity of what Malphit Doom just said.

One of the wizards with the gold trim spoke, his voice awe filled. "Master, how is this possible? The threads of all magic are protected by the equilibrium, how can this be?"

Malphit Doom looked to the wizards and smiled a mirthless smile, his voice suddenly loud. "We can and will destroy the very threads of Light, we shall make a book and into that book, we will pour our combined energies, once completed, we will use the incantations in that book to destroy the very Arcane threads of light and to that Light Magic will be poisoned, that book will be like a poison into a vein of a man, reaching the heart it will stop it and Light Magic will forever be killed, then the Guild of light, powerless, will be hunted, and each member head will go there." He pointed over to a wall where there were dozens of heads; on the end was the head of Blazak, a look of terror in his cold dead eyes.

Several wizards looked to each other with shock on their faces for no one has ever been able to access to actual Equilibrium let alone destroy any part of it. Another wizard in Black robes with Gold on his hood and also on the cuffs of his robe spoke quietly, "Dread master, how may we serve this end, what shall your bidding be for we serve you? We serve the Art."

Malphit Doom smiled, for his assembled five were his darkest and vilest wizards. They were also his most loyal, and he knew the value of loyalty. He looked at the groveling pig before him, his contempt for this wizard was heavy as he spoke. "And you Zarkam, will help solidify these plans. Are you up to this dark task?" A murmur of shock ebbed through the other wizards, some were shocked at this young wizard's inclusion into this crucial plan for he had no gold on his hood. Malphit Doom seeing this spoke irritated, "Silence you all, where were you my five when these plans were being hatched, these two were the ones that were in the Usurper's midst, and for that he will be of service where you will not?" When he said these words the others silenced their rumblings as they knew to not cross their Master.

"Ye, yes, master, I... I am ready..." Zarkam said in a shaky voice prostrating himself onto the floor, his trembling with fear visible through his robes.

"Good, very good, as already the attack by the usurping magic users has begun, for already one hundred of our Guild has been killed; the Guild of light is working with the common folk to hunt us down."

The other wizards with the gold trim looked to each other with outrage in their faces, it has started, and they were shocked that it had actually begun."This must be stopped" said one wizard with dark skin, his eyes bulging in rage, flecks of spit flying from his mouth.

"We must have our revenge" echoed in the dark room by another wizard, his blond hair and fair skin making him look more like an Amarian scribe then a dark evil wizard. Malphit Doom smiled as he knew if successful it would not matter.

"We have time, and you, Zarkam, will work with Croneter and he will know what to do, I have given him the required books and tomes, he has the Dark Tome, the Tome of Vileness, that will help in the creation of the book, and remember nothing else matters and Croneter knows what to do if something goes amiss, don't you, my vile little friend?"

Stepping forward, an old wizard with yellowed long nails smiled his sharp toothed smile, looking as evil as he indeed was, his wrinkled skin gray and pale, his hunched back straightening slightly in pride, he glared at the others in contempt knowing his master with this task, announced he was the favored one. "Master as I serve you, I serve the dark, I know what you have told me to do and your bidding is my goal, it is my life."

Malphit smiled this time with a pleased grin knowing that this wizard was his most vile, his most dark and evil follower. "Go to your tower and pour everything into the book. Zarkam will serve you as you serve me; Zarkam do as I tell you; Croneter, he is your master, his words are to be followed for now and even over mine." Shock again registered through the room at these words, how can their Master say this, no one is to be above the Master. "Yes it is time to put aside vanity, our order is at risk, and we must do everything to protect it. Once this book is done bring it to me, and I shall once and for all end this for I know what power is needed to use the book. However, I am limited in its creation as the one who creates it cannot wield it. Now, go make haste and bring me the book once it is finished." The two wizards gathered their things and bid their master farewell, and to this the two wizards left the stone tower and headed towards the old wizard's tower to begin the final ending of light magic.

Several Weeks past the Late Summer yielded to Fall and that to Winter; the hour was late, darkness laid over the area like a thick blanket, no moon showed as it was snowing outside. The wind was cold blowing against the glass of the small window that was set high into a tall stone tower. The tower's thick block walls were black and pitted with age; inside the tower in the flickering fire light, a man lay on the floor dead. His black robes lying around him like a cold death shroud the silver piping around the hood of his black robes trimmed with strange runes.

Another old man was at a small wooden table his back hunched over a book; a candle, its flame flickering shadows across its pages and the gold runes that trimmed his hood glowing like fire. He momentarily looked at the body on the floor grimacing with contempt, his eyes passed over the body and no pity fell unto his heart for the dead man he was looking at, he spoke with contempt in his voice. "Zarkam you are a foolish idiot, your stupidity and weakness paid with your life, and you shall miss out seeing our Master's great plan completed." He then turned his attention back to the small book that laid in front of him.

The old man sat at a table in a round room, the room was small with a small smoking fireplace on one wall, its hearth filled with nothing but glowing coals and a slight spitting fire; shelving surrounded the room, dark books lined some of them, on others were small jars with strange things in them, some moving against the glass their tiny little yells and screams not heard through the glass. Their little fists clenched some in fear, some in anger. The old man closed his eyes as he was stooped over the book, his lips moving, his voice raspy and dry, strange words coming from his old cracked lips. As he spoke the strange and complicated incantations he wrote with an old worn quill onto the pages of the book, his gnarled fingers grasping the quill carefully. With each word written its ink glowed hissed then burned into the pages.

This night was the culmination of many hours of dark work with his fellow wizards succumbing to the power and danger of the dark book's creation. He could feel the excitement in his chest build as he was on the last page of the dark book, he smiled at the emotion almost foreign to his wrinkled features as he wrote the last vile word then placed the smoking quill down on the table, a drop of ink falling from the tip onto it, hissing and burning the wood where the ink fell. He leaned back arching his back as it was aching from the days of being stooped over the book; stretching, he closed the old book, placing an age worn hand on top of its warm leather cover, smiling to himself... almost caressing the book.

"Yes I am finally done, tonight it begins for I will go down in wizards' lore as the one who was the most dedicated, most disciplined." The book that lay on the table was made of brown leather with various words and symbols on its pages, the spine of the book stiff and firmly holding the pages, its cover adorned with an odd symbol, an orb yet not an orb, its many faceted sides each holding a different dark arcane symbol, the symbol of his Order.

As he sat there he thought of that fateful night so many weeks before when the Great Master called him into his laboratory, telling him of his great plan and placing in him the trust that he had on the table now. Malphit Doom decided to create the book that if successfully made would allow him to call upon the deeper dark powers of the Underhalls and Deep Dark; with these powers, he would be able to destroy the very strands of Light Magic thus forever cementing their order in the Realms. The old man sat there looking at the strange book and then again, to his fellow wizard and felt no pity for the dead man, for the book was done, and he knew he was hours from being the one, the one who forever tipped the magical balances. He leaned back again stretching and knew he had to sleep, he was tired, his last incantation that finished the book drained his magical powers so much that he knew he would need to sleep before sending his familiar to the others so they could come and witness their triumph.

The tower was silent; as he sat there his mind was numb, for twenty days he had been awake almost constantly pouring his magical energies into the book, his only respite from its dark creation was the occasional rest to restore his magical powers. He needed to teleport to his Master, he could not trust any other way, he was far too weak to perform such a difficult spell. He needed the help of the others; earlier that day he summoned three of them to aid him in performing the spell.

Once the others arrived, they could combine their energies and teleport him to the Master directly, then the Master would use the book to forever destroy the usurpers. Turning in his seat towards the fireplace he pointed a shaking finger at the pile of wood that was next to the dwindling fire in the fire place, "Lerrian" he spoke and two pieces of wood floated from the wood pile into the fire, hissing and sparking, they caught immediately, the fireplace quickly throwing out a warm glow. He felt dizzy and it irritated him that this most simple of incantations made him feel thus.

He then stood up, his bones aching from being sat at the table over the book for so many long hours, and walked stiffly over to the shelving, his robes dragging on the dusty floor. Pulling a small tome off its shelves, dust covering the light green leather, he smiled opening the book with a gnarled finger, slowly reading the page when suddenly he heard a loud "Crack" then an echoing "Bang" ran through the room coming from far below in the tower, a small sliver of dust fell from the ceiling, the tower shuddered. He was startled. However, quickly with an unnatural nimbleness, he threw the book to the floor, closed his eyes muttering "Keil, las onra deuverey nectum" as he whispered these words, he felt his mind floating, going through doors, down halls and narrow stairs lined with smoking torches to the outside where he saw a large crowd gathered, shovels in hand, some with large sticks and clubs, some with knives, torches in hand, yelling, and in the front were a large group of men in a mixed assortment of armor with a battering ram. "Bang" he heard yet again, the tower shaking as the battering ram slammed against the stout door to the tower.

As he pulled his mind back his heart raced and fear flickered in his chest. He knew he was not rested enough to repel them, he spent far too much time and energy making the book, he must think... "Think, dammit, the book took so long to complete, so long to get ready. How can this happen now? I must think, I must make sure it is protected."

Suddenly he heard a hollow crash then a large bang, he knew the outer door was now breeched. He licked his lips, dry and cracked, his mind racing. "Deuco render obstrucum" he whispered feeling the magic flow from him, his knees almost buckling as exhaustion came over him. He hoped the magical invisible wall he just placed in front of them in the entry hall would hold; he felt tired, weak and he knew his magic was failing. He needed sleep. Why couldn't this happen after he rested, he could easily defend his tower if he could just rest and his familiar a small vulture sitting in a perch eating a small cat would not be able to reach the others in time for them to help? It was too late for that, what mattered now was nothing more than the book. He took a deep breath knowing he had several minutes as the magical wall would block the peasants for a bit, however it was weak as his magic was failing him. He took a deep breath, calling on his training in the dark arts. Calm washed over him and he knew he must use his last bit of magical energy to do the unspeakable.

Would it work?, he wondered... He had no choice he had to try, he could not allow this book to fall into the hands of these cretins, he had no choice. He was so weak, so tired, standing up he walked quickly to the book and picking it up, he walked over to a large shelf, pressed a small catch on the frame, a loud "Click" sounded and then a scraping as the shelf popped away from the wall. He then, before entering the dark stairway, pulled a small red tome off a dusty shelf. Opening it, he looked at the strange angular symbols and on the page was a pendant shaped drawing, he opened the front of his robe pulling out a small amulet on the end of a thin pewter chain, ripping it from his neck, the chain cutting him but ignoring the pain, he took a deep breath for once this was done there was no stopping what was to happen next.

He then placed the pendant on the page over the drawing that matched its shape and size; when he did this the page glowed, then hissed. He then felt the book become heavy, the small amulet glowing red and bright melting into the page, then the tower shook again this time from some unseen magical shift, the book dropped to the ground with a hollow thud, the pages slowly dissolving, closing his eyes and smiling to himself. Feeling better as the amulet worked, he pulled open the secret door exposing a small narrow set of steps, he then entered the stairway pulling the secret door shut behind him. As he walked down the dark steps into the musty velvety darkness, he felt more at ease, his feet falling knowingly on the steps not needing any light as he walked these steps thousands of times over the past two hundred and thirty seven years.

He walked down the narrow steps, and he heard the town folks through the wall, he stopped momentarily and looked through a peep hole and could see several dozens of them, torches in hand, ransacking the entry hall, one of the larger men in the front was yelling orders,

"Find him, find the wizard! His evil stops tonight once his heart stops beating, take what you can!" at this several men yelled in agreement, several peasants were banging on the invisible wall in frustration others were going through drawers filling their pockets and burlap sacks with whatever they could steal.

He smiled to himself in a knowing, self satisfied manner. "They know not of the power they miss; yes, my ignorant invaders, destroy what you want for you miss the greatest prize, and you will feel my revenge soon" He continued to walk down the steps, the air getting cooler and musty as he knew he was underground now; his knees were shaky and he felt so weak. He walked to a small door set in stone, there was no lock on the door nor were there any hinges as the door itself was set into the hard dark stone. However, he placed his weathered hand on the face and there was a slight "click" and the door opened exposing a small dimly lit chamber lit by a pair of ruddy torches.

He walked into the chamber and placed the book on a small table in its center. The room was small and round, no more than twelve feet wide. The table in the middle of the room was the only furniture except for a wooden shelf along a wall. He stood there, his breathing deep as he was close to exhaustion. He let his robe fall off of him exposing his frail old naked body, his hunched back stooped and bony, he raised his hands in the air chanting loudly, and he felt his chest burn where the amulet used to lay and he knew he had not much time. Chanting and whispering arcane dark words, he walked around the table, he felt the cold stone on his feet, but he didn't care as he knew this was his final act so the book could be saved, so the book would have another chance one day in this world to finish its purpose.

As he chanted the earth shook and the doorway into the chamber melted into solid stone, he smiled at his sealed fate then walked over to a shelve and removed a stout iron cask from it, placing the cask on the table and opening it, he placed

16

the tome into it and placed an iron lock onto the hasp. Closing his eyes, he placed both hands onto the cask, still chanting, the casks lock then went "Snap" and glowed brightly, the searing heat burning into his hands causing his pale skin to bubble and hiss, screaming in blissful agony he let go stumbling back. The cask suddenly had many glowing symbols along its sides, the wizard's tears of agony becoming tears of joy as he saw the glowing symbols upon its iron surface gradually fade the cask becoming dark and cold.

He knew the book was safe now, and he knew in moments it would be done. He stood there for a few moments then felt it, his chest heaved, and he felt himself falling, he closed his eyes in anticipation as he felt himself, his consciousness being pulled from him, his last thought before darkness enveloped him was that in moments the villagers would be gone and his Order plans would one day be realized. He smiled in painful contentment, and then he saw nothing.

Malphit Doom lay in his bed with his eyes closed; he was not asleep as he felt that the book had been completed, the amulet on his chest was cold, so very cold and that was a sign that the task was done. Suddenly, he felt something more, like the amulet had been ripped from his chest! Jumping up from his bed he stood there grasping at the amulet it was still there. However, he knew something wrong had happened. Fear and panic ripped through him as he realized that the book was now far away, and he ran to his Seeing Well. Looking into the clear water he concentrated. He saw Croneters' tower under attack, and then he knew that Croneter had done something. He saw a flash of light then his knees buckled feeling like someone had punched him in his stomach, he collapsed to the floor grimacing in panic more than pain.

"No, I must get the book!" His voice panicked as he stood up shaking; moving towards his desk he took down a scroll and reading it quickly he felt the magic of the scroll activate, he suddenly felt warm, and he saw the book. However, dread filled him as he saw the book moving far away out of his reach, and he knew it was gone until he could find a way to regain it back. He sat in his chair and knew he had to now hide. The Usurpers of Light Magic would be coming to his tower soon, and he would be killed. He made a decision to hide as it was the only way, until he managed to gain the book back. It was by far not over yet.

Ten leagues away in the small village of Smolt a woman was feeding her pigs, the night sky was shrouded in clouds, snow falling heavily, the bitter cold wind was blowing against her thin cloak and dress when suddenly an unnatural light blazed in the distance, then, a moment later she heard a deafening roar as if the earth itself screamed. The earth shook and she fell to the ground, panic licking at her heart, her hands stinging in the deep snow; her pigs squealed in fear and a dog ran under the porch with its tail between its legs. She laid there, her face in her hands, her heart pounding in fear, and her mind racing,

"Gods, what could this be?, please do not punish us," she prayed as she knew the only thing in that direction was the old wizard's tower. Moments later a warm wind rolled over her smelling of burning and death, then there was only silence except for the sounds of her pigs and cows.

Days later as the men who went to the tower did not return, word reached the Village that some vile evil visited the tower for it was gone; several women went to where their men and sons left to go to, and they saw the tower was no longer there, instead only scorched earth and sheared trees were left. The days came and went, days turned into weeks and weeks into months, and rumors floated in the winds. The tower was gone and eventually a peace settled over the Realms.

Malphit Dooms plans were delayed. But only for awhile.........

Croeneter hears the villagers

Dark as night......
Dark as a Man's Soul.......
Dark Magic infects all that it touches.........

                    - From the Book of Light

1

DISCOVERY

The horse whinnied as the farmer lashed at it with the stick, "Move your butt now Dixie," he yelled, the sweat dripping off his brow. It was midsummer and hot and there had been no rain in weeks causing the fields to start to dry up and wither.

The old farmer was not in the mood for a stubborn horse, he needed to get this well dug or his crops would most definitely die and that could not be allowed to happen. The horse reluctantly moved, its bridal and straps biting into it as it slowly moved the large rock. The farmer smacking the horse on its rump in the hot sun his patience wearing thin. Finally moving the rock the farmer looked, the earth under the rock was dry and cracked and his heart dropped as he was hoping to see damp earth.

"Well, what the hell do I do now?" he muttered to himself wiping grimy sweat from his forehead. "Guess I need to start digging," he said to himself in frustration and at that he broke out a shovel and started digging. His digging went on into the early afternoon; he was getting angry as he kept running into large black stones that were pitted and rough.

"Damn stones, where the hell are these things coming from?" his wife came walking out across the dusty field the hot dry wind blowing around her the bun her hair was falling out causing her brown hair to blow about her and into her sunburned face.

"Herm, you need something to eat and drink," she said as she approached the small hole her husband was digging. She was holding a couple of sandwiches wrapped in wax paper and a pitcher of lemon aid. Mary Beth was Herm's wife, a woman in her early fifties. However, she was very pretty and looked in her early forties, her dark hair long and blowing in the dry dusty wind.

"Mary Beth, I am aware what I need to do!" He said irritated as he looked up squinting due to the bright sun at his wife the sweat rolling down his neck. Herm was in his late fifties and looked it, his dark skin was sun dark and wind weathered, his bright blue eyes standing out in stark contrast to his dark weathered features, his sandy hair now favoring grey. It was common talk in the area on how Herm landed Mary Beth, and what she saw in him as in high school the now local Doctor courted her, and she declined his advances in favor of Herm, who everyone knew would be a simple farmer.

"Well, don't get snippy with me Herm, it's not my fault there hasn't been any rain, nor is it my fault you aint' getting any water." He looked at his wife standing there, her country dress and apron fluttering in the hot dusty wind and smiled at her and decided to just eat and drink. While he drank from a glass of lemon aid, he picked up one of the black rocks turning the rock over in his hand, puzzled as he never saw stones like these around here.

He had farmed this land and area since a small boy and in his fifty eight years never saw anything like it, as normally in this area one found nice round rocks of granite varying in colors from red to green to blue to gray.

Oddly, this stone was black and square; however, it looked almost melted, like it underwent some hot fire. The surface was pitted with bubbles and this wasn't the only one, he had been removing lots of these stones out of this well pit for hours. He tossed the rock on the small pile that was growing off the strange stones. He finished his sandwiches, thanked his wife and started digging again in the dry dusty soil. As he dug, he felt his shovel hit something solid,

"Dammit these confounded rocks are getting on my last nerve!" he stooped over the sweat rolling into his eyes, irritating them in the heat and dust. He tried to pry the rock out, but it was larger than the others, so he took his shovel prying along the edge, the object bending out of the hard dry soil the farmer seeing it as a rusty box, staring at it. "Mary Beth look at this, it's a metal box." His wife looking into the hole at her husband,

"So what, Herm it's an old box you need to worry more about finding water; our South field is going to be burned by week's week's end if this heat don't go away..." she said this squinting up to the sky, the suns unrelenting glare burning into her pretty face.

"No honey look at it, it has a lock on it, maybe there is a treasure in it! What if there are jewels?, we can leave this place and become high fluting folk," he looked at the box a million fantasies running through his head. The box was small about the size of a bread box, it was rusted heavily, its old lock rusted to its side, its hinges not visible. "Hand me that pick, honey," Herm said holding his hand out to his wife and she bent over picking up the heavy pick, handing it to her husband, his calloused hand grasping the heavy wooden handle. He hit the lock once, rust popping from its surface. In the distance there was a rumble, his wife looked to the East.

"Herm, you hear that, was that thunder?" she said looking up into the bright cloudless sky.

He looked up at her from the hole he was in, the sun beating into his eyes. "Thunder, you mad woman, this is August, we don't get no rain in August," he then struck the lock again, the old rusty lock snapping off, as he looked at the box he felt a chill, and it occurred to him that it was becoming overcast, he looked up and sure enough dark clouds were suddenly scudding in the sky,

"Herm look! Where did those clouds suddenly come from? It looks like rain, by God could it be?" her voice was excited.

He looked out the hole, there were indeed dark clouds rolling in, rolling and turning in the sky, he felt relief like he hadn't felt in many weeks, "Woman, I think you may be right, we just might get rain, you smell that?, it smells like rain is in the air."

Mary Beth looked around taking a deep breath the smell of dampness reaching her nostrils her heart racing filling with excitement. "God sure does work in mysterious ways," she said smiling.

Herm looked at the box, a drop of rain hitting it and quickly evaporating, he placed it on the edge of the hole, and then he took out a stout pocket knife from his old blue jean pants pocket and pried the lid open, a slight sucking sound emanating from it as the lid old and rusty snapped off onto the ground.

Suddenly there was a large crack of thunder startling the farmer and his wife. Looking inside the box he was surprised to see the inside was intact, almost brand new looking, its smooth iron sides not rusty in the slightest. He felt disappointment when all there was in the box was a leather book, he picked it up and opened it, there was some foreign language in it with writing and symbols on the pages that he couldn't read.

"Well honey, what is it? Oh it's a book, what kind of book is it?" his wife asked peering at the book in his hands. The farmer irritated looked up at his wife from the hole,

"I think it's some book in German or something from the Quakers who settled this area, it's a damn crappy book, no jewels honey." There was a crack of thunder then darker scudding clouds, the air temperature dropping from the high nineties to the high seventies within minutes causing goose bumps on Mary Beth's arms; without thinking she rubbed her arms in the much cooler air. "Herm it's getting oddly cool, this isn't normal." Herm looked at his wife from the hole he was in. Looking at her rubbing her arms, her apron blowing in the wind he smiled. Mary Beth seeing her husband's grin smiled back.

"Honey we best get inside its gonna rain cats and dogs, I can tell," Mary Beth said to her husband and at that the farmer climbed out of the hole and taking the book in one hand and his wife's hand in the other they walked hurriedly back to the small farm house, the sound of thunder above them.

As they reached the old farm house it started raining heavily and for a moment, they both stood on the front porch looking in disbelief at the torrent of rain coming down, lightning flashed in the air the dark clouds scudding along low and ominous.

"Do you think we are going to have a twister?" Herm's wife asked, with a concerned look at the dark skies and flashing lighting in the air. The air had an odd feel to it as if something was coming. She was worried and Herm sensed it in her voice.

"No, it isn't that kind of storm, hun. This one's odd, leave it to this confounded summer to bring strange weather!" Herm said. Smiling reassuringly at his wife he sat down on the porch swing, his wife sitting next to him placing her hand on the book that was sitting on his lap.

"Honey, let me see that book," she said as she grasped the book off the lap of her husband. Looking at it opening the cover looking at the strange angular writing she was perplexed. "Do ya think it's worth anything, hun?" she asked.

Herm looked at her smiling, he spoke with an air of hope to his voice. "Well, with this rain we can take the afternoon and maybe go into town and talk to the lady at the Library, she will know if it is worth anything." Mary Beth smiled back at him, looking at the stormy weather she figured they had time to go to town, and at that they got up and walked to their new car, a 1927 Model T they bought brand new not a year before.

Cranking the handle in the front of the car, it rumbled to a start, and they headed into town down the old mud soaked road with the lightning and rain around them.

They got to the Library in Smithfield, which was about twenty miles from the farm, pulling up, the rain was coming down in sheets; they ran up the narrow wooden steps, rushing through the flimsy screen door, which squeaking as it swung open, and making a smacking sound as it closed. The Library was small with wooden floors and several shelves with old books on them, a few light bulbs glowing hanging from pull chains from the ceiling, and it was stifling hot and muggy in the building.

"Hi, Mary Beth," a small elderly lady said, she was short with her hair rolled into a tight bun on top of her head. She stood behind a small wooden counter its surface worn from use.

The farmer and his wife walked up to her. "Well, hello Abby, we got something for you to look at. I dug this up in my field earlier today," Herm said placing the book onto the worn counter.

The Librarian looked at him with a smile on her face shaking her head in disbelief. "You were digging in this rain, the heat got to ya, did it Herm," she said this laughing.

Herm, looking embarrassed, glanced to his wife who was also smiling. "No, no Abby... it started raining just as I found that book," Herm said pointing to the odd book that he placed on the worn counter. As the book laid there a large clap of thunder struck, the single light bulb hanging above the counter flickered briefly.

Abby looked at the book, turning it over in her hands examining the strange design on the cover, then opening it, she looked puzzled as she leafed through its pages. "Well, I'll be, I don't know what language this is. Looks like its Dutch or German, Herm? Plus it has odd symbols in it. I am not sure this is anything, it most likely is some old settler's ledger and these books are all over the County, all settlers kept financial records. I think you have an interesting read if you knew how to speak German." She said this smiling placing the book back on the counter in front of the couple.

Let down, Herm had an idea, "Well, what do you make of this symbol on the cover then, it looks like a funny ball all these symbols on it and all?"

Abby looked at it for a long moment, her brow narrowing in puzzlement, placing it back onto the counter she smiled. "Peters nose if I know, it could be a design the settler carved into the leather or the maker's own symbol? Who knows, maybe it is the family's crest or something?"

Abby said smiling again, wanting to get back to her cataloging. Herm and his wife stood there for a few minutes talking to her, then looking at her husband Mary Beth said sighed, wiping the sweat from her forehead.

"Blazes hot in here!" She looked at Herm with her famous "no more arguing" look. "Well let's get back to the house, I have pies to make. We got our rain thank the Lord, and we have things to get done instead of worrying about a worthless ledger."

Herm, taking his handkerchief out of his pocket wiping his sweat covered face, sighed a knowing sigh. Looking at his wife and feeling a bit let down he agreed. "Yes, we do have things to do, I have to get that damn horse shoed and get the other one out of the field before it washes away in this rain," he said chuckling.

So, at that they headed back home in the rain. On the way home Herm could not get the book out of his mind, he decided that once he had the chance, he would read the thing. Or at least try to. Maybe he could make sense of it. Getting home, he placed the book in an old chest that he kept old papers in and got busy getting his chores done. That year was 1929 and was the wettest summer on record it rained for thirty straight days.

Several weeks later Mary Beth was in bed, sleeping. The weather had been so much cooler, and her husband said earlier that he was going to stay up and take a better look at the strange book he found in that field.

She awoke after midnight with a start thinking she was awoken by a clap of thunder, or was it a cow's yell. As she laid there half awake wondering if she had dreamed the noise she realized that Herm wasn't in bed with her. Thinking that he'd better get in bed, she laid there, and it then occurred to her that there was a strange humming, sort of off and on. After a few minutes it went away, and she decided to get up and tell her husband to get in bed as they both had things to do early in the morning.

She got out of bed, her bare feet making slight noises on the old wooden clap board floors, and entered the kitchen. She stood there for a moment looking, her eyes adjusting to the lantern light, blinking she saw the kitchen chair turned over and laying on the floor, the book was closed on the table, along with a glass of milk that was spilled across the worn oak surface. Herm was nowhere to be found. Mary Beth walked outside onto the porch, the cool night air causing her to rub her arms, her hands running over the goose bumps that appeared on them.

She yelled his name several times and thought about going out to the barn to see if he was there. Instead she shook her head, "Spilling milk all over leaving a chair turned over. When I see that man in the morning he will hear of it!" and at that she went back upstairs to bed feeling pretty upset at him and is seeming not caring. The next day when she looked for him around the farm he was nowhere to be found. She called the police and the local Sheriff and a few locals looked for Herm thinking he may have wandered off and had a heart attack or something. However, after two days they didn't find him and the search party gave up. Mary Beth placed the book and a few of Herm's belongings in that same chest and waited for her Herm to one day come home.

Mary Beth stayed on that farm for another year hoping one day to see her Herm, but he never came back. With the fields growing and the crops rotting from not being taken care of, Mary Beth sold the farm and went to live with her oldest daughter in Michigan. Her belongings and the old chest were placed on a truck along with some furniture and pictures and taken to Michigan with her where the old chest was placed in an attic of her daughter's to be forgotten for almost sixty years.

Mary Beth died of a stroke in 1950 and after her funeral her daughter forgot about that chest in that attic.

The strange book inside that old chest sat waiting, as if it knew its day was coming soon.

Herm and Mary Beth's Farm

Although we do not have him with us here, He will always be in our hearts.

One day our paths will cross and I shall say....
Herm, where have you been ?

...... From Herm's Funeral

2
THE GAME SHOP

Spring came early, and Don was excited as he drove down the road to Pat's house. Hutch and James were in the back seat, playing a quick round of the Raven Crest card game. They had plenty of time to get Pat and then get down the road to Kalamazoo, to the new game shop that was having its grand opening this weekend.

The four men were best friends, and had been so for years. Ranging in age from twenty eight to forty five, they had one thing on common: Gaming. Scrabble, Ravens Crest, Guild War, and every Friday and Saturday night they would gather at one of their homes and play the Alterverse Role Players game, one of the hot games to get that Summer.

These four friends were very close, yet their playing styles were as different as their personalities. They all loved playing Alterverse; however, they approached their play very differently. Don tended to be a thinker, and liked to talk things out amongst the group, but if they took too long wrangling over his Crusader or Paganis[1] character would move on in the game. This tended to get him into hot water with the other players.

[1] A Divine magic using class that can cast spells

Hutch was also a thinker. He usually planned the adventures and ran the sessions as the Game Master, but when he ran a character he always wanted to hang around and help the damsel in distress. Quick to offer assistance, which was not always popular with the group, he favored playing the healer, but always with a quirk in his character and a joke to lighten the mood.

Pat liked strong, straightforward characters. Northsman[2] or other Barbarians whose problem solving skills were mostly limited to "get a sword and chop it down to size," were his favorites. Hot-headed and quick to action, his impulsiveness had saved their group several times, but it also put them in jeopardy on a regular basis.

James was the sly one of the group. His character would lurk in the shadows, gathering information or watching over the rest of the party, a final card waiting to be played when all seemed lost. Sometimes his characters acted unpleasantly, but always came through in a pinch. Their varied playing styles not only made for interesting game sessions, it also allowed their characters to succeed in their adventures.

The Saturday morning sun cast long shadows across the road. With Pat again canceling due to problems at home, last night's gaming session had evolved into a gab session, ranging from the plot of Don's new book to the online Game Wizard Spell to the new expansion for the Alterverse RPG[3] scheduled to be released today. This morning they had moved on to discussing the store they were going to visit.

"Better be a decent place," Hutch said. "I'm sick to death of the crummy shops we have around here."

[2] A class where the player is from a tribal society similar to a Barbarian
[3] A Game released in 2010 by 2 Moon Games using the Task Level System

"Yeah," Don agreed, "I hope they have a decent selection of dice. And maybe an area to do some gaming in."

"Andrew Jackson here says it's a shit hole with crap in it," James said, pulling a twenty-dollar bill out from his pocket and waving it.

Looking up from the cards laid out on the seat between them, Hutch grimaced, "Man, you ever positive? Here we are, going to the first new game shop in this area since I was a kid, and you gotta be all negative."

James glared at Hutch, a response on his lips, but deciding against it.

"Man, you two need to give each other a hug!" Don threw back from the front seat, laughing, as he pulled into Pat's driveway.

They got out of the car and walked up to Pat's door and went in. Pat was just getting his coat on and his wife Lee was watching TV. Pat was tall, his six feet six frame was slightly buff, his big feet carrying his large frame easily, his sandy colored hair long and in a pony tail,

"Hey I'm getting my coat on, sorry about last night, I was trying to handle something," Pat said tossing a glance at the couch where Lee, his girlfriend, was sitting with her back to the men.

"Yeah, right slacker, bet you were sick all right, bet ya were so sick ya stayed in bed with Lee night, huh?" James quipped looking over at Lee and smiling.

"Yeah right." Lee popped off with an upset look on her face. Don looked at her and saw the tell tale signs of a red face; she had been crying.

"Damn, maybe we should have gamed here last night." James said laughing... pushing it as he always seemed to do.

Hutch seeing Pat's dark look and Lee's face nudged James and gave him one of those "Shut the hell up" looks.

Lee got up and smiled at Don, Hutch and James. Things were bad, Lee and Pat had been having a lot of problems, and with Pat losing his job at Nation Tech where he was an IT guy they had been on hard times also. What made matters worse was that Lee had been spending a lot of her evenings with, she claimed, her friends, and Pat thought she had been having an affair.

"Let's get to the shop, ok... We have some gaming to do, plus let's do a cook out this eve. Lee, you are coming also right?" Don asked with a smile hoping Lee would agree.

"I might, then again, I might have to take care of something this eve," Lee said giving Pat a quick look. Pat gave her a dark look, shaking his head in disgust as he walked past Don,

"Let's go guys, nothing more to do here." and to that he walked out the door not waiting for the others..

They all then got back in the car and started the drive to Kalamazoo to Otto's Game Emporium. The weather was ideal for a nice road trip, sunny and in the low sixties. The sun sat high and bright; Pat's dark mood seemed to go away quickly now that he was away from his wife, and the friends all discussed the weekend's activities.

"Yeah, it's supposed to stay sunny and mild all week no rain, whoo hoo!, we all still cooking out today?" James asked excited. James loved to BBQ out especially when it was not at his place.

"We could, I guess," Don answered. "Call Bri on the cell and have her get some potato salad made and maybe Pat you can get Lee to make some of that macaroni salad she makes."

"Yeah Lee makes the best Mac salad, oh and get Bri to also make some of that pretzel stuff while you are at it," Hutch interjected.

"BYOM? What the hell is that?" James asked puzzled. "We always go half on the drinks, I mean I have a six of Pabst in the fridge at home, I could get Bri to bring that.

"Hey Moron, BRING YOUR OWN MEAT. Sheesh as well as cheap." Hutch joked. The bantering went on as several calls were made to the ladies, as this eve's BBQ was planned and placed into motion. As they got into Kalamazoo from I-94 and exited onto Westnidge, they searched for the shop and finally found it on a rundown street on the outskirts of town.

They all were disappointed as they pulled up to it as it seemed to be a small run down little place, not new at all. There was a new banner hanging on the side of the building that said "GAMES AND MORE" and below that in smaller letters was, "GRAND OPENING TODAY!" further they saw that the "Grand Opening" as was advertised must have escaped everyone else as they were the only ones in the parking lot.

"Now isn't this the shit, I'm impressed, oh yeah", James said sarcastically.

"Ya know, I gotta go with moron on this one", Hutch said, as they sat in the car looking at the place. As they sat in the parking lot, their hopes were falling fast as this was not what they at all expected from what was advertised.

"I think we just crapped away ten bucks in gas" Don said with a sigh. "Well we drove here, let's go check out the Grand opening and be amazed." Don said with even heavier sarcasm as he opened his door and got out of the car, stretching.

Otto's Game Emporium was a small building with split and cracked brickwork on its face and small, dark dirty windows. The only other thing signifying that this was a business besides the large banner was a small rickety wooden sign hanging over the front door that said "BOOKS" and behind the dirty glass was a small handmade cardboard sign saying, "Games For Everyone Inside."

The front door was made of wood with a large window in it, the door was painted bright red as was all the trim around the windows, and all the wood trim and the door had a strange gold filigree on it. As they opened the door to Otto's a small bell that was hung over the door twinkled, and they immediately noticed that this was more like an old book shop than a game shop.

The shop was filled with shelving with all manners of books on the shelves. Old dusty and cluttered, large cardboard and wooden boxes were stacked here and there filled with dusty books.

On one side of the old shop was a single counter with a new sign hanging over it that said "Otto's Game Emporium" and behind the counter were many new game books and card games, there were dice and all manners of gaming materials. A young man maybe twenty or so stood behind the counter and greeted them while smiling.

"Hello, welcome to Otto's. I'm Patrick, I'm the one running the game part of this store." As he said this an old man came out from behind a small door.

"Yes, and that's all you are running here boy," the old man said in a dry dusty voice. He was old and walked slowly, his shoulders hunched over a stout cane in one hand, thick glasses on his nose. "Welcome my friends, what manner of books may I provide you?" He stopped, looking at the guys his eyes large and unblinking through those glasses.

The young man behind the counter made a face and shook his head in a mocking manner.

"Hmm we are here for the new game shop sir, the paper said you were having a grand opening." James said to the old man.

The old man looked at James balefully and turned around and started walking back through the door, as he turned, he said sarcastically to the young man behind the counter. "Some customers of yours Patrick."

Don and the rest walked up the counter to the young man standing behind the new glass display cabinet, "This is the game area, I take it?" Don said to the guy.

"Sorry about Gramps, he's not happy with this game area, he thinks it's a waste of time, we haven't sold a book in months here, and he just doesn't get it. And yes this is it so far. I am hoping to draw players from the College and such, and one day make this a full line shop."

Don looked around, then at him. He seemed like a decent guy, as they looked, they saw that the shop had the latest edition of the Alterverse Role Playing Game, and the price was ten percent off list.

"How many manuals ya got? we need four Players tomes and four Masters tomes" Pat said to the young man who smiled at his question.

"I got them, no problem," the young man said reaching on a shelf in back of him taking the manuals down and placing them on the counter, "also I have the new edition of Raven Crest the card game, if interested?" he said this as he pointed to a shelf behind him, which had several boxes with Ravens Crest Edition Deluxe blazoned on them.

"Hell, let me have six packs" James said stepping forward to the counter reaching in his back pocket.

Hutch leaned over to Don whispering in his ear, "He has twenty bucks to buy cards but whines about bringing his own burgers for the grill?"

Don smiled at Hutch then walked over to the right and saw what he was looking for. At the end of the display cabinet was a dice display with several colors of polyhedral dice in tubes.

"When you're done there Patrick, I will take a set of the red 'glow in the dark' dice."

The young man walked over after giving James six packs of the card game and taking James's money, he smiled at Don taking a set of red dice from behind the counter handing them to Don. "These are only eight bucks a set, most other places sell em for twelve; also I do appreciate the business and please let everyone you know who games I am here. I am hoping to expand once gramps retires."

Hutch was walking around the shelves in the book shop area looking on them, he leaned over a wooden trunk and reached in pulling out an old Bible. "Hey, these books for sale?"

Patrick looked at Hutch then at the door the old man went through. "Just a second, let me check," and he went through the door, a few moments later he came out. "Gramps is in his chair asleep, and they haven't been cataloged yet by him, but tell ya what. Go ahead and dig through them if ya find something ya want, I will sell it to ya, no problem." Patrick said smiling while eyeing the door the old man went through.

Looking towards the door Don could see that it had a curtain across it, and he could hear a television going on through it.

"Thanks, this place is actually kind of cool," Pat said looking over the dusty shelves and wooden boxes.

"Yeah, pretty cool indeed," Don said looking through a pile of books that sat on a table, covered with dust.

They spent the better part of an hour looking through the various old musty books that were in the various boxes when Hutch moved a box aside to expose a steamer trunk. The trunk was of average sized, with old leather bindings and a brass hasp keeping it closed. Opening it he sifted through papers and letters and an old musty quilt. Picking up one of the papers he could see it was a letter, yellow with age, in old ink writing to some chick named Mary Beth.

Mixed in with all the papers and such was a small brown book with an odd design on it, the design looked like a Twenty Sided dice. "Hey guys check this out, it has a D20 on the cover,"

Walking over quickly Don looked at the book that Hutch was holding. "Dammit Hutch! You always get the interesting things, that's cool!, what kind of game is it?"

Hutch opened the book and Don saw a puzzled expression in his face, he thumbed through the old cracking pages. "Man, I don't know. Don?, it looks like some weird language maybe Hungarian or something."

Don looked into the book and saw it was old, and had strange symbols and even some glyphs in it along with strange writing whose symbols and letters were strangely looping into each other. "Hutch, that may be some old chemistry book in Latin," Don said loudly so his voice would carry to Patrick. "Don't act too excited", Don said in a whisper to Hutch, "maybe the guy will sell it cheap."

Hutch walked over to the young man who was standing at the counter talking to James about the cards he bought,

"Hey Patrick, how much ya want for this old chemistry book?" he said this holding up the small book in one hand.

Patrick walked over looking at the book looking at it then looking over at the curtained doorway he shrugged. "Tell you what, give me ten bucks and its yours, I don't think Gramps will miss out on one of his precious old books."

Hutch smiling like a Cheshire cat, reached into his pocket and handed the guy a ten dollar bill. Outside there was a slight crack of thunder.

Walking over to one of the dirty windows and looking out it, Don saw it was getting overcast and saw low dark clouds scudding across the sky darkening the shop even more, "Hey look!, it's getting ready to freaking rain." Don said to the guys squinting through the glass into the suddenly grey sky. He turned to them in the shop and the shop suddenly seemed darker and colder.

"Awww, hell, no it better not be. I want me some mac salad and potato salad!" James said concerned.

Pat looked at James with a smile, shaking his head, he started to laugh. "Yeah always your stomach, never your brains," he said looking up from the Player's tome he was reading at the counter. However, he did look at the window and the encroaching darkness that was overcoming the shop.

After another twenty minutes of browsing the guys decided to leave. They all paid for their books and things and then left the shop and got into the car, a few rain drops spattering the windshield of Don's black Grand Prix.

"You know, that wasn't too bad a place. I think overall we made a good trip," Pat said happily while everyone seemed to agree with him, there was still a slight let down as the BBQ they were planning to have was not going to happen as it the sky seemed to open up just then, pouring rain.

"I thought you said it wasn't supposed to rain, Don?" Hutch said a little irritated wiping the fog from his glasses as it suddenly was very humid outside and in the car.

"Hey, don't shoot the messenger! I checked online this morning, and they said it was supposed to be nice. Don't blame me for Michigan's weather."

As they pulled out the rain started letting up some, talking of the strange shop and the odd combination of cool kid, and crazy old man, they agreed to still have a BBQ as they would just grill in the garage and after eating while the women did there thing they would spend a Saturday night gaming and relaxing.

When Hutch was dropped off at his place, he got his gaming stuff around and sat down to take a look at the new Alterverse RPG books he bought. After reading them for a bit, he picked up the old leather book. Looking at its cover he saw that the D20 on the cover didn't have numbers on it, instead it had on each facet of the dice a strange symbol.

"This is so cool" Hutch said to himself as he flipped through the pages. The rain outside increased and lightning flashed. "Emily, can you turn my computer off and unplug it please, it's thundering out now," Hutch yelled into the next room,

"Sure will" his girlfriend responded.

As he flipped through the pages he started to get excited: he knew this book was going to come in handy with the game he had set up for this evening. Hutch was, it seemed, always the Game Master, the one who actually ran the games.

He had an innate sense of creativity and could always be counted on to create the most involved and interesting situations for the games he ran.

Leafing through the pages he got a good look at his buy, the pages were yellow with age and were written on only one side, he could see the ink was from a real quill pen and the strange symbols and writing in it were formal and old.

"This may be Latin of some kind... interesting," he said to himself aloud as he leafed through the pages. "I think this eve's game is going to be a very interesting one," he said aloud to no one in particular.

"Whatcha got there? You get your books you been craving for finally, hun?" Emily said as she walked in the room, her hair wet and combed straight. She walked over to Hutch, her slight frame wrapped in a damp towel, her large brown eyes curious and a smile on her small mouth.

Hutch looked up to her smiling. "Yeah I got my fix, also I got a really cool old used book. Oh! The shop was a letdown, it was actually just a book store," he said looking up at her, his eyes going to the towel and of how much leg shown on her.

She looked at Hutch amused as she knew he was staring at her, so she tightened the towel smiling at Hutch's let down look. "Oh really that's a shame, a long way to drive for nothing then", she said with that same devious smile.

"No, I got what I wanted and this also," Hutch said holding the old leather book up smiling turning his attention back to the book.

Suddenly, a crack of thunder struck, flashing a bright light into their living room, startling them both.

Smiling at Hutch, Emily leaned over giving him a quick kiss on his lips. "Hey quit trying to peak down the towel, you were the one who wanted to go to the new game shop." She said in a teasing manner. "You missed out on an interesting morning." She laughed as she turned walking back towards the bedroom.

Stopping and turning, she seemed to remember something. "You know, Lee called and she said we are having a BBQ this eve. Are you sure that's a good idea in this rain and lightning?" she said this as she looked outside at the cracking thunder and down pour of rain that was causing the gutters to over flow.

Hutch looked at her and smiled. "It will be OK, we are cooking in Don's garage." He said this in such an innocent way causing Emily to shake her head smiling.

She then got serious, "Lee was talking today about divorcing Pat." Seeing Hutch's shocked look she went on, "She also told me that Pat hit her last night."

Hutch looked at her incredulously, "He did WHAT! I know he is a hot head, but hitting Lee... No way, I mean he actually hit her... Man those two are disintegrating. What a damn shame, they used to be attached at the hip." She nodded, sighed and turned then and went into the bedroom.

After Emily got ready, Hutch packed up his books and gaming things, went into the freezer grabbed a couple of steaks, and they got into the car and drove over to Don's house. When they arrived, they saw that everyone was already there except Lee. Walking in, the ladies started chatting and Hutch saw that Bri, James' wife and Pat were already in a heated game of Raven Crest, and they were arguing about some of the rules. Seeing them Pat said he was done and would resume it later, this caused Bri to start taunting him.

"Yeah, chicken out wimp, I am pulling the rules off the net. I am allowed to play a Level card in my turn, with a Turn the Tables card. And if I am right... and I am right, then you lose."

Pat looked at her laughing, "Yeah, right Bri, your play style is as bad as your memory. Pull the rules, I am right. You know it, you just get pissy when you lose. And you lost sweetie."

Bri took a deep breath in getting ready to most likely loudly respond when Emily broke in. "You two are as bad as my little kindergartners. Come on Bri let him think he won; we women know the truth."

Don, looking at Emily, opened his mouth to say something then Emily looked at him smiling, "Yes Don, you have something to say? Oh, and also when are you going to find a nice woman to settle down with? You need a good woman, you are the odd man out here. I have a nice cousin..."

Don looked at her with a feigned look of shock on his face, then smiled in a wicked manner, "Hell no. I am not saying anything, and as far as a woman, you drop one at my doorstep and I will take her, but I will pass on your cousin. I know her and I am not interested in a woman who has hairier legs than I do."

Emily looked at him, smiling, "One day Mr. Bachelor, you will find a woman to settle you down! Make ya a good proper husband,"

Pat looked over to Don, seemingly oblivious to his wife not being there, "Aw, come on Don, Hairy legs are great, just think of all those romantic evenings combing her legs," at this Hutch broke out laughing so hard the milk he was drinking spurted out of his nose, even Bri laughed. And at that the women started getting things ready for the dinner and the guys sat down at the table pulling their books and dice out, excited to be getting ready and prepared for another night of adventure.

The thing was that they had no idea exactly what the adventure was that they were going to truly go on with each other. It was going to be a very interesting evening for them all.

A Journey Begins

Woe be on your soul. For you have stumbled into my Dark
and vile home. For it is one that you will learn to loathe.

...... From the Hafarian Book of Dread

3
MAGIC UNEXPECTED

Their outside BBQ was canceled due to the rain and lightning, and the women decided to simply order pizza in. There was a pounding on the door, Emily got up opened it. Standing there was a rain soaked pizza delivery boy who looked thrilled to be out on an eve like this.

"Here ya go ma'am, that will be twenty seven eighty." Emily took the pizzas and handed them to Bri.

She looked into her purse taking some bills out, and handing them to the young man, said, "Here, keep the change." The man thanked her and walked off the porch into the hard rain.

The smell of pepperoni and cheese wafted through the dining room as Bri placed the three pizzas on the counter.

"Hey, sweet food!" James exclaimed hopping up from the table where they were arguing whose D20 was better.

"James, can't you wait till they get the plates, sheesh." Pat said looking up from the D20 he was holding up to the light, admiring it.

"Yeah, James, sit your butt down, we will bring it with the rest of the chow," Brim said good-naturedly as she smacked James's hand lightly with a spatula as he was lifting a pizza box lid.

"Damn, I'm starving now. And I gotta wait longer. Your mean!" he said smiling as he turned and walked back into the dining room, sitting down at the table.

As the evening wore on, the rain became stronger, it hit the windows like sheets. However, they all relaxed for about a half an hour, eating pizza and gabbing. Pat and James were still having an issue over their D20's.

"Yours isn't lucky, you couldn't roll over a ten 4 out of 10 rolls if your life depended on it!" Pat said poking his jaw out in a mocking manner.

James was holding his D20 between his fingers, it was orange with red spots on it, it was well worn and James claimed that a Pagan priest actually blessed it once many years ago. "Your dice is a heretical dice, mine has divine guidance. You're just jealous that mine was blessed."

Pat laughed out loud in a mocking manner, and Don and Hutch smiled with a familiar tolerance, as James told this story at least three times every game session.

"Divine whatever my butt. Tell me Roth God Jr., who was the priest, what is his name? Come on, and where was this done!" Pat chided James.

"I've told you, the man doesn't want his real name..."

Pat interrupted in a firmer mocking manner.

"I know he doesn't want to be exposed. HAH! Your dice is a fraud, that's why it can't roll a 20 if you rolled it thirty times!"

Don broke in, "Ok, Ok come on, let's get the game going you two. We got better things to do than..."

Hutch then interrupted. "Yeah let's get the game going ok, we shall be amazed at the Divine O' Dice and its rolls. See ya happy I am sticking up for you." Hutch said this with a Cheshire Cat grin on his face.

James was not pleased. He sat there upset. "You guys are going to see Crits galore rolled this evening you watch."

Pat rolled his eyes but kept his mouth shut. And to that they settled down for their game.

Hutch was the Game Master and had his adventure all planned out, and as night fall settled in they started their game.

"OK, you all are standing outside a large walled city, its tall walls sloping, a stout gate allowing entry with two bored looking guards at its entrance, both with rusted armor and conical helmets holding short halberds, half asleep." He stopped talking referring to one of his manuals.

There was a muttered quick talk amongst the players, then James spoke, "We are going to approach the guards, we are making sure our hands are away from our weapons and each of us take out a single gold piece from our pouches." And this is how the game went for the next couple of hours. As they played the rain continued outside with the occasional crack of thunder and flash of lightning. Emily, Hutch's girlfriend, looked out the window concerned,

"Don does you think you guys need to put up the patio furniture? It's pretty windy outside."

Don glanced out towards the patio door at the wind and the rain beating against it; he shrugged looking back to his manual that he had been open in front of him, "Nah, I think it will be OK, if they move around at all I will go out there." And the game continued.

About twenty minutes later Emily walked into the dining room and up to the table with her purse in her hand,

"Hey, me and the girls are going to the store; anything you band of heroes want us to bring back?" she said smiling.

James pulled out is wallet looking into it with a grimace, and then to Bri his wife. "Yeah bring back some of those cheesy curl things, the nacho flavor kind, Bri you got any cash on ya I am broke, I left my cash at the house on the kitchen counter." James patted his jean pockets, "And also bring back something to drink, maybe some ginger ale. I am craving ginger ale BAD,"

Emily looked around at the other guys at the table, "Well you two, you want anything else?" Pat and Hutch said nothing else was needed, and she left with Bri and left the guys to their game. As the game went on Hutch would tell the players what they ran into, or the situation they were in.

Dice were rolled, the clicking sounds that they made being rolled on the table, a welcome chime in the players' ears. The players would tell Hutch what they did or how they handled a given situation. The new books got a firm work out early on and everyone was having a good time. The women came back and placed the pop and snacks on the table, James immediately ripped open a bag of Cheesy Whips and reached in, grabbing some.

"Hey, don't put your nasty paws in the bag, ya'know someone else may want some." Hutch said to James.

"Yeah, damn James! that's nasty, I bet you didn't wash your hands after taking a leak earlier." Don added in with a smile.

James looked at them both, "Yeah I picked my nose also, enjoy," he said placing the bag on the table. Getting up he walked into the kitchen getting a large bowl down, he walked back in, sat down and poured two thirds of the bag into his bowl. He tossed the near empty bag back down, cracked open a bottle of Ginger ale and took a swig if it.

Hutch grabbed the pretzels and to that the game went on. After about twenty minutes they got back to the game; however, Hutch had a surprise for the players, now was the time to add some real flavor to the game.

As the game went on Hutch opened the old leather book he got at the old bookstore, and he opened it to the first page, the yellowed pages were brittle with age and they seemed heavy in a way, odd for a book. The strange writing in it gave him an idea, its unusual curved writing looped inside of itself twisting and running into each word. His idea took an immediate form and he ran with it.

"The old man you are facing is in the road, he is wearing a hooded robe, the hood is open and laying around his shoulders over his back, there are strange glyphs on the sleeves, he looks angry, and as you approach. he orders you to stop."

Don looked into his manual, as did Pat. "Ok, I am going to try to talk to him." Pat said looking at his Character record sheet. He spoke in his Characters voice, "We only want to pass my friend, we do not mean any ill will or intention."

Hutch looked to Don and James at the table, "You shall not go by as this is Dramark's road and no one may pass, unless they pay homage to his greatness!" Hutch toned in a firm loud voice.

James then spoke, cleared his throat and in a forceful tone said, "Move aside old man, or you will feel the sting of my sword."

Hutch raised an eyebrow. Knowing James he figured he would fall into his plans, and he smiled to himself.

"Hey moron, look, Hutch is smiling, you know what that means, he has something up his sleeve. Why are you threatening the old guy, he is obviously a wizard or mage." Don said to James in his Character's voice.

Hutch smiling and unconsciously rubbing the strange leather book ,spoke. "OK, the old man you can see has covered his head with his hooded robe, and you can see glowing runes on the edge of the hood, they seem to be moving." Hutch said smiling to the group.

"OK, I have a mage, I am stepping forward, and am going to prepare a shield spell," Pat said to Hutch as he looked into his player's tome in the spell section.

"OK, that's fine, as you step forward the mage in front of you in the road sees you and says, go back apprentice as you know not whom you stand before." As Hutch said this, he opened his Game Masters tome and read up on the Fire blast spell he was going to have his character cast at the group. Reading it and seeing what he needed to see he said to the group.

"OK Pat, we need to roll each a D20 to see who casts first." They then both rolled their D20dice, the dice clattering across the table and the papers that covered it and read up on the Fire blast spell he was going to have his character cast at the group. Reading it and seeing what he needed to see, he said to the group.

"Sweet! I got an 18 and you got an 11, I cast first," Pat said with glee as he won the roll, "I cast my spell. A Shield spell and I am a level 7 Mage so I can extend it thirty feet, so I am going to do that to cover my fellow adventurers."

Hutch smiled knowing the fire blast spell would cause at least half damage, not enough to kill them, but enough to make them sting a bit, "Your spell envelopes you with a shimmering glow as the protection spell surrounds you and your companions. You now see the Mage in the road chanting, you hear him say…" and at that Hutch looked at the first page in the book, now was the time to add some real flavor to the game, he started to read the first page of the book out loud.

"Luchar amentra seedol krail ethrenumer kal drakmart seek!" As Hutch was saying this a crack of thunder clapped louder than anything so far this eve with a flash of bright light startling the men, causing Don to jump in his seat, the lights flickered. Looking at the door Pat seemed concerned.

"Man, do we need to call one of the women on their cell phone; I don't like this weather and them being out in it."

Don looked outside again at the rain pounding against the patio door, "Yeah maybe one of you guys need to call the ladies and tell 'em to just come back."

James looked at the rain and lightning outside, "Nah, they will be ok, it's just raining, plus we don't have them interrupting us, they will be ok, and I am sure they will be back in a bit." He got a few dark looks at the table but no one said anything to him.

Hutch went back to the book. "Solararis darkum gringfor past incluserary momentum." after reading this passage Hutch heard a slight sound like a crackling tone, it seemed to be coming from somewhere very close, ignoring it, he felt odd as if he was a little dizzy and his fingertips felt warm.

"Man, can you turn on the ceiling fan Don, it's getting warm in here" Pat said to Don as he shifted in his seat.

"Yeah, I am feeling a little warm myself also a little woozy." Don got up and turned the ceiling fan on. The blades started spinning causing a slight breeze to fall over the players.

Hutch holding the book firmly in his hands went on to the final word, "OMARK" he raised his voice for dramatic effect.

Once he said that something odd happened, there was a bright light erupting from the book; shouting a yell of alarm Hutch attempted to drop the book. The rest of the guys tried to jump out of their seats. However, they were unable to move, the book glowed bright for a moment then went dark. Hutch's arms felt weak, the book felt so heavy, his arms fell to the table the book face open, his hands riveted to the book.

Hutch looked in fear at it, he wanted so badly to let it go, it seemed alive, pulsing in his hands, it was as if he felt it breathing. Fear soaked into him.

The book sat there for a moment, everyone's eyes locked on it. No one could move, let alone tear their eyes from it. The book shimmered, its open face then turned black, a low undulating hum came from the book like an alternating low and high tone and the book seemed to pulsate. Fear went through the table as the men sat there unable to move.

Don thought for a moment he might have blacked out and this was some strange and horrible dream, then a sucking sound came from the book and the men could feel themselves being pulled, their bodies seemed to shift and squeeze. They felt their faces being pulled, pain racked their bodies, and then they saw nothing but darkness as unconsciousness hit them.

Don awoke and felt groggy. He was on his back as he laid there his eyes blinking in an attempt to wake up. He was cold and his back and arms were wet. He laid there for awhile and looking to his right and left, he saw he was lying in grass. He looked up and saw that the stars in the sky were bright and a bluish silvery light enveloped him.

His head hurt badly and he had a hard time focusing his eyes. However, as he lay on his back, he came to the odd realization that he was outside, for some odd reason hit him funny that he just realized it. Blinking his eyes in an attempt to get the grogginess out of his head, he tried to sit up. As he leaned up to a half sitting position his body screamed to him, and he felt a wave of wooziness. He felt the chips and pop from earlier that evening hitting the back of his throat, he leaned to his right and threw up, the bile sour in his mouth.

Every bone ached and every muscle was sore. "What the hell happened" he muttered to himself, rubbing his arms and face, he saw Pat Hutch and James lying not far from him, he also saw his surroundings better now.

He was in a large field, dark trees were on one side and to his back, and another field was to the other side of him. However, between him and the other field there was a small dirt road he could see in the bluish silvery light. He sat there leaning, feeling the sick sensation finally leaving him, his arms shaking from the cool air, and then it occurred to him.

Panic struck him as he realized something, and he quickly looked into the sky again. There were two moons, one Silver the other one a bright blue. Both moons seemed close to each other like they were in orbit with each other, his heart dropped and lurched, and he got nauseated again,

"How in the hell is this possible?" he spoke out loud in amazement and fear, "there are two moons... this can't be. What the hell is going on here?" Looking around more he saw nothing else odd or strange, he realized then that he was wet because there was dew on the grass, and he could see steam coming from is breathing and his friends' breathing.

It was midsummer? "Why was it so cold outside? Also how in the hell are there two moons... what the flying hell is going on here?" he said to himself as he looked around rubbing his face and eyes.

Don slowly stood up his legs feeling like jelly, he stood there for a second the blood rushing to his head, his evening dinner almost coming back up yet again, he clenched his jaw holding it back.

Closing his eyes he thought, "This has to be a dream, this has to be something, this isn't real, I must be asleep or drugged. That pizza guy must have drugged our pizza," he walked over to Pat who also seemed to be waking up, "Pat ,you ok?" Pat was on his back opening his eyes wide trying to shrug off the grogginess,

"What the heck happened?" Pat said sitting up slowly. "Damn what the hell did Emily drop me a Mickey or what?" Pat said, then looking up at Don, he saw the moons over Don's shoulder. With a start. he jerked his head, "Don what the heck is going on here?, there are two moons in the sky!" He tried to sit up falling back on his butt on the ground, holding his head in his hands.

Don looked at Pat, concerned, "I know to man, I know something is going on Pat. I am not sure what, but we are not in Michigan, I don't think... I just don't know what is going on." Don helped Pat to his feet helping him steady, as Pat went through the same thing as Don did. In the next ten minutes, the other two guys woke up, with similar effect and results.

"WHAT! Is that two moons? Is this some joke," James said loudly as he looked into the sky. They were all looking around in various states of shock and disbelief, as Pat went through the same thing as Don did.

"Man I don't know what the hell is going on, are we drugged or what?" Hutch said as he kept looking at the twin moons in the night's sky, "why is it so chilly it's August, we are supposed to be hot as hell. Did that storm bring cooler weather or what?" Hutch said aloud while holding his stomach.

"Man, Hutch I don't think we are in Michigan, don't you see those moons I don't even know what planet we are on, what the freaking heck?" Pat said afraid looking around desperately.

Don cleared his throat, he was panicked but was settling down a bit."Look we have to get our bearing here, we need to find out first where we are and what or where the hell this place is, two moons, cold outside... there's a road there," Don said pointing to the road that sat there like a scar on the field. "maybe it leads someplace? We need to find a house... anyplace and ask the home owners for the closest police station or whatever, maybe use their phone, so I can call my sister's cell. We need help but panicking like little girls paint gonna get it."

Reaching into his pocket with a worried expression James spoke. "I aint panicking Don, but this is not like we are stuck in Detroit with a flat; have you looked in the freaking sky," his voice raising an octave or two. He was patting his pockets, "Plus my cell was in my pocket, and now it is gone, it may have fallen out or something. He said this and started to look around the grassy area where he was laying.

"I have looked dumb ass, and I am scared to freaking death James, but this yelling back and forth isn't going to fix this, I don't know what the hell happened or what went on, but we need to work together".

Hutch then stepped forward between them, "Look guys, we all are friends, before we do anything let's think dammit! What was the last thing we all remember?" He said this while rubbing his face.

"You were reading from that book then a light, and I am here," James said he was patting his pants pockets again and his shirt pockets. "I got my keys, and cigs and lighter that's it." James said.

"Yeah you were reading I heard a weird noise the thunder clapped, there was a light, and then I woke up in this field." Don said, then thought feeling his pants pocket. "Wait a sec, I got my cell, some cash and change. Maybe my cell... I will call my brother." He then opened the cell, the blue light illuminating his face in the strange darkness, he stood there waiting for a sec, he then got a disgusted look on his face. "Nothing!, it's dead," He looked at the lit face of the phone. "Yeah it says no service."

"My wallet isn't here, I left it on the table, but I got my keys and a pack of Wiggles gum, HEY, I got a flashlight on my key chain." He said this as he pressed a button on it, a thin beam illuminated the ground, he then clicked it off, "What the heck, what happened here?"

"Well then it's the book that did it?, what the hell I only read a few lines felt odd then it did all kinds of things, could it really be magic, I mean magic isn't real.. Right?" Hutch said this with fright in his voice. Hutch then patted his pocket and with a huge smile pulled out his cell phone. "I got mine also, we can make a call, I am calling Emily, just a sec." And he then opened his cell, hitting the send button he sat there for a few minutes listening then tried it again several times. "No bars and no signal. Let me check my voice mail." He then reopened the cell phone hitting some buttons, the cells light illuminating his face. "No voice mail, no nothing my cell won't work here. What the hell?" Then patting his pockets, he pulled out a D20, a set of keys and a pocket knife, and about twenty bucks in cash.

Don looked to the group with concern. "Man, Hutch I don't know, that book went off once you read those words, magic isn't supposed to be real, I would think this was a prank but the sky... those moons... Those are real, man, I am frankly scared to death here, but we gotta figure this out." He was afraid they all saw that, "What the hell are we going to do," Don asked to no one in particular.

Hutch spoke up, "We need to find out where we are, and also what happened, let's get our asses moving, someone has to be around here."

The group muttered an approval to his plans, and then Pat pointed something out to the group. "Hey guys.. Hutch where you were laying, look.. the book is laying there," they all looked and on the ground was the leather book it was just sitting there, the four men looked at it, as if they expected it to come alive grow legs and arms and attack.

"Man, heck with that thing, let's leave it, that thing is something I am not sure what, but it's something?" James said pointing at the book with a look of revulsion on his face.

"Look, we need to take it, if it got us here, wherever here is then maybe it can get us back home." Pat said looking around in the silvery darkness, "I also think we need to talk to someone."

"I agree we need to bring it with us, that damn thing got us wherever here is, and I bet it can get us home or at least maybe someone knows what it is, man this is too unreal... it's like some movie. James did you put some LSD in our salsa this eve?" Don said looking at James with a forced grin.

The friends stood around for a few moments while the effects of their trip wore off fully, they all started looking around their surroundings, they saw they were in a field and there were woods to one side and a narrow dirt road to the other side. The air was cold and Don suddenly wished he had pants on, his legs were suddenly very cold, and he had goose bumps. Then as they looked around they heard a low howl from the wooded area followed by some snorting sounds and a light rustling noise.

They were all startled, and James felt a lick of panic hit him, "Let's just get the damn book and get the hell out of here." He said eying the woods apprehensively. They agreed and Hutch volunteered to carry it as he was the one who read it and got them here in the first place.

Looking around they made a quick agreement to stand by each other Hutch placed the small book in the cargo pocket of his camo pants and then the group approached the road.

The road was a small one lane track, it was rough and pitted, and it winded into the dark distance; the group of guys started walking down it looking for a house or a store or gas station. Anything that they could maybe find out what was going on and where they were exactly.

The Road to Who Knows

Do not fret lost traveler..
For you are now my guest and are welcome...

- Amarian Proverb

4
A FRIGHTENING SITE

They traveled for about thirty minutes down the road in the dual moonlit, the road was rough with many ruts and holes causing the men to trip on some of them in the darkness. They crested at a small rise, and they saw about fifty feet off the road a couple of tents and a small fire with about six people around it, off to one side were several horses and a wagon with several large burlap bags in it. The people were dressed funny.

"Look, there are people there let's go talk to them," James said and started towards them at a fast walk.

Grabbing James by the arm lightly Hutch cautioned, "James let's take this one easy, we don't know who they are, and what they may think of us. And look at the clothes they are wearing, they are wearing leggings and cloaks." James looked at him angrily for being pulled back but did stop and looked closer.

"You know something isn't right here, they are carrying swords, and look at that big one he has a chain mail shirt on and his sword is out next to him. I don't like this at all guys something doesn't fit?" Don said quietly standing in the cold.

As they stood there one of the horses whinnied and shuffled its feet and the large man stood up looking into the darkness. He was tall and had a rough beard, he grabbed his sword and stepped out of the fire's light peering in the general direction of the group of men.

"Down!, he is looking this way." Hutch said in a hushed voice kneeling down, and they all laid down on the edge of the road hugging the dirt, their hearts pounding in their chests with fright. The large man said something to the others, and they laughed then he went to the horses checked on them, walked around them a bit then went back to the camp and sat down where he originally had been.

"Let's leave now!" Pat said and everyone quietly agreed, they hunched down and quickly moved away on the other side of the road, cold and tired they walked for another hour not running into anything, then decided to settle down and talk, and get something more firm in the way of a plan worked out.

"This isn't working at all, I don't know what's happening here but those people were dressed like Ren fair goers and the big guy was dressed like a berserker or something." Don said aloud in a worried voice nodding his head back towards where the camp was.

"You know I don't know what to say Don, Pat what do you think here? They don't look like Larpers, they look like they are real, like real people doing what is normal for them." Hutch asked looking at Pat in a pleading manner.

"It's like we are in one of our games living it, the only thing missing is a goblin and a troll to come by and try to eat us," Pat said with a nervous laugh.

"Hey guys, I'm taking a leak, be right back," James said and walked about twenty feet away the others looked at him, Pat looked at Hutch and shrugged.

"Well we need to get smart here and at least look the part, this may just be some community like the Amish or something, you know the type of people who live their religion or something?" Hutch said.

"Umm hey guys come here..." James said his tone kind of off. Hutch looked at him in irritation. "Just a sec James, we are trying to get this planned out."

James spoke again.

"Umm, guys get your asses over here you want to see this... NOW" James said, and the panicked tone in his voice made everyone come over to him. James was standing there urine on his leg, he had a really frightened look on his face and was pointing across the road into a small field.

The others looked and saw what James was looking at. A man was standing in the field across from them; he did not see them but had a very long sword trailing behind him. He was making a strange hooting sound waving his arms. The group knelt down quietly trying not to make any more sounds or make themselves seen by the strange man,

"It's a guy James. What's the huge yank?" Hutch whispered to James. Then as Don looked and his eyes adjusted better to the odd light he saw what James was talking about, it was not a sword trailing behind the man it was a large tail, and it wasn't a man, it was manlike but shorter, and it had tusks and a snout, its hooting caused others like it to come out of the forest along the edge of the field. They walked with their hands holding evil looking curved weapons, also they had more of a hunched gait than a walk, and they stood there smelling the air pointing their faces to the air.

"Oh, my God!" Pat said fear gripping him. He looked over to James then to Don with fear in his eyes; the fear was felt by all seeing these things.

"Stay down don't make a sound." Hutch said in a hushed panicked voice, causing Don to look over at him and seeing fear in Hutch's face that he had never seen before. They all laid down hugging the ground, looking at the hideous creatures through the grass. The monsters gathered for a few minutes then hooted as a group and took off running down the road back from where the group just walked.

"Oh, my God, what if they smell us and follow our scent back?" Don said, fear sprouting from him as his thoughts went to visions of seeing his guts yanked out by one of these creatures.

"Man, I say we run like hell and get out of here NOW!" Pat said while starting to get up,

"NO!" Don said grabbing him and pulling him back down. "I think we should stay put right here on this spot and not move till daylight." Pat with fear in his voice whispered with a pleading look to his friends. "Those looked like Orc's man, freaking Orc's from my Critter catalog, they had damn tails, did you all see that!" Pat said scared pointing down the road at the monsters who by now were disappearing into the strange dual moonlight.

"Yeah I saw that and they had pig snouts, they took off in a hurry, why?" James asked. "Man this is way too fricking much, I want to go home, this is just out there man," James said visibly upset.

The group stayed hunched beside that road afraid to move, as if afraid that by moving, they would call the monsters to them. They laid there till the next morning with sleep coming fitfully in the cold night air as each man was afraid to go to sleep in case the monsters came back. They curled up cold, each one hoping they would wake up in their own beds.. However, after a mostly sleepless night they awoke to frost on the grass, their breathe steaming in the early dawn. They were still there.

The morning was cold and as they sat there in the early dawn hour cold, hungry and still afraid. The gravity of their situation seemed to hit them all. "I am beat and hungry as hell," James said looking around yawning rubbing his belly.

"You know bud I have to agree with ya, I am so hungry I can eat a plate of Pats old ladies goulash." Hutch said in an attempt to be light. It didn't do much to ease the mood among the men.

Don stood up in the cold morning air stomping his feet trying to get his legs warm, in the night they started cramping due to the cold and laying on the cold wet ground. "Where are we? I don't get it," he said looking around with a worried frown on his face. "we have to find out where we are, I say we go back to that camp back there." Don said pointing down the road.

"What about those things that went that way Don? Here we are, we don't know where we are. Or really even when we are, no food, no clothes, is it fall or spring? It's cold and what if winter is setting in? We don't have any money, have no clue to the customs... we are seriously screwed." Pat said with consternation in his face.

"I agree we go back that way," James said pointing to back where they came. "I mean, its daylight or getting there, we can now yell to them from the road, maybe they won't take it as hostile as walking up in the middle of the night?"

The men talked about the idea, they hoped the campers would at least offer some basic news of where this place was. And to that they all agreed to go back the way they came as it was getting daylight and they could see in the cold mist of early morning their surroundings better. They saw they were surrounded by fields and forest, so they knew they could see any problems before they happened, so at that the tired group headed down the road.

As they walked, they talked of many things, of home wherever that was, of the monsters they saw last night. Their first night here, where ever that was exactly was not a good one. Don had a habit of getting headaches, really bad ones. And this morning he had one. Pat looked at Don and saw his face.

"Got a headache, dontcha?"

Don looked at him. "Yeah couldn't have been lucky to leave those behind huh." He rubbed his face sighing. "This is going to suck, I know it."

They walked and as they came around a bend on the road, they saw the encampment. It was about two hundred yards away, sitting there in the misty cold air, a thin wisp of smoke from the camp fire pit slowly rising up into the hazy cold air.

As they approached the encampment they saw that the fire was almost out, its grey blue smoke slowly wafting up in the cool air. The horses were gone. The wagon was still there, its contents seemed to be all over the ground. The tents were collapsed and there was debris all over. The men stopped looking around themselves to make sure nothing was going to jump out at them.

"Something isn't right here", Hutch said in a whisper.

"You know, I wonder if those monsters came here, maybe that's where they were headed, no one is around. I say we go to it." Don said looking closely at the camp area and the smoking fire.

"No, not all of us just one or two of us in case the owners are around or worse... those things." James said.

Hutch looked at him with a smirk that really didn't have any humor in it. "And are you volunteering James?" Hutch said. Hutch looked over at Pat then to Don and coughed in the cold air, clearing his throat, he seemed to almost say something but did not.

"Look James, you want to go with me?" Don said looking at James seriously, "let me and you go there and check it out, if shit goes south we can run like hell and not draw attention to everyone," Don said with a worried look.

James looked at him then at Pat and Hutch who were looking at him seriously, shrugging James smiled "What the hell why not, after all the worst that can happen is we get eaten by Orc's."

"Look you two, be careful, this doesn't smell right at all, that camp is really close to the woods, be careful ok, you Don don't have a widow to bury ya, and you James... we argue, but you are still my bud," Hutch said. James and Don smiled at Hutch and started to make their way to the camp.

As they approached Don was looking all over the place, his head hurt badly, and he wished he had some aspirin. Slowly, they approached in the misty cold air, and Don started to get Goosebumps on him. He knew this was real and didn't like it one bit. He thought to all the times while in a game that he ran into similar situations, the worse real worry, he had then was to get a bowl of chips to snack on. Now as he walked doing this for real, he worried he was going to be the snack.

As they got closer there were a couple of swords on the ground with caked on dried blood on them, and also one of the tents was splashed with blood. The ground was trampled and there were items from the tents scattered all over, pots and pans, leather cups, a lantern. Bags ripped open lying about and clothes were all over the place. There was even a small child's doll lying on the ground, it looked so forlorn just laying there, and Don had a ping of sorrow at the thought of one of those monsters carrying off the doll's little owner.

It was obvious that there had been a huge fight. They walked around the ruined camp, both men were quiet, their thoughts to themselves. As he walked to one side of the ruined camp James called to Don waving him over to him.

"Don" He said in a hushed voice, "Come here check this out, I found one of them." As Don approached James, he saw James was wiping his mouth, he looked down, lying along the edge of the back side of the camp was a woman. She had been slashed and stabbed several times, her dress ripped open and blood soaked, Don felt a need to vomit like James just had, and it took a lot to hold down the bile that was hitting the back of his throat. He looked at James, and then to her, and then they both seemed to notice it at the same time.

"Don, her eyes... they are gone, look! They have been cut out." Don shook his head feeling sick and he looked away.

"This is bad James, it is obvious they lost the fight; if the men were around, they wouldn't have left her lay here, not saying I am right, but I don't think those men are alive, and I found a small doll. James I think there was a little girl here."

James looked at Don with a surprised look on his face. "A little girl? Are you serious? What could they have done with them all? And this woman... I know we in our games talk about this, but she looks so bad." James said to Don looking around with his face red, and his eyes red also. Don, for some reason also, felt tears welling up.

"Also, there is heavy frost and the only tracks are the ones we left." James said looking even more closely around. Don forced a smiled to himself as he was glad James was finally thinking and not panicking. James walked over to the edge of the encampment and yelled the OK to the others to come over his voice unusually loud sounding as it echoed in the clearing.

The others started walking toward the encampment, and as they approached, they seemed to have the same reaction as Don and James had.

"Look guys, there is a dead woman over there, she is pretty hacked up and her eyes are even gone. So don't freak when you see her, ok?." Don said. Hutch walked over looking at her then leaned over and threw up,

"Man, we got to do something about her, we need to bury her or something," Hutch said wiping his mouth with his sleeve.

"Look, I bet all of these people are dead, but we can benefit from this. We need to gather everything up we can, we need clothes, weapons, anything we can find and use. We don't know how long we are going to be here, and we stick out like a sore thumb, we need to blend in." Pat said to everyone.

Everyone agreed and as each one looked around and started gathering things, Don and Hutch dragged the dead woman off away from the camp. Don went back, grabbed a torn blanket and covered her up. He stood there for a moment looking at her covered body and decided he hated this place. He also decided that gaming was not for him anymore. How could he Role Play a scenario where something like this happened? He sighed, his head feeling like it was going to explode, he hurt so badly... but had to move on. He decided also that he would find a way home, and then started to look around.

"Hey look, I found one of the monsters!" Don heard Hutch yell from over by the wagon. Don ran over to Hutch, who by now had James and Pat standing there. As he ran up his nostrils were hit with the smell of what only could be described as a cross between a wet dog, and a dirty cat litter box.

"Ugly bastard isn't he." James said quietly, taking his boot and nudging the dead thing.

"Yeah you got that right, he also smells like cat shit, and look at his fur, it's all matted." Hutch said covering his nose.

Don stood there and felt again like he was going to puke, his headache was not helped by the smell, and he also felt suddenly woozy.

"Yeah, he is dead. Wow see his skull it's all crushed in, his tongue is hanging out, reminds me of a dead deer on the road." Pat said smiling.

"How can you just smile, you are looking at a freaking monster, this isn't a deer. I mean shit!, we have to be the first humans to see something like this." Don said irritated. For some reason, his friend's blasé attitude over the monster laying there pissed him off.

Looking back at the monster laying there, Don saw he was big. His fur was lightly covering its pink skin and he was reminded of an Armadillo skin. He had no armor or weapon, and his face had indeed a pig snout and a single horn coming from his forehead. Curving up, curling.

"Well I guess they strip their dead... huh?" James said quietly, he wasn't wanting to agitate Don, he knew he had one of his headaches.

Don had suddenly a cool idea, he pulled out his cell phone, "I'm taking some pics of this thing. NO one is going to believe a word of this when we get home." There was a muttering of an agreement. He pressed some buttons aiming the cell phone at the thing on the ground. Smiling he folded it and put it back in his pocket. "Well at least they are good for something here." He said smiling suddenly.

"Man I gotta get pics of that from you, ok." James said. James then peered over Don's shoulder as if seeing something. Looking to his right across the field he saw it.

"Look there is one of the horses!" James exclaimed causing everyone to about have a heart attack. Sure enough about fifty yards away the horse was standing eating grass, his head bowed, steam coming from its nose as it breathed in the cold morning air. Pat walked towards it and as he got closer the horse stomped its foot and snorted; Pat closed slowly and laid a hand on its neck, patting it lightly, the horse looked at Pat and nudged him and Pat lead it back to the camp.

"Does anyone know how to hook a horse to a wagon?" Pat said with a perplexed look on his face.

"Are you joking, I am a software engineer." Hutch said smiling, and at that they tied the horse to the wheel of the cart and continued to forage. After about an hour they had in the wagon a nice pile of items: clothes, a few swords, a shield, the lantern, three flasks of oil some leather bags that were intact, and several sets of boots. They managed to salvage two of the tents that did not have any blood on or in them. They also managed to salvage a huge pile of yams that had been scattered about. They placed these in the cart also. Hutch took the time to get the fire going again then pulled out some cheese and a few loaves of hard stale bread to eat that was found in a large box - it seemed the monsters did not have a taste for bread and cheese. They divided it up and ate quietly. They all stood around the fire getting warm and worked out a plan.

"Look, we use the wagon to travel by, and we change into the clothes we found, then we now will look normal. The problem is that night time around here doesn't seem like a good time to be out and about, so we will need to find someplace safer like a town or village." Pat said while chewing a mouthful of bread.

"Yeah, I agree with Pat We also should figure out about these yams, we will need money, and maybe we can sell them at the next town, get a hotel or something?" James said hopefully.

"We become Wagoner's, wow! from paupers to proper merchants in a flash, I am impressed." Don said cynically with no humor, and at that they changed into the clothes they found, as Pat walked out from behind the wagon where he was changing James laughed. Pat was standing there and was not happy his wool pants were about four inches too short.

"Man, Pat you look like a medieval Erkel," Hutch said laughing hard, causing the others to also laugh.

"Yeah, laugh it up funny guy, your belly sticks out the bottom of your doublet." Pat said to Hutch, causing Hutch too look quickly down.

Seeing his belly wasn't sticking out he looked at Pat, "Yeah, funny guy you are Pat," and at that they gathered up their clothing they had taken off, placing all of it in a burlap bag, they placed the bag into the back of the wagon. Don and James put on brown wool pants that were loose, Don also put on a set of leather tall boots tucking the pants into them and a dark green doublet over his shirt. His legs were finally thawing out, and he felt suddenly very tired. His head still pounded, however, eating something made it feel a little better.

"How's the head?" Hutch asked placing a hand on his shoulder.

Don looked at him, smiled. "It's better since I ate." He said with a forced smile.

After moving the yams around in the wagon and also the equipment they salvaged, Pat and Don got the horse hooked up the best they could figure out, and they took the tents and the rest of the things they found, and placed them neatly in the back of the wagon and Hutch and James climbed in the back while Don and Pat climbed into the wagon's front seat.

"Hey guys, what about the lady, we need to bury her, right?" Hutch said aloud looking in the direction of where she laid. Looking up at the circling birds over the camp Don spoke up,

"Hey buddy, look up there, those are vultures, and they are letting everyone and everything in a ten mile radius know something is dead here." Seeing Hutch's look Don decided to just get it over with. "Fine, who is helping me bury her?"

Hutch jumped out of the wagon. "I will, she is a woman and deserves to be at least put to rest." And to that the other two men jumped out. They dug a shallow grave with a shield and a sword as best they could, Pat and James gathered some rocks.

They placed her lifeless body in the hole. Pat asked the question. "What should we do, say a few words. I mean is she Christian or what?"

"I don't know, I can say something I guess..." Hutch said sheepishly. He stood there for a second then cleared his throat.

"Although this woman will walk through the shadow of death, may no evil harm her..."

James interrupted him. "Hutch, that isn't the right way to say it. Let me..."

"Look I got this ok... Man just let me do this." Hutch said with irritation in his voice. "Let no evil touch her, and may the child that was with her be safe. Amen."

The rest of the men feeling awkward said Amen, they stood there placing rocks on the grave. Pat walked away, and then came back with the doll. He brushed the doll off with his hand, then placed the doll on the top of the grave.

"Maybe it was her kids. If so I think she would have wanted it there." The men stood there for a brief second, all four men's eyes were welling up with emotion, clearing throats and wiping their faces, they walked away from the forlorn grave in the morning light. One last time they went over the encampment looking for anything of use, finding nothing they got into the wagon.

"Well, I am sure this is far from being over." Pat said looking at the vultures circling, and at that they took off down the road and into what they had no idea, but they hoped that they could get home soon, their loved ones were on their mind, each one thinking of what the women were going through and thinking.

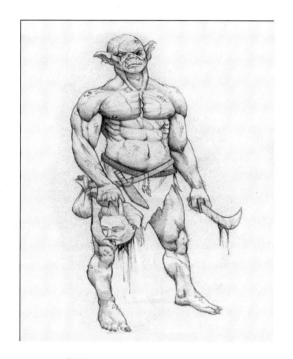

They come for the
unknowing camping Adventurers

Do not worry for when death comes....
You will not care for you will be dead.

...... Hafarian Proverb

5
STRANGERS

They rode the wagon down that road for about an hour the wagon seeming to find every large hole and bump in the road, its rattling wheels clamoring and banging, causing the men to wish they had a car. When they crested at a small hill and saw a rider approaching them on a skinny bone thin horse, the rider had no shoes on, and he was old and had a yellow stained bushy beard. As they approached him, he moved his horse over to make room for them. "Let's talk to this old guy," Hutch said over Dons shoulder from the back suddenly snapping out of his melancholy and James murmured an agreement.

"Yeah I agree to just sit back and look uninterested, so he doesn't freak out." Pat said over his shoulder. The group slowed the wagon down to a stop and the rider stopped next to them,

"Good Morn me Masters, how can I help ye?" the old man said in a scratchy voice, he seemed sickly thin and like he didn't have a care in the world.

"We are looking for the nearest village or town good Sir" Pat said. Chuckling the old man replied,

"Good Sir, he-he... now no disrespect but I never been called that", he looked at them for a second, "The Great city of Dark Home[4] is near ten leagues over towards those mountains", He said pointing to the players right. "And the Town of Drakmar[5] is near three leagues over there" he said pointing to the left of the group. He looked at them a bit closer, "No disrespect good masters, but if you are wanting to get rid of those yams ye may try Dark Home, it's on the great river just West of the Spikey Peaks so ye may get better prices, that's where me master sells his cabbages and hogs."

Don looked at the old man, "Thanks to you old man, you have helped us a lot, I think Dark Home it will be."

Then James leaned over the wagon's edge and spoke up.

"Tell me old man, are there any dangers on the road? Anything we should be worried about?"

The old man looked at James a little surprised. "Do ye mean more dangerous than the Orc's that infest this area? Not really, I mean Goblins come down once in awhile from the mountains, but they tend to only come in little groups, cowards more than anything, and we aint seen no Cave Creepers out yet, it's a little early in Leave Turn for that. But if ye keep a big fire then the Orc's usually stay away. But be careful the closer ye get to the mountains as there be all sorts of critters creeping around them areas."

James and Hutch sat back in the wagon, "Orc's, Goblins, what's next?" James said afraid and at that they bid the old man farewell and rode for a bit then had a small meeting, they stopped the wagon and everyone got out stretching their legs.

---

[4] The second largest city in Amaria, only outsized by Loc-Amar itself
[5] Located in the South Eastern area of Amaria

Pat was pacing around obviously irritated. "Goblin, Orcs, and what the hell is a Cave Creeper! I don't care how, I don't care what, but we need to get home. THANKS! Hutch for doing this."

Hutch walked forward and for a moment Don thought he was going to hit Pat. "Blame me all you want! I don't give a shit! I am not going to become the whipping boy here by any of you just because the fricking book was magical. Tell me something, and I mean all of you… When was the last time on the news you heard of magic!"

Don stepped forward, "No one is blaming you Hutch, we just…"

Hutch interrupted. "He is!" he said pointing a finger at Pat angrily.

"We all need to calm down ok, this is no one's fault. But I do want to go pay that game shop another visit when we get home." Don said with a scowl.

"Are we going to ever get home guys?" James asked quietly in a melancholy voice.

Calming down Hutch turned to James. "Yeah, we will. We just gotta find out where we are, and what the hell happened."

Taking a deep expansive breath, then letting it out James perked up. "OK, are we going to the big city or the small town, we need cash, so I vote the closest town, also it will be better info, and maybe we can sell this wagon also do ya think they make one with shocks on it." James said looking at them all.

"Sell this wagon, hell no!, are you going to fricking walk James", Pat said frustrated looking at James angrily. "No offense but a league is three miles, so that city is thirty miles from here and that's if the old man has his mileage right that means we stay outside for another night maybe two. Hell no I say we beat feet for that village" Pat said.

"Look I say we think this out guys, maybe we ride towards that city, if it's a city then there's also a chance we may get help with this damn book.", Hutch said holding up the leather book in his hand. "Also we can stop by a farm or something maybe ask to stay in their barn, pay 'em with Yams hell anything to get off the road!" Hutch said.

"Did anyone hear that old man say Leave Turn, he said it was still early Leave Turn? Maybe we are in the Fall here? I say we do Hutch's idea and go to that city, help could be there and frankly the sooner we get help, the sooner I am in bed with a warm Lee." Pat said to them all smiling. He looked at Hutch then, "Look I didn't mean to blame ya, I know it isn't your fault."

Hutch looked at Pat still seemingly angry. "Whatever, but don't blame me again. I didn't do this, the book did."

Deciding to break the tension Don then spoke up, "Yeah I think the city is the best, and also we can get more info and also some help with that book Hutch is carrying, but I say if we go for the city then we also try to get shelter. Maybe stop at a farm, Hutch had a good idea; we can barter barn space for yams. Big fire or not I don't want to tango with any of those Orcs, Goblins or whatever the hell a Cave Creeper is" So at that they agreed to go to the city and see if they could find help, they all agreed, that is except James.

"Look. Why is it, you all always disagree with me, my opinion matters here also you know?" He said indignantly.

Hutch looked t him angry, "Look James this isn't us ganging up on you. It's called a majority vote, in case you aint figured it out where ever the hell we are having REAL things that go bump in the night!"

Then Pat chimed in, "Yeah did you hear that old man, Orcs, Goblins and what the hell is a Cave Creeper? Anyway, get pissed all ya want but the sooner I am home the better. If that means I go to this city through an Orc den then I say let's do it!"

And at that they got back onto the wagon and headed towards the huge mountains in the distance, their snowy peaks high. They could see snow on the faces and large hills and smaller mountains in the distance also with a large forest.

They rode on that bumpy old wood wagon until they came to a small track that seemed to go towards the mountains that the old man pointed out to them, it was mid afternoon and the sun was warm on their faces and Don's headache finally was gone. They rode for about an hour when the track ended at a large forest, the trees yellow red and gold and some of them were a light sky blue.

"Man, do you see those leaves, I gotta get some of them for Emily." Hutch said eagerly.

"Do you really want to pick something from this place?" Don asked causing Hutch to change his mind.

The small track they were on entered the forest and disappeared into darkness into the cool woods. "Shit, if we are going to follow this then we are going to have to go into the woods," Don said concerned squinting as if trying to see if there were anything hostile in the wood line. They looked at the woods and the trees looked like any tree they would see at home except for the blue leaves, they heard birds chirping, and it smelled like Fall in the way that it does when the leaves turn and start to fall to the ground.

Hutch hopped out of the wagon, looking at the road in front of them, "Look there are ruts in the road and also some horse hoof tracks, and they look fresh?"

James then also hopped out followed by Don and Pat. James stood there looking at the woods then turned to everyone "You know you're right, also now that we are close those woods look like any normal woods, the problem is we should have asked that old man more about those Orcs and where they live at. I know in my books they live in caves, not woods."

There was a muttering of agreement and to that they got back into the wagon. Don slapped the reigns to the horse, and it slowly pulled forward and they entered the woods. As they entered the confines of the woods. they noticed it was much cooler, the trees were mainly what looked like a mixture of Maples and Pines with a smattering of a strange looking tree with a bright red bark and maroon dark red leaves, they could hear birds chirping, and also they could hear the scurrying of little things in the fallen leaves. The path opened up a little as they entered, and they could see mottled sunshine on the floor of the woods and path along with the tracks, the road they were on went into the woods several hundred yards then veered off to the right, they traveled for several hours and as the day wore on it got cooler and then they entered into a small clearing just as dusk was starting to fall.

The clearing was shrouded in trees. However, there was a small brook running through it, the sound of its splashing on the small rocks echoing in the wooded clearing. There were low bushes and some stumps where one could tell someone cut down some of the trees most likely for firewood. They could see that the area was well worn with many old fire pits where evidently travelers spent the night.

They rode into the clearing and stopped the wagon. Hopping off, Pat spoke first. "Look stay here and let me take a look around; those things if I remember didn't have shoes so let me see if I can see any tracks."

James hopped off also stretching and arching his back, moaning, "Yeah let me go with ya, my legs are killing me," and at that they took a look around. A few minutes later, they came back and reported to Don and Hutch that they couldn't find any tracks. After a short talk, they then decided to make the clearing there home for the night.

"You know I think we are going to be in these woods for who knows how long, so we might as well make this our Alamo for the night." Don said to them as he hopped off the wagon.

"Yeah, I will go gather fire wood. There seems a lot of dead fall in this place, we can make a big fire and at least stay warm," Hutch said while reaching into the wagon for a sword.

"Yeah a big fire, remember what that old man said about the Orcs, I don't feel like ending up like that lady," Pat said. And at that they went off to the edges of the clearing and started gathering wood. Don and James started removing things from the wagon James shifted pulling at his pants,

"You know these pants are riding up me, I don't know how they got by in old times?" he said grimacing as he pulled at the crotch of his pants. Don simply smiled and at that they set to camp up as best as they could. Soon they had a good fire going, and they sat around it with their meager remaining bread and cheese.

"What about food, stale bread and old cheese isn't my bag man." Hutch said to them all smelling the bag that held his share of their meager provisions.

"Yeah, I agree maybe we could find some fish in the brook." James said hopefully looking at the small narrow brook that was bubbling not far away.

"No there isn't any, it's fresh water and drinkable though, I checked: no fish or snails, crawfish or anything, which sucks, maybe we can look for some roots or something." Don said to James. And so they settled down and quietly talked for the next few hours. Soon they got tired and decided to take turns at keeping watch and to that the night went on, no one really slepvery well tht night as they all worried about the creatures that may be in the woods. However, their first night in the woods went by without incident and the next morning, sore, tired and hungry they packed up their meager things and got back onto the wagon and continued on.

As they continued through the forest, they saw more of those red barked trees and James soon had to pee. "Hey, pull over I gotta piss bad," James was shifting in his seat.

"Yeah, I agree, I have to take a leak also" Pat said. So they stopped. James walked into the edge of the forest and went to pee on one of the red barked trees, as he stood there peeing he looked around he saw a squirrel run up one of the red barked trees and then saw the tree open a mouth and swallow the squirrel whole. James jumped back and yelled. "WOWA", the other ran over to him, James ran to the guys zipping his fly up,

"What's wrong, what happened?" Don yelled as they ran to him seeing he was white with fright.

"Man those red barked trees, I just saw one of them eat a freaking squirrel, seriously the little bugger was running up its bark and then GULP and it was gone!" James said this out of breath and looking over his shoulder. "Also I was pissing on one of them when it did this." Suddenly he felt his groin as if to make sure it was all still there.

"What. It ate a squirrel, how?" Hutch asked looking around worried looking at one of the trees then stepping away from them.

James still feeling his crotch and with a wild eye "It was walking up the trunk, then a mouth opened and that was all she wrote." James said. They all looked around and it was suddenly clear that there were a lot of these red barked trees in the forest.

"You know I think it's time to get the hell out of this place, there are far too many surprises here for my liking," Pat said. And at that they got back on the wagon and made their way down the path. As evening approached. they ran into another clearing, it looked similar except this one had no brook running through it. However, there were the remnants of many camp fires.

"Look, another one, it's like these are rest areas in this place, maybe travelers use these things or like merchants use them," Don said to them all.

Hutch looked around carefully, "Ya know, you may be right Don, there are a lot of fire pits here and there, also look to the right, there is a lot of horse crap, so it's obvious they pen their horses there." They settled in for another night and gathered wood and then Hutch made an observation.

"Hey guys, did you notice of all the wood we gathered and also gathered last night, there is none of that red barked stuff, I bet those trees defend themselves in some way besides a mouth,"

James looking at the red barked trees that suddenly seemed everywhere agreed, "Yeah maybe they are like Trents, they can move and fight,"

Pat looked concerned and started looking around the ground.

"Look let's make a rule, no pissing on any of those things, and let's stay clear of them. I don't like the idea of being eaten by an Orc or a Tree. Plus, Lee, I am sure wants me back in one piece, and I plan to get back that way." And at that they settled down for the night and realized only Hutch and James had some bread and cheese left. They divided that up and sat there, depression setting in.

"Well we need to gather food or fry yams for now on," Don said looking at the last bit of cheese he was holding up before popping it into his mouth.

The evening went without incident until sometime late when Hutch smelled something. He sat up from his bed roll looking around. "Hey you guys, smell that, it smells like bacon cooking?" Pat sat up and so did Don,
Smelling the air Don looked at Pat and Hutch said. "You know, you are right, I smell bacon cooking... What the hell, I think there's company close,"

Pat stood up and peered into the woods and then walked to the dark road just out of camp fire range. He came walking back a few minutes later. "Two of us need to take a sword and then take a walk down the road, maybe go a half mile or so down the road and see if anyone has camped out, recon it and report back. We can smell it, so they are close, I bet. And I bet they are not off the road too far? And maybe they will have word about the road ahead?"

"I will go with ya," Don said standing up. Don and Pat took one of the swords and went off down the dark road leaving Hutch and James there by the fire. Don noticed that as he walked down the road it was dark, the darkness almost felt like he could touch it. He felt a moment of panic as he wondered what was also in the dark with them, behind him? He saw Hutch and James standing there looking. However, he knew the darkness enveloped them, he saw Pat next to him a dark shape the sound of his breathing odd and almost distant. They walked for about a quarter of a mile down the road then took a sharp turn to the right, and as they went around that turn they saw, in the distance, about a hundred yards ahead a camp fire, they approached slowly and saw it was a man and a woman.

The man was large and the woman slender, he wore fur boots going to his knees bound with leather cord, and had heavy wool pants. His sword was in his lap as he was sharpening it with a stone, and he had a large tunic on. Next to him was a piece of breast plate armor dented and heavily worn and on his face, he had a huge black beard tied into braids.

The woman, however, was very slender and slight of build and very pretty. However, she did have a nasty looking scar below her right eye, it went from the edge of her nose to her ear. She was wearing leather pants, and she had bright red hair, and tall leather boots. She also had on a heavy wool over jacket with a cloak that was fur lined. She had next to her a quiver of arrows and in her lap was a medium sized bow, and she was oiling the bow string.

They stood there quietly and noticed he looked battle hardened and rough, and she looked very feminine yet had a look that showed she was someone to be careful of. Don and Pat approached them carefully, and as they got about fifty yards from the pair they could see that they were alone, and they were both laughing and talking.

A fire was in front of them and there was a pot that had something in it as there was steam coming from the pot, the smell of bacon and something else strong in the air. There were a pair of horses picketed not far away, one a large heavy war horse, the other a smaller more slender one. There were no tents. However, there were a pair of saddles on the ground, and the man and woman seemed to not be worried or on alert.

Don and Pat stopped and they talked in a very hushed tone leaning into each other ear.

"What do you think, are they friendly or not?" Pat offered to Don whispering.

"Hell, I don't know why don't you walk into their camp and introduce yourself and find out," Don said sarcastically in a whisper.

"Yeah, right where is James when we need him." Pat said with a smile looking at Don in the darkness.

"Well, look, they seem like common adventurers, they also seem like they know how to fight, and they may be of help, or maybe we can follow them at a distance to see where they are going to?" Don said whispering to Pat.

Pat looked at Don and then at them, licking his lips nervously he spoke. "You know the only way we are going to find out is to say hi so to speak, maybe we can call to them from here, take it from there. They don't seem to be too worried about these woods so maybe besides the trees that like squirrels this place is pretty safe."

Don looked at Pat for a moment, "Look I agree, but if they freak out, we need to run like hell, it will take them a few seconds to get adjusted to the dark, so we should have time to get to camp and if need be grab what we can and keep running."

Pat looked at Don. "I cannot believe this shit Don, two days ago we are gaming, going to Kalamazoo, and now we are here in this weird place and about to possibly piss off two warriors. This is crazy but you are right. Remember if we run, we go back to the left and run like hell."

Don nodded in a silent agreement, licked his lips, took a deep breath and stepped forward. They both walked to within thirty feet or so of the camp. Don looked at Pat, he could see Pat's face now as the camp fire from the strange pair was lighting his face just enough to make out his features.

Don then took a deep breath and spoke. "Hello, we are friends." and at that both the man and the woman jumped up, the man grabbing onto the sword and the woman notching an arrow in her bow pointing it into to the darkness directly at them.

"Who is there, speak now or feel my sword!" the man yelled looking. The woman was slowly moving to the right her eyes peering into the darkness, and it seemed right to where Don and Pat were standing.

"We are lost and need help. We are unarmed and mean no harm. There are only two of us." Don said aloud.

The man said something to the woman, and she nodded. "If you are just two then show yourselves but know if you try anything you will feel my arrow in your chest!" the woman said. Her voice was feminine. However, it had an edge to it that said she had no problem shooting a person in the chest. Don and Pat slowly moved forward, and Pat dropped the sword he was carrying. As they approached and the pair saw them Don and Pat noticed that the pair's eyes were everywhere.

"Are you alone? Be truthful as if you lie then you will be the first to die this eve!" the man said harshly.

"We are just us two. However, we do have a camp about a mile back and have two others there waiting for us, we are friends and harbor no ill will," Don said holding his hands up where they could see they had no weapons.

"What do you want, speak or die" the woman said harshly glaring at them while aiming her arrow at Don's chest.

"We are lost and are not from here, we are tired and do not know the area, all we want is to talk and get help if we can," Pat said looking at the man and then to the woman.

"Well, speak! You heard Freya, speak you have our ear now!" The man said slowly approaching them his sword still drawn. Don looked at Pat and felt like this was not going like they thought; it looked like they might have made a huge mistake with these two.

Freya Aims her arrow at Don right before the Goblins attack

I'm a horrible shot...
After all isn't it horrible when
my arrow pierces your chest...

.... Freya

<u>6</u>
<u>GOBLINS</u>

Don and Pat slowly entered the lit area of the encampment; they walked slowly waiting to see if either of the strangers just suddenly attacked. As they approached the large man looked at them carefully, "You are Merchants?" he asked them looking at their clothing.

"No, we are lost travelers and are only looking for protection and also a safe way to the city of Dark Home, we are no danger to either of you." Don said looking at them both, sweat coming off his forehead even though it was so chilly out one could see your breath in the air.

The woman spoke looking at them, "Lost traveler aye, you both have an odd look to you and a strange eye. How do we know there are not twenty more like you hiding out of fire site?"

Partially due to being overtired and also overwhelmed with events, Pat stepped forward a little his hands held up so they were in clear sight, "You know we do not as if we did then we would not have approached in peace we would have easily attacked and overcome you. It is as my friend said. We are lost travelers from very far away and only ask for help, nothing more." Don looked over at Pat with a look of shock in his eyes as he could not believe his boldness.

The large man seemed to relax a little. "Then tell us your tale and we will decide if you are in need of our help but fair warn you be, if you lie to us then your lies will be the last your lips mutter!" Don and Pat moved a little more into the fire light and as they walked into the actual camp they could see that these two were most likely very seasoned warriors, as their camp was neat and tidy and set up so they could easily and quickly move on if need be.

Don decided that the need to just be blunt and honest was in order as these two especially in this world would probably listen and think it was normal everyday magical stuff. "I can lie to you both, but I will be honest, our story is strange and how we came to be here is not only hard to believe but has uprooted us from all we know, you see we…………"

Just then there was a crash of bushes and from behind the lady with the bow jumped out three small yellow creatures about five feet tall, they had large domed heads large jaws lined with teeth and small pig like eyes, they had a mismatch of clothing and armor on and carried short knives. They grabbed the woman from behind grabbing and pulling on her surprising her. She was arching back let loose her arrow, the arrow went whizzing into the trees above them, screaming. she tried to escape their grip reaching for a boot knife.

The warrior yelling spinning as four more dove into the clearing screaming a high pitched scream attacking him, he immediately swung his blade lopping off one of their heads, one from behind jumping on his back. Don jumped in surprise to one side, Pat ran into the darkness where they came from and for a moment Dons heart dropped thinking Pat ran off.

Don quickly picked up a cast iron poker that was next to the fire and ran to the woman. She had stabbed one of the little creatures, it yelled and scurried off into the bushes holding its side. The other two were trying to drag her into the bushes, one had wrapped a leather sack around her head, slashing at them wildly she fell back kicking wildly, and when she fell back, they both were on her. The others were busy with the warrior, suddenly Pat was there with the sword they dropped and stabbed one of the ones that was attacking the warrior in the back.

As Don ran towards the woman the creature that was slashed came back into the clearing carrying a nasty looking jagged short sword. He saw Don and smiled, he raised his sword and ran at Don. Panicking, he stood there frozen in fright, his legs wouldn't move, he raised the bar just in time, diverting the hard swing of the creature. He then swung wildly and got a lucky hit. His iron bar struck the thing in the head, causing it to fall to the ground laying there squeaking, Don then stabbed it with the poker, it yelled in pain then became silent.

The other one was quickly slashed with the knife the woman was yielding, the woman tearing the bag off her head, wild eyed and angry looking just in time to see saw Don stab one of the creatures through the back its body arched back in pain, a shrill scream leaving it lips before died.

Pat and the warrior were fighting off the remaining creatures; the woman grabbing her bow quickly let loose an arrow, the arrow striking one of the creatures in the back of the head, and as the arrow struck it the creature stiffened then fell. The final one had its belly and chest splayed open by the warrior's sword, wheeling around the warrior saw they were all dead, he turned on Don and Pat, the woman running over to his side.

"Who in Hades name are you and how do you come to help us, we are nothing to you?" The warrior was sweating in the cool air, the woman's hair was disheveled, and she took one hand attempting to straighten it somewhat.

"Yes, who are you and why do you help us when you could run easily?" She was looking at them breathing heavily, she was obviously wound.

Don looked at them breathing heavily bent over with his hands on his knees then looked around at the bodies of the dead creatures,

"We didn't know what else to do." Don's heart was beating hard he was scared as he never saw anything like these things outside his game books, and had never killed anything or anyone in his life.

Pat was in a state of shock it seemed, and was staring at one of the creatures. "What are they?" he asked nudging one with his boot.

The woman looked at him oddly seemingly irritated at his question. "You don't know a Goblin when you see it? How is that, as they infest these lands and infest the entirety of Da'Naan?"

Don looked at her then looked at the small dead little creatures bleeding all over the place, "Goblins... like I said we are not from here."

The large man walked to Don spitting into his hand, he offered it to Don, "Knowing these vermin or not, you saved Freya and helped me and this is not ever going to be forgotten. I am Kord and she is Freya we are adventurers, we hire out our sword to anyone who has the Gold or Silver to pay us. You paid for our loyalty with your help and bravery tonight. We can be called friends by you now." And at that he shook Don's hand, his large hand closing around Don's the grip crushing.

"Thanks to you both your help is needed, we need help with getting home," Don said between clenched teeth grimacing at Kord's handshake.

Freya then spoke placing her disheveled hair into a makeshift pony tail, "That is no problem, we know the all of the realms[6] as we have traveled across the frozen wastes of the North to the sweltering depths of the Southern jungles. We have sailed the pirate infested waters of the Oaken sea and walked the bases of the spine mountains which are the home of the largest clans of dragons in the world. Where do you hail from?" she was looking at Pat and Don.

Pat looked at her then at the Goblins littering the ground, his face was red, and he had a small scratch on his forehead, "Freya I am Pat and we are not from this place, we are from a place called Michigan, in a city called Homer, it is very far from here we regretfully think."

She and the man looked at them with a questioning look. "What part of Da'Naan is that village?" Kord said to them, he had an expression like he was thinking hard. "I can go get a map you show us." He turned to go to a pack that was laying on the ground.

Don looked at him then at Pat, "There is no need. Michigan would not be on any map of yours," Don had an expression of just plain being ready to give up, and he kept looking at the wood line where the Goblins jumped out of.

Freya seeing his look spoke. "Don't worry they won't be back. They were a raiding party, Goblins never attack outside in large numbers, they came to grab me as I am a woman, they thought I was an easy take, so they could mate,"

---

[6] Realms is a common term used when referring to Da'Naan, and means essentially the whole of the world.

she looked at one of the dead Goblins at her feet and spat on it as she said that.

Don looked at Pat and due to being over tired and hungry and frustrated he decided to just come out with it. "We are not from Da'Naan. Some magic brought us here from our home, we are far from it, and we need to find out how to get back home." Seeing Kord's and Freya's look he spoke again.

"I know it's hard to believe but please know we are telling the truth. We are not from this place, we were in our homeland and found a book one of my friends who is back at our camp read some of it aloud and we all felt some kind of magic hit us then we awoke here two days ago. We have the book but don't know anything about it and need help to find someone who can help us get home." Pat muttered an agreement looking around at the Goblins.

Kord and Freya stood away from them for about ten minutes quietly talking and discussing what Don and Pat thought was what they would do with them.

"Don I ran a sword into that one there," Pat said pointing at one of the dead Goblins. "He yelled when I did that, it shrieked in pain, I killed it man... I murdered it." He looked crushed.

Don looking at him patted his arm laying a hand on his shoulder, "Pat look, these aren't human, they are monsters, they were going to carry that lady off and do god knows what to her, also they would have probably eaten us or worse. Did you see the hooked knife that the one was carrying that came after me? You did the right thing here. We both did the right thing."

Pat looked at Don and smiled slightly, "I hope you are right, then again, I hope I wake up in your living room on the couch and bitch about this bad dream over your crappy waffles,"

Don smiled, "You know man if we stick together Lee will be making us breakfast again. But buddy we gotta stick together and do what we have to do to get home." Pat nodded a quiet agreement then wiping his nose with his sleeve stretched and yawned.

Kord and Freya walked over. "We will go with you to your fire and your friends, we will travel with you and take you to the City you seek, and there I know someone who may be able to help you with your problem. However, be aware if you are lying, we will not take it kindly, as we do this out of gratitude for helping us this eve."

Don looked at him, "yes let's go back and get some sleep we will explain fully tomorrow on the road how we came to be here, and we will tell you more about us and our homeland." And at that they watched the two warriors pack up and Pat offered to carry the steaming pot looking into it, he saw it was a stew with vegetables and meat floating in it, and suddenly he realized he was starving, they then walked to their camp leaving the bodies of the dead Goblins laying on the ground where they fell. As they approached their encampment James and Hutch were waiting for them and saw the two companions, James stepped back.

Don held up a hand, "They are ok, they are going to help us." James stepped back and looked over at a sword that was standing against a log that they dragged from the woods to sit on.

"Don, who are they? Are they ok?" James asked looking over at the sword.

Kord eyed James suspiciously seeing him looking towards the sword. "I am Kord little man, and uninjured, Goblins are of no concern."

James looked at Don with a surprised expression. "Goblins. What is he talking about and who are they?" Don looked at James eyeing him,

"Like I said these are friends, they were attacked by Goblins just now, and we helped them, "Raising his hand to hold off the hundred questions that were about to be asked by Hutch and James." They can take us to the city, and they know someone who can help us." James and Hutch said hello and the two warriors hesitantly looking around closely seemed to relax a bit.

"Let's eat and rest, we can clear many things tomorrow." Kord said sitting down in front of the fire, "I will take first watch," and at that he pulled out his sword and settled down, looking as if he planned to sit there for a long time. Offered food the group gratefully ate from Kord's and Freya's pot with little discussion other than James occasional question about the Goblins, then bellies full and feeling safer than they have since arriving, they slept till morning the cool night passing by without further incident.

The next morning they awoke. Don laid there and was so comfortable, he slept so well that evening, and as he lay there for a moment, he thought it was all just a dream. Then hearing the fire pop he leaned up, his back hurt badly from sleeping on the ground, and he felt so dirty. He needed a shower badly, and his teeth needed brushing so bad, his mouth felt like he had been chewing on an old sock. He looked around yawning seeing his friends waking up and found Freya and

Kord already awake and tending to the horses, including their old one that pulled the wagon. Freya looked to them smiling,

"So, you all are finally awake? Do you always sleep so late in this Michigan you are from?" James looked at her with a confused look on his face.

"Umm no it's early isn't it?" he looked at the low dawn sky, the mist thick and damp the air cold and crisp.

Kord laughed heartily. "Early it is my friends, and far we have to go, let's get on the road and let's talk as we have much to talk about," and at that everyone gathered up their things and as Kord and Freya got on their horses, the intrepid band of friends got on their wagon and set off as a group down the road in the woods. They passed the camp site where the battle took place and saw the dead Goblins, vultures were there eating what they could, their wings flapping as they ate fighting over the carcasses,

"Those are Goblin then, ugly little buggers," Hutch said as they passed, he took out his phone to take some pictures, but Don looked at him, glancing to Freya he shook his head, causing Hutch to nod and place it back into his cloak.

"Yes they favor nothing and they are more pests than real threats, unless they are in large groups, but you usually don't run into large groups, unless you are in their caves." Kord said over his shoulder riding his large war horse. Freya was riding next to the wagon keeping pace and was talking to the group.

"You say you are not from here and how you got here was strange, tell me how then you came to be here?" she was looking intently at them and Don could tell she was not one to lie to. She had piercing green eyes, and those eyes he thought had seen a lot of pain in her years, the scar on her face in daylight was red, and he could tell the cut that gave it to her must have been vicious and painful. Seeing him look at her face Freya unconsciously held a hand to it and smiled.

"My present from a Hafarian Pirate many years ago, he thought I would be willing to welcome his advances, when I declined. he gave me this," She said touching the scar again with a smile. "However, don't worry he paid with his hand. He sliced me in the face, and I sliced his hand off, his present was more keenly felt than mine."

Don looked at her for a moment feeling pity then said, "I'm sorry"

She looked at him with curiosity than a smile.

"Why are you sorry? He lost his hand and it was his right one at that, he will forever be an outcast. He fared worse than I," she said this laughing, and Don and Hutch and James laughed. Pat was sitting quietly in the wagon not paying attention as he was sharpening a sword with an odd look on his face.

Don proceeded over the next two hours to explain the book and what happened to make them be here, and also explained a little about his world, he left out things like modern technology and such as, he felt she would really think he flipped his lid, he instead just kept it similar to her world, but that in there they didn't have monsters and magic. Freya asked many questions and seemed surprised that there were no monsters or magic in Michigan. Kord would occasionally chime in with a question and between Don, Hutch and James and occasionally Pat they seemed to make Kord and Freya at least believe that they were not from Da'Naan.

As noon approached, they broke from the woods and entered a large rocky plain. Low hills could be seen with the mountains towering high above them, once they exited the woods they could see how dark it was in the woods as it was very bright out and warmer. The sun made them all squint as their eyes got used to being in the bright light. To the North were pine trees in small patches and there was a small stream close by tricking clear and cold.

"Well Dark Home is just West of us about ten leagues, we should have one more night and be there by morning." Kord said looking around and taking a deep breath.

Freya was looking around smelling the air also. "We will have snow soon I can smell it."

Kord looked to the East and grimaced. "Yes you are right, we might want to make a stout fire this eve, maybe if we can find an outcropping to shelter us from the wind if we get a huge blow from the mountains. At the minimum we are going to have a hard frost." Don and Hutch sniffed the air,

"Do you smell anything Don?" Hutch asked leaning over to him in a whisper. Don looked at him with a shrug.

"No I don't, but I think those two are a little better at it than us." And to that they rode on into the afternoon as the afternoon progressed, dark clouds started coming on from the mountains, dark and forbidding.

"Well, it seems we have snow coming much sooner than we thought." Freya said pulling a cloak from her pack and putting it on.

They rode until dusk and as darkness fell the first flakes of wet sticky snow started to fall, large and lightly falling through the cold air. Don, Pat and the rest bundled up with another layer of the clothes that they salvaged, huddling in the back of the wagon shivering James was not happy, he looked around and whispered to Hutch.

"Look this is stupid. Why are we riding in this crappy wagon going to a city, we are trusting some old man to, also. How do we know these people, far as we know they are taking us out to kill us?"

Hutch looked at him angrily leaning in close almost nose to nose, "Listen moron, if they wanted to kill us, we would be dead, I think they are willing to help for what Don and Pat did for them, chill out, ok. Tomorrow we will be at the city and maybe get home to boot, plus shut up, they might hear ya!"

James looked at Hutch with agitation and went on, "Look they have two horses, let's steal them tonight then at least we can get out of this stupid hard wagon?"

Pat overhearing James suggestion leaned back turning and glared at James. "Pipe that shit up now, you don't like this then hop out and do your own thing, I am sick of your whining complaining and frankly we're not going to let you piss off the ONLY two people in this world that are willing to help us. Sit back, shut up, and no more, unless you want to get out and walk and do your own thing!" Pat then spun around angrily.

James glared at Pat for a moment then sat back forcefully. Muttering to himself no one heard him say. "You all think you know it all, we'll see.. We'll see."

They stopped about an hour later, the air was cold and Don was miserable as he had another one of his headaches. Kord made a large fire, and it helped warm them a lot. The eve went without incident, and they talked more of Michigan and Da'Naan and of many things. The next morning they awoke to about two inches of snow on the ground, Don opened his eyes, and saw it everywhere. As he sat up he saw he saw that the blanket that covered him was also covered in snow, and it was cold and breezy making things worse. Irritated he stood up and walked over to the fire that Kord had gotten started again. His friends were awakening with similar looks, and obvious thoughts. They stood around the fire warming up, miserable and cold Don was rubbing his arms, so was James and Hutch, Don was commenting to them how cold it was and how they needed to do something about it, hearing them Kord walked over to them.

"You all are not dressed for this weather, here." He tossed a pile of furs onto the ground, they were rough fur cloaks and were warm, each one of the guys put one on, and offered thanks. Even James found nothing to complain about. They packed up yet again and set off across the rocky plain, then about an hour into their ride, they crested at a small hill and saw it. A winding road that stretched like a brown scar on the plain and a huge flowing river. Along the river, they saw the City of Dark Home.

It was huge and had a high wall all around it, the falling snow made it look indistinct and almost not real. The road went right up to the main gate, and Kord raised his hand ordering a halt. Kord became very serious and looked at them all.

"This is Dark Home, it is one of the most famous and dangerous cities in the whole of Da'Naan, be careful and stick by us as we have been here many times and know how to navigate its ways."

Hutch looked at Pat smiling,

"Can't be any worse than Battle Creek at ten at night right?" and to Pats laughing, they rode down the steep hill through the low scrub brush to the road and turned towards the great walled city of Dark Home.

Gate Guard of Dark Home

Tarry not after dark
For the City watch suffers no fools...

......Sign at the entrance of the city

7
DARK HOME

Dark Home was a walled city, it seemed to have at least three main gates as the road split the closer they got and led up to each one, the guys were sure there were most likely more gates around it. The city walls were about fifty feet tall made of large grey granite blocks the size of small cars, with large towers about two hundred feet apart. Each tower had a catapult on its top with many arrow slits and strange slotted openings starting about thirty feet from the ground. The snow that was falling was settling on the walls and Don thought of a Christmas card when he saw it.

The walls had large knocked out chunks and pits in them, and it was obvious that this city knew what a siege was and most likely repelled several rather easily. As they approached the gate, there was a small wooden shack and four men, the men wore well taken care of armor and had swords at their waste. However, they looked like they were at ease as the party approached. One of the guards walked to the edge of the road holding up a hand to them,

"Hold, what is your business here?" he asked in a tone that indicated he had asked this question already many times today, he also looked into the sky distastefully at the falling snow settling on his cloak and helmet.

"We are here to visit this great den of sin my friend, and to have some of the best mead and ale in the realms" Kord said laughing. "Plus maybe someplace warm wouldn't hurt either."

The guard looked at him for a second seeming to become at ease even further, "Are the woman and wagon with you also?", Kord shifted in his saddle looking up at the falling snow then back to the men wagon and Freya,

"Yes they are, and can you tell me where an Inn is as me arse aches from being in the saddle far too long. And we have some good yams if you are interested? And we will make you a fine deal on them if you want to buy a few for your dinner," The guard scowled at him. However, Kord continued on. "They have been kept by a warm fire every eve so they are not frozen yet," the guard walked over to the wagon looking in it and eyeing over the men, saying nothing he looked at Freya winking at her and smiling his yellow rotting teeth contrasting his brown beard.

The guard cleared his throat pulling his cloak about him, obviously he was very cold and miserable with his duty. "Go on, go ahead, there is an Inn called the Cracked Flagon on the main avenue you can't miss it. They have clean beds and very few bugs, and the mead and ale usually doesn't have anything floating in it."

And at that he turned and went back to the shack placing his hands over a glowing brazier with coal in it and resumed his talking.

Kord motioned at them to move on,

Freya looking up to the falling snow said "Let's go, we got lucky with the weather, and I wish to get warm." And at that they all rode through the main gate into the city. As they rode through the gated area they saw that the wall was incredibly thick, it was about twenty feet thick at its base, and there were a series of portcullis and gates that welcomed those entering the city.

Dark Home, as soon as they entered, was a surprise, the roads were paved with stones and there were all manner of buildings made of wood and stone. Some had tall roofs some had towers, and some were low squat buildings with no visible door. The place was jammed with people and wagons, and it was noisy. It seemed everyone was yelling and bumping into each other. Don noticed that his nose was hit with a myriad of smells, there was the strong smell of rotting hay mixed with a noble woman's perfume, he smelled cooking food with spices some familiar and some very odd. They rode close to one another Kord nudging people out of his way with his large horse, and they slowly made their way down the street, the deeper they got into the city the less crowded it became, it seemed the deeper you got the more orderly it was.

Kord slowed down until he was even with the wagon and Freya, "Before we go to an Inn let us get rid of your vegetables, we can do that at the Merchant square,"

Freya agreed and so did the men and to that, they followed Kord again. As they rode down the main road in the city they saw that this road seemed to go from one end of the city to the other, and breaking off from this road there were other smaller streets and alleys, with the same congested buildings on the side of those roads, that was until they rode for about almost thirty minutes when they came to a large clearing.

GAMERS SAGA - DONALD SEMORA

The clearing turned out to be a huge square with a large fountain the middle and total chaos in it. This was the central market as best as the men could tell, there were merchants selling everything from spices to blankets, there were yelling men and women haggling price over carrots, lanterns, leather good, chickens and other small creatures that everyone didn't even recognize, to one side, there was a butcher chopping meat. The ground was slick and once in awhile someone would fall and this would result in a raucous laughter from those seeing it.

"Stop here and I will be back shortly," Kord said to everyone, and he dismounted giving the reins of his horse to Don, "I will see if I can do this quickly, the price won't be as good but we do not have time to tarry," and at that he walked into the mess of people and seemed to disappear. They all sat there quietly for about fifteen minutes when he suddenly reappeared with a short very skinny man.

The man had a narrow face and large pointed nose and he walked up to Don and Pat, he was wearing a long bright red doublet and a short pointed dark brown hat folded over at the top. "Good morn fine merchants, I understand you have produce to sell?" he was oily and reminded Don of a slimy used car salesman; while he was talking, he was eyeing the back of the wagon on the burlap bags of yams that were in there.

"Yes, yams, they are of good quality and are fresh," Don said not knowing in the slightest how to do this.

The man looked at the contents of the wagon, picking up a yam, smelling it, and then he took out a small knife sliced into it. He stood there for a few moments thinking, "This appears to be about a hundred weight, right now the market is flooded so best I can do is twelve silver sovereigns." He suddenly looked very busy, and like he was waiting forever for an answer.

Don looked at everyone, saw some nods and shrugs, and looked back at the man, "We will do that, do you want them now?" The man looked surprised at the agreement, shrugged and spoke.

"Take them to the right side of the market to a man named Drollmar, he is my payer, tell him Akbar said twelve silver, he will unload you and pay you," and at that he turned and disappeared into the crowd.

Pat laughed, reaching over patting Don on the back. "I think we just got ripped, I bet he would have gone higher, then again, how much is twelve silver whatevers?"

"Yeah, maybe but it's something, and we have cash now" Hutch said.

Kord was laughing and so was Freya sitting on their horses looking at Don and Pat, "You are truly not from here, I don't think Akbar there knew how to deal with you; he is used to fierce haggling and dealing, plus the price was low but not too bad, if you haggled over you might have gotten eighteen or twenty from him." And laughing, he and Freya led them to the payer where they unloaded their yams and collected their cash without any problem. They divided three sovereigns to each man, and gave Kord one for his help, smiling Kord offered his thanks.

"We need to get an Inn, I think you should let me and Freya for now on talk price," he said this laughing, and he led them down the main road. Their empty wagon suddenly bouncy and bumpy from being empty, its wheels clattering on the cobbled road. They rode for about ten minutes and saw Kord stop in front of a three story building, it was made of wood and stone and had a wooden sign nailed next to its door, on the door it said.

"THE CRACKED FLAGON, NO SILVER - NO SERVICE !"

There were two boys out front, and Don could see that there was a small alley to the right of the Inn, where he saw the stables.

One of the boys approached them and offered to take their horses. "Sirs, it will be three coppers for one night tending to yer and we will even brush 'em and water 'em," the boy was about fourteen and was dirty and the smock he wore was torn and grimy.

Freya approached the one boy, "You say three coppers? If you take care of our horses and give them clean hay, I will feed ya bread and cheese tonight and give ya an extra copper in the way of thanks, but only if you do as I say." She said this smiling, and the two boys, also smiling broadly, agreed and promised to give the horses the most royal of treatment while in their care.

Kord seemed to get irritated for a moment. "You encourage the rabble to do their job by paying more. I say they do it or get a firm back handing!"

Freya looked at Kord and smiled a tolerant smile. "Better to pay a copper and some food and make sure our mounts are well cared for. You know what these places sometimes do. Let your big arse walk for a bit due to a sick horse. I will throw you a copper in the way of compensation then."

Kord looked at her with a straight face but said nothing. The party got off the horses, taking their weapons with them and a few bags with their possessions. They stretched, feeling the road leave them and walked up the short steps to the entrance of the Inn while the boys led the horses into the stables.

Turning, and suddenly very serious, Freya spoke to the men. "You have to be careful in places like this; if they think they are not going to get something they will mistreat your animals and also possibly steal your horses, even though to do so in this realm is death." Freya said looking at them smiling.

Suddenly, Hutch wondered if the wagon horse was branded, and if so how would they explain them having it. He had visions of being dragged from the Inn kicking and screaming and being strung up.

They stood at the entrance for a moment; it was early afternoon and still snowing, as they opened the heavy door and entered the Inn a wave of warm air hit them, and it seemed hot and stuffy. The warm air smelled of food and hay, and also of smoke. Suddenly, Don realized that they indeed had been out in the weather for a few days and this would most of the time, be chilly to them inside. The Inn had a large central room with a huge fire pit in its center, with huge logs blazing in it. There was a bar or more like a large counter to one side, and the windows were grimy and sooty and offered only a grayish brown light into the place.

There were several men and women in it already drinking sitting at several benches that were scattered all around the place, a few glowing iron lanterns were hanging from low beams throwing off a golden glow. As they entered through the door a cold wind seemed to come through the entrance causing the lanterns to flicker in their iron cages; people looked up for a moment but not seeing anyone they knew they went back to their drinks and talk.

A huge chested woman with black hair approached them, "Well, warriors and wenches seem to be the order of the day, how may we serve ye?" her voice was throaty and full of friendly mirth. However, she had a small knife tucked in her belt.

"We are looking for three rooms, food and drink and privacy!" Kord said harshly.

The woman looked at him for a moment smiled and said to him laughing, "Oh, you're a strapping one, I am Doreen and I can help you with all that." she winked at Kord and leaning to him, she whispered a hardly hidden invitation. "I will want to talk to you later," and to her tinkling laugh, they followed her to a set of benches and a narrow grimy table made of a wood that long ago surrendered to the food and drink spilled on it.

They sat down and Kord spoke to her, "What do you have to eat and drink here that doesn't have a rat floating in its cask?"

The woman looked at him and momentarily seemed irritated at his comment. "We have the cleanest rooms and freshest food in Dark Home bearded one, no one gets sick off my sisters or fathers cooking or brewing." She stood there with her hands on her hips as if challenging the group to say otherwise, "We have Ale, wine, cider. Plus we have Bear stew, Amarian pickle, bread and Cheese. What will it be?"

Freya spoke cutting Kord off, "We will all have stew and bread, and bring a pot of ale and cider."

The woman looked at Freya seemingly like she was still insulted, "That will be two Silvers," she said with the hint of a challenge in her voice.

Don thought quickly and said to them, "We will pay this," then looked at Hutch, "poney up, James and Pat get the

124

next one." Hutch gave one and Don added one of his to it and gave it to her. Freya and Kord looked surprised and offered their thanks.

Hutch looked at James and Pat. "Look, cheap skates you got it next time, or better yet, you two pay for the rooms."

The Inn remained pretty steady for the next hour or so as they sat there eating the stew the lady brought, by and large, the food was good and the men ate their stew without many comments. It had been several days since they were well fed, warm and felt safe, and it was catching up to them. James and Pat sat there half nodding off their heads in their hands, Hutch was sitting and leaning back, his eyes feeling heavy, and Don also was feeling like a warm bed and a good night's sleep.

"Well, we have a question to answer?" Freya spoke waking the men up. She was looking at them all intently. "We said we would take you here and help you get settled and introduce you to someone who may be able to help. The problem is what will you do once you find out or should I say if you find out how to get back home?" She was staring at each one of them and Kord next to her spoke up.

"Yes indeed, you four men are fish out of water I can tell that much. Your world must truly be odd," his voice was low and gritty, it seemed oddly out of place in here as he always was so loud and clear when talking.

Doreen came back to the table looking at Kord in a seductive way. "So, are we staying the night? We have the cleanest beds, and quietest rooms at that." She looked at Kord smiling and winked then looked at the rest.

"We will take three rooms, and that's all!" Freya told the serving wench with an edge to her voice the wench caught.

Doreen looked for a second like she would say something more but seemed to think better of it. "That will be three silvers for the rooms, and add a copper if you want fire wood during the night."

Freya looked at the wench; she seemed to have something on her lips but evidently decided to not say it. Kord reached into his pocket pulling out the money, throwing her an extra silver and smiling at her.

The serving wench spoke at Kord directly. "I usually am done cleaning by midnight, and will be sure to get you all good dry wood," she smiled at him. Laughing, Kord smacked her on her bottom and the wench giggling pranced off.

"Go ahead be stupid like when we were in Moordeep, go ahead but I won't save your arse the next time," Freya told Kord sternly with a serious hard eye.

Kord looked at Freya with a look of feigned innocence, "What? the situation was blown out of proportion Freya, I had purely honorable intentions. Her husband mistook my help, is all." Freya looked at Kord sternly then broke out laughing causing the table to also break out laughing.

They sat in the Inn quietly talking for another hour about the four men's situation and how they would handle it, and then as the early evening pressed onto the city and the windows became darker and as more lanterns were lit by the serving wenches they decided to go and explore a bit of the city. Kord and Freya said they were going to go and talk to someone and would be back before midnight with hopefully news for them on this person who may have information on getting them home.

"Be weary and careful as this city is well patrolled by King Malricks[7] guards, and they do not suffer fools, and there

---

[7] Known as the Dread Usurper King. Murdered his father in 4352 to gain the throne

are other elements in this city that are more dangerous than simple Goblins, you will hear once outside the tolling of the hour, these are large bells in the large spire in the city center and they sound the time every hour. If it is five you will hear five bells and so on. Be careful!" Kord said and at that him and Freya got up and left quietly.

"This is stupid" Pat said in frustration as they all sat in the Inn's common room watching Kord and Freya walk of the Inn. Pat seemed suddenly frustrated catching the rest off guard.

James was sitting there leaning over the table with his hands waving, "I say we go ahead and do our own thing, I don't care what you all say, I DO NOT trust those two. You guys are falling for a pretty face and kind words."

Hutch was draining the last of his ale; he let out an expansive burp. "Look everyone, I can see James' logic here a bit, but James, you gotta chill out a bit. Kord and Freya may indeed help us, and I have the book anyway, so no one is going to do anything without me giving it to them."

Don leaned forward his face pensive with deep thoughts. He took a drink from his cup of ale then cleared his throat, "I have a question for you all. Hutch you read the book then bam! we were here, right?"

Hutch looked at him, "I didn't read the entire book, only the first page then suddenly BAM, and we are here."

Don sat up more in his chair, "Yes, you read some of it, now the magic that brought us here is in the book, wouldn't it stand to reason that there is magic in there that would maybe get us home?"

Pat coughed, then James spoke up, "Yeah, read the thing, I mean let's see what the entire book says. You know I think that-" Suddenly Hutch interrupted.

"Look, I see where you are going with this Don, but we don't know what that book will do if anymore is read, if I go reading it who knows what could happen. Some of those Orc things could appear, hell, we could be taken to another world, or worse, James may grow a personality." This caused everyone to laugh except James, who sat there shaking his head angrily.

"Why is it you have to always carry the book Hutch, I mean, don't you trust any of us?" James said suddenly catching everyone off guard.

Hutch looked at James for a moment, Don though he was going to say something to him, but instead he smiled pulled out the book and tossed it on the table. "Here ya go stud, you carry it."

James looked at the book on the table then at Hutch. "Yeah, I wasn't saying I wanted it, I was speaking for the rest. Someone may want it."

Don started to speak and Pat interrupted him. "James, you always have to have something to complain about. Tell ya what I will carry it this eve, give ya a break Hutch, OK?" Hutch said no problem and Pat placed the book in his cloak giving James a dirty look.

The four adventurers talked a bit longer and seemingly getting nowhere they decided to do some exploring, they agreed to break into two teams, and explore a bit. They would meet back at the sound of ten bells.

"Me and Don will go one way and you and James go the other, is that cool?" Hutch asked, there was a murmur of agreement, and they stood up,

"What if one of us has a problem?" James asked, "What if we run into something bad and need help?"

Pat cleared his throat leaning forward in his chair. "We then we beat feet for this place, get the room, go in and lock the door and wait for the rest of us. If we act normal we should have no problems," he said.

Don looked at Pat and then to Hutch and James. "Wanna tell me what normal in this place is?" they all chuckled at that and walked out into the early evening. When they walked out into the snowy nightfall the sky was turning a pinkish tinge giving the snow that was falling around them an odd, almost glowing quality.

"I wish I knew the time exactly, and what Emily is doing right now." Hutch said in a pensive voice to no one in particular. Just then they heard a low booming BONG, then another followed by four more.

"Well, ask and ye shall receive good masters, it's six in the evening." James said in a fake wheezy old man voice. The men laughed at that, and they walked into the street with one group going right and the other left.

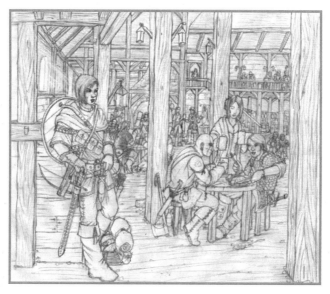

The Cracked Flagon

Best food, Cleanest rooms and no rats in their Ale

8
A FAMILIAR PLACE

Don and Hutch went to the right, and as they walked with their cloaks pulled tight around them, they realized it was getting a lot colder than they remembered. Maybe it was that they had spent several hours in a warm common room filling their bellies with warm food. Don felt like his belly would pop. They saw that as evening approached the streets and the cobblestones were getting slippery, it was still snowing very lightly and there was a good layer of snow on the rooftops and also the fences and other stationary things sitting out.

They could see faintly through the falling snow the mountains in the distance, pink hued and cold looking, and Hutch pointed out how the snow on the peaks was having their snow blown into the sky, as it was obvious there were huge winds up there.

"Yeah, let's hope two things, one that THAT snowy weather doesn't really hit us that hard like up there," Hutch said jabbing a thumb to the snow-covered peaks,

"and also that in this fiasco we won't have to traverse over those damn things." Don said interrupting Hutch, eying the blowing snow on the peaks with distaste then sticking his tongue out catching a few snowflakes on it.

"Yeah, I know bud, I know..." Hutch replied looking not much happier. They walked down the street, and even though it was cold there were still a lot of people out and about. The people had their cloaks tightly about them, and walked quickly with their heads bowed in the falling snow. The alleys that jutted off to each side of the street were dark, and they could see occasionally windows lit down them, or shadows of people in them. They walked to a small building and outside it there was a wooden sign hanging over a narrow structure, its windows were stained with candle soot. However, they had a warm glow and on the wooden sign was.

OTTOS BOOKS AND SCROLLS

Don looked at Hutch with an incredulous look, and Hutch gave him one right back. "You got to be fricking kidding me, no way. I am NOT seeing this!" Don said suddenly feeling sick with nausea and butterflies.

Hutch spoke quietly with a bit of awe in his voice, "No this can't be, it can't be what we are thinking, I mean if it is then we just solved our problem."

Don looked at Hutch riveted to the spot in the street staring at the sign and the windows, the snow falling around him collecting on his shoulders and hood; he could see someone moving around in there. However, the windows were so stained with candle soot he couldn't tell who it may be.

"Look if that little bastard Patrick is in there I am going to reach across that counter and beat the truth out of him," Hutch said angrily, looking at Don.

Don looked at Hutch with a serious frown, "Let's go on and say HI, if it is that little punk me and you both are going to be reaching. Hutch this is too much of a coincidence the name and all, plus the selling of the same thing... What the hell is going on here?"

Hutch looked back at Don, his face features sharply outlined in the fading light, the snow lightly collecting in his brown colored cloak, his breath coming from the hood's entrance in steamy wisps, "I know this is odd, but I swear I am going to be kicking that kid's ass if we walk in there and he is standing by the counter."

Looking to the door Don said, "Well one thing for sure, it's time to find out." And at that they walked up to the door grasped the brass handle and turned it opening the door to a warm wave of air that hit them and there was a winkling of a little brass bell; they looked at each other, Don looking at Hutch with butterflies in his gut, and then walked in.

Across town, Pat and James were at the large central market walking around the various stalls and tents, most were closed at this point but there were a few die hard merchants staying open late in the falling snow, their tents and booths made up of a myriad of colors covered in snow.

"Let's look around and ask some questions about this place, tell everyone that asks we are from that small town... what did that old man call it?" James said to Pat.

"Drakmar, you dolt, the old guy called it Drakmar and yes we can do that," Pat said smiling. The market was thinning out as evening approached and some of the merchants already had their carts closed for the night, and some that had tents had their flaps tightly closed, their fabric outer shells glowing with the warmth inside. Others who were desperate for business were still yelling at passersby's hawking their wares. James slipped on the icy cobblestones falling on his butt, and cursing the ice he got up slowly. "Damn I think I broke my tail bone that time, they need to spread some salt, morons!" Pat smiled asking him if he was really ok, and seeing he was they continued on. They walked in the falling snow, passed by one merchant who was selling what looked like leather goods, the merchant smiled broadly, then seeing the two men not stopping scowled and went back to warm his hands over a small fire brazier. They had been walking around for about ten minutes when they ran into a stall selling old books, Pat stopped looking at the opening to the stall, the merchant looked at him hopefully.

"Yes good sirs, how may I help you, I have the finest Amarian[8] religious texts, and even some from the far off lands of Hafaria," he said to them, smiling as he spoke.

Pat smiled at the merchant, while James was looking over some of the books, "I have a question maybe you can help me with? You say Amaria and Hafaria, do you have any maps of the region?"

The merchant looked at him still smiling, "Oh, no sir, I do have some tomes that have maps in them. However, accurate maps are hard to find, and very expensive. Nevertheless, I may have a source if the master has gold?" He said this half leaning over the entrance as if in anticipation.

"Umm... no I don't have much money... but I have a book that I am trying to find information about." While saying this Pat was taking out the book from his cloak, holding it up to the merchant.

The merchant placed a pair of narrow glasses on his nose peering at the book, "Hmmpff, no it appears to be of Amarian binding, although the symbology on the front is nothing I am aware of, let me see it?" at that he held out a thin hand, taking the book from Pat, opening it, he glanced inside

---

[8] One of the three kingdoms. This is where Dark Home is located at.

then with a disgusted gasp almost threw the book back at Pat. "Where did you come across this disgusting thing, that I can tell you easily is Dark Mage script, it is of Dark Magic. Dangerous and not predictable, you should not have that book! I can see you are no Dark Mage, or are you?" the merchant was looking at Pat then to James intently.

James spoke quickly, "We aren't Mages, we are simple travelers who are lost that is all, if you can tell us where it is from, you will be of a great help,"

Pat looked at the old merchant, "Sir, I know this book is dark and dangerous, but we have to know where it is from, and what it says, can you tell us anything about it?" his voice pleading in the cold night air.

The old man looked at them as if they were infected with something. "I am sorry, I know nothing about that, I can't help you. Please leave, you are blocking my paying customers,"

Pat looked around and saw that no one was standing in line or even around the stall then pleaded with the merchant again, "Please sir help is all I want.."

And at that the old man raised his voice. "What you hold is blasphemous, and I don't want it in front of me, leave now or I will call the city watch!" And at that he pulled a curtain that cut off his booth from the two men.

"That didn't go over well at all." James said to Pat looking around hoping they didn't cause too much of a scene, they saw that no one seemed to take notice of their exchange with the merchant.

"I guess not but we at least know it is magical but the magic is something that scared that old coot," Pat said looking at the book, he then placed it back inside his cloak and suggested they go back to the Inn and wait for the rest and tell them of how the merchant reacted.

"Maybe, just maybe Kord and Freya will know what Dark magic is and if so then where they should go next, or at least it will be help to whomever they get to help?" James said, and with Pat grunting in agreement, they then headed back to the Inn, the snow falling more heavily the large cold wet flakes settling on everything they touched.

Pat looked at James and reached into his cloak grabbing the book. "Your turn you carry it to the Inn, I am sick of this thing already. And next time you want to volunteer someone, volunteer yourself!" James took the book and placed it in his back pack, and they walked off in the falling snow. Meanwhile as the two men walked away the merchant left the back of his tent, bundling himself from the cold night air he made his way to the City Watches shack on the edge of the square. Knocking on the door a man in polished breast plate opened the door. "Yes what do you want?" he asked in a bored tone, chewing on some food from his supper.

"I have something you should know," the merchant said to the City Watch officer.

Don and Hutch entered the book and scroll shop looking around as they walked in for the counter and someone familiar, however, they were surprised to see a middle aged woman. She had long raven black hair braided over her right shoulder, she was dressed in a leather corset over a white cotton loose shirt, and her skirt was bright red with a wide leather belt. "Well hello, two handsome men in my shop and walking in so serious about that and at so late an hour, should I be worried my wares may be not safe?" she said this in a throaty voice that Don found oddly fitting for her.

"No we thought for a moment we might know the proprietor of this place." Don said looking at her then around the shop, there was no sign of the young man or anyone else.

The shop was filled with shelving and the shelves were covered with books; there was a counter that the woman was standing behind and hanging from the pale wooden rafters were several large lanterns with ornate stained glass that gave off a strange multi colored hue to the room and its walls.

The woman looked at them for a moment with a strange expression on her face, "Well, I am the owner, Constance Quinlin is my name, and I have owned this shop since I was twenty, the old owners died in the great Death Siege way back that Lantern Lock." She looked at Don and Pat up and down then spoke again, "What can I do for you, you two are standing there soaking up my warm air with that door open?"

Don turned and closed the door. "Sorry I didn't mean to leave it open," Hutch stepped forward clearing his throat while looking around to see if Patrick would be lurking around somewhere in a corner.

"My name is Hutch and this is Don, we both are from very far away and are lost. Do you by chance know of anyone who may be able to look at a book and tell us what it is, and where it came from?"

The woman started laughing, "Know what a book is and where it came from. Do you think just because I am a woman I am some Dolt? I can tell by a book's paper where it originated from and by the leather covers smell what part of the cow it came from!" She was looking at them both sternly as if offended at what they said. Hutch looked at Don then at her feeling awkward and Don felt that things were going downhill quite fast.

"This may be a very rare book though, it also may be enchanted or magical in some way." Don interjected hoping a new voice would smooth her bruised ego.

She smiled at them looking back over her shoulder at the curtained off room that was in back of her behind the counter."Well let me tell you something, I am familiar with most tomes and have an extensive library of materials that may shed, however I also know of some people that may be able to help if I cannot decipher its origins for you. Do you have this book?"

Don then stepped forward clearing his throat, "Ma'am we don't have it here, but we can bring it back tomorrow; that book is why we are lost, we were home, opened it, and it was read by a companion, then we found ourselves here," Don didn't mean to go into such detail but something about this woman told him she was not only someone who could help, but also she was someone whom they could trust. Maybe it was just the events and his desire to need someone, but he decided to throw caution to the wind and be blunt.

"You bring me that book tomorrow after twelve bells and I will look at it for you. If it is something that needs further looking into, we can then talk about price. I am fair and honest, and I tally no lies in my business but also I expect the same in those I deal with." She said this looking at them both and Don and Hutch felt like her eyes were going through them and seeing into their hearts.

They both offered their thanks and agreed that they would be back the next day so she could look at the book and hopefully tell them what it was and maybe how to fix the predicament that they were in. As they turned to leave, she walked forward and cleared her throat and then spoke. "Come to think about it can you tell me what language it is in, or what it looks like?"

Don looked at Hutch who shrugged then Don spoke, "It is small about two palms in width, made of brown leather and has an odd symbol on the front, the language in it we are not sure of."

The woman looked at him for a moment, "An odd symbol you say, what does it look like? Is it a bird or something?"

Don cleared his throat, "No it is like a twenty sided... I mean, its round in shape and has many faceted sides with strange symbols on each facet. It also-"

The woman interrupted him holding up a hand looking suddenly very interested. "A many sided faceted orb with symbols all over it. Are you sure?" Her look was direct, and she seemed to almost lean forward when she spoke the words.

Hutch cleared his throat, reaching into his cloaks pouch he grasped his D20 dice and pulled it out. It was Red with yellow speckles. "The symbol looks like this but with different symbols on its facets."

The woman looked at Hutch then at Don. She rubbed her jaw as if thinking.

"I may know of it, I will have to do some reading this evening on it, but I am sure I can help you. It may be a very old family crest that I have seen, if so the owners will be of great help. Where do you stay at, I will do some checking into that kind of symbol as I have a huge library," she said this waving a hand expansively around the many thousands of books that lined the shelves surrounding her. "I will be glad to help and my rates are fair."

Don looked at her then at Hutch, he looked at Don and shrugged his approval. "We are staying at the Cracked Flagon, do you know of it?" She looked at them smiled and said she did, they then walked out of the woman's shop into the cold air. Once they walked out of the door the woman looked to the back room, the curtain parted and out of it stepped a small man in black tights and grey doublet with a black cloak.

"Interesting, do they have anything we want?" the small man said with an oily grin on his face, the woman looked at him.

"I am not sure, this book they speak of may be something I have heard of a long time ago, and if it is what I think it is then yes we will want it, the thing will fetch a great price with the right people. This book... Kain, this book... if it is the book I have read of then we need it at any cost including their lives!" "Follow them, do not let them out of your sight." And to that the man smiled and walked back into the back room chuckling to himself in anticipation.

After they walked out of the building Don was looking at Hutch with a smile, he felt an excitement in his chest. "You know, this woman if she does know as much as I hope she does, then she may be able to get us the info to get home."

Hutch looked at Don, stopping in the street. "Don, what if she is some charlatan and somehow steals the book, I don't want to stay here forever, I like gaming but after this, I might decide to take up video games instead of pen and paper games."

Don looked at him, he looked around the dark lantern lit street, the snow was falling slowly and the flakes glowed as they passed by the lanterns, some of the flakes hitting the hot iron tops hissing as they evaporated. "Ya know I agree, for some reason living an adventure is a lot different than playing it, but also I think Kord and Freya will make sure she doesn't do anything like that,"

Then Hutch seemed to have an idea that cheered him up. "You have to admit that she was hot did you see her cans, they were huge,"

Don looked at Hutch with a smile shaking his head, "Yeah, I did, and I will tell Emily to get a corset because you found a woman in another world who is hotter than she is,"

Hutch looked at Don and smiled then realizing what his friend just said. "Hey man don't do that, Emm will cut my Tonies off if you do that, plus I would hate to lie and tell everyone at home you made it with an Orc wench." Don looked at Hutch and smiled.

"Tonies?, what the hell are Tonies?..." and laughing, they walked towards the Inn in the darkening snow fall, their spirits higher than they had been since arriving in this strange world, and their talk of the book and of the pretty woman who they thought may be able to help them. As Don and Hutch made it slowly back to the Inn the bells sounded eight o'clock and they both saw an old man with a candle on a hooded stick lighting the rest of the lanterns along the side of the roads and walkways.

Looking up at the snow that was now falling more heavily Don grimaced. "It looks like they are going to get a good ole Michigan snow fall," Hutch looked around then raised his face up to the descending snow opening his mouth letting the flakes fall on his tongue, he looked at Don the snow sticking to his eyebrows and encroaching beard.

"Yeah, it's getting thick isn't it?, let's get back to the Inn maybe have something to drink, I think a beer sounds good about now." And at that they made their way back to the Inn in the falling snow with the encroaching darkness surrounding them.

Pat and James heard the bells toll eight and saw the Inn far down the street. Walking down the street towards them were many people wearing their cloaks pulled tight in the heavily falling snow; the lanterns were lit along the street and walkways giving off an eerie strange glow in the landscape. Along with the people, they saw three men also that stood out, they had bright blue cloaks on and had polished copper breast plate armor on, they also had conical helmets with pointed spikes of the top of them. They were walking slowly casually and their swords were at their sides within easy reach. James and Pat moved to the side to walk past them when one of them spoke.

"You two, where are you headed?" he was taller than the rest and on his robe was a gold star embroidered, and he had the same gold star on the front of his helmet in polished brass. James looked at him then at the other two.

"Who are you?, our business is our own," at this the three men shifted, their hands going to their swords the man with the star on stepped forward with an angry look on his face, his two companions also stepped forward one to one side of the pair and the other to the other side blocking all chances of escape.

"I am Kralgar[9] and I am an Officer of the Watch, that is my authority, and my business is anyone's I choose to ask of!" He was looking very angry,

Pat broke in quickly and took on a wheedly almost pleading voice, "I am sorry good sirs about my friend here; we are not from here and are not familiar with your laws and

[9] Officer of the Watch is a commander of up to 12 City guards.

customs. We are mere merchants just selling our yams today in the great market, we mean neither harm nor disrespect."

The large man looked at Pat relaxing. "Your friend has a large mouth and one he needs to keep in check, he has an unseemly look about him. What Inn are you staying at?" Pat looked at the man, but before he could speak James spoke.

"We are staying at the Inn right there," he said pointing down the street to the Inn. "It's called the Cracked Flagon; are we breaking any laws?" Pat gave James a withering look and so did the guards standing in front of them,

"You sir are someone we will be watching, it is late, and you need to get off the streets, honest men seek warmth of their beds and ale pots this time of eve!"

Pat looked at the man, "I again am sorry for my companion's mouth and rudeness, we are going to the Inn now and will be of no problem to you or your men," the large man grunted, gave James a dirty look and the three guards wandered past them and moved down the street into the falling snow.

Pat turned on James, "Are you INSANE MORON?", James giving Pat a hateful glare shot back.

"No I am not, dork, I didn't know what else to say. Also how in the hell would I know they were some police or guard, hell you all are always on my ass, it isn't my fault we are here. I didn't buy that book or read that book. I am here and stuck like you all!"

Pat, steaming mad, gave James a hard look. "Next time why don't you try being polite. Also, no one is saying it is your fault, but you are the only one whining and doing ignorant things. Suggesting we take Kord's and Freya's horse, don't be saying dumb crap like that anymore, and don't go pissing off the locals, especially the ones that can throw us in a dungeon."

James glared at Pat but simply turned around and headed back to the Inn, which was right down the street. Looking after him as he walked Pat shook his head in disgust, looked back to make sure the three guards were gone, then muttering to himself, he slowly walked after James to the Inn.

Standing across the street in a dark alley watching them was a man. He wore a black cloak and had long greasy hair. He smiled as he watched James storm off. "That is the one." He smiled and muttered to himself, watching James walk into the Inn he turned and crept back into the darkness of the alley disappearing into the blackness.

Constance
of Ottos Books and Scrolls

Driven and Devious
a bad combination in anyone.
Doubly so for her, for no one knows
her true motives

9
THE OLD MAN

Don and Hutch arrived at the Inn, and as they walked in they saw that Pat and James were already seated at a table. There were some mugs on the table and they both seemed to be upset.

"Hey you two, I take it no luck?" Don asked as he sat down grunting slightly as his knee was sore from the cold.

"Oh no, we had luck, we know what the book is now and that it freaks people out... OH and also Mr. Personality here," he said jabbing a thumb towards James, "almost got us arrested and thrown into a dungeon." James, who was looking into his mug of ale with an upset look on his face looked at Pat, scowling.

Hutch looked at them both, "Well you are here let's move on, you said Pat you knew what the book was?"

Pat looked at Hutch, "Oh yeah it's a book of Dark Magic? Evidently, this Dark Magic is heretical or something, also its bad stuff. The merchant we talked to said we didn't look like Dark Mages, whatever the hell one of those is."

James cleared his throat looking up from his cup of ale he was staring into, "You know I have an idea, maybe the book is trying to get back to something or someone. If it is some kind of evil magic then wouldn't it be something like that maybe, I mean why would it take us here, unless it had a mission?"

Don looked at James with a cynical look. "You mean like it has an ego or a conscious?"

Pat took a deep breath in, "Maybe it's like it has a spell on it, the spell brings the book here and someone is supposed to get it, or maybe we are supposed to deliver it to someone and there are clues as to who it is in the book?"

Hutch looked at Pat, then at the other two. "Hell no, I am NOT going to be reading through that book looking for clues. We talked about this earlier and agreed. So I say we wait for Kord and Freya and see what they say." There was a general murmur of agreement and at that they waited for twelve bells, so they could talk to Kord and Freya.

James, seeming to remember something, spoke while removing the book from his pack. "Here you can have it back, I don't want to even see the thing." He then tossed the book at Hutch, who picked it up and placed it in his cloak.

The evening went slowly while they all waited as they hoped that the news and information they had would in some way make things better so they could get home. They sat quietly watching the Inn's patrons some laughing, some arguing and even once a fight broke out between two very old men, turning over a bench in the process and knocking Doreen to the side. Doreen angrily broke it up by pulling out her knife and threatening to cut some of the old men's more important parts off. Aside from the excitement, everyone's thoughts went home and the women they left behind, and of how they would get home.

Around eleven bells Kord and Freya came walking in. Kord's face seemed ominous in the dark lantern lit room; as he approached, Don was reminded of a stalking hunter coming to get his prey. The newcomers sat down both looking at the men strangely.

"Did you find anything out about the book?" James asked quickly. Kord looked at Freya for a moment and then spoke.

"We found out little other than to say that the book you have maybe something more than we thought. The person we talked to says that he will need to see the book and that if it is what he thinks it may be then it is something that many people will be after, and also you may not have much time to fix your problem, or you may be here forever."

The men looked at Kord with disbelief looking also at each other as if to get some form of support. However no one offered any as what could one say to that. "You mean to tell us that not only is this book something that if word gets out a lot of people will be after? And also that it has a timer?"

Freya looked at Don, "It's all is not as bad as you may think, no one knows you have it, so we have the advantage thus far."

Pat looked at Freya and cleared his throat. "Someone does know."

Then looking at Kord then to Freya he spoke up a bit sheepishly, "Yeah, make that two people."

Kord looked at them sharply, "Who knows, exactly who have you told?"

Don spoke up to the two warriors quickly trying to avoid another problem, "We met a lady at a book shop, we asked her about it. When you left, we split into two groups, we both went our own way into the city. Me and Hutch met with a woman in a book and scroll shop named Constance something or another, she wants us to bring the book back tomorrow."

Freya looked at Don, "Who? Where is this shop?",

Don looked at her, "Ottos Scrolls and-"

Freya interrupted. "Books! I know the woman, Constance is very well known. She isn't to be trusted! That one always is trying to further her agenda. Stay away from her, trust my words on that!"

Pat then spoke giving James a dark look, "We also met with a merchant, he saw the book looked at it and told us it was something called Dark Magic, and that it was blasphemous, and then freaked out and told us to leave him alone and threatened to call the City Guard on us."

Freya looked at Pat sharply. "Did he call them?", she leaned forward looking intently at him.

Pat looked at her and sat back a little surprised at her sitting forward and having such an intense look in her eyes. "No he did not, we left him alone after that. Pat then told them both about their meeting with the City Guard and how James acted.

"You need to be more careful little man, if you are arrested your trial will be quick and your punishment slow; when you cross the Guard in this city you take your life in your own hands, more than once justice was dealt out with a sword in an alley without a Captain's verdict." Kord said this to James with steel in his voice, steel that it seemed James heeded.

James looked at Kord and everyone was surprised his response. "I'm sorry, I will be more careful for now on."

Kord then informed them that they were to meet this mysterious man the next day at twelve bells and that everyone needed to go to bed and get a good night's rest as they had been on the road. At that they agreed to meet back in the Inn's common room in the morning.

Freya offered a parting bit of advice. "You are far from home, you are overwhelmed, we both can tell that. However, know we are helping you. Go to bed get sleep, tomorrow will be a day of much information and hopefully good words." And at that they all retreated to their rooms, and without many comments went to bed with thoughts of home.

It was well past Midnight and Constance walked down the snow clogged street her cloak open exposing her bodice to the ice cold wind that was blowing in the narrow street, snow flying up into her face, she merely waved it away as if she was waving away a bothersome bog fly. She walked quickly for she was running late this and late was not something she wanted to be, as she had a meeting with someone very important. Someone who could make her very rich. She was hoping to strike a deal with this person, but she had to be careful as she knew of this character, and this was someone who would sooner cut her throat then put up with any games.

She turned yet another dark lantern lit corner and saw a large man standing there. He looked at her, a grin coming to his ugly pitted face in the glow of a large iron lantern he was holding. "She is waiting and you are running late. What? Having some problems, are we Constance?"

She shot the man a look filled with venom, "Late or not it is not for a mere hired dog to concern himself with, so stand aside so I can take care of my business with your leash keeper!"

153

The man sneered at her with anger leaning forward he pointed a stubby dirty finger at her, his greasy black nail long and pointed. "So be it for now wench, but things change in this City, trust that." And to that he stood aside exposing a small set of brick stairs that lead down into what appeared to be a basement, the steps were covered in thick wet snow, and as she walked down them she almost slipped a few times, cursing to herself the heavy snow fall.

She made it to the bottom of the steps and there was a door. The door was small and narrow made of simple wood planks. As it was dark she could see through the gaps in the boards, cursing to herself inside as she worried what laid beyond those wood planks, she took a deep breath of the cold air, the cold stinging her lungs and opened the door and stepped in.

The room was small and dark save for a single candle that lay on a table that was giving off a slight glow that covered the table top. There was a doorway to the right and the room was as cold as a tomb. Sitting at the table was the person she had arranged to meet on such short notice. They were sitting there calmly looking at her with a warm smile on their face. Their cloak was tightly about them, however the hood was down exposing the woman's direct look. "Well you have something I want, and I can get something you want. Question is, how much gold can you give me?"

Constance smiled and tried to put on a flattering face to the lady at the table. "How much do you want for it. Simple as that, tell me how much it will cost?"

The lady at the table smiled, "Constance, the real question is how can you come up with the fee for it? I can get the book yes, however, I want five thousand gold sovereigns for it. Not a copper less."

"I can get it to you but it will take me a little bit, after all that is a sum of significance. The question is also if I can get the gold can you get the book, and also can you wait for a bit for me to get the gold." Seeing the person about to speak, Constance spoke again holding up a hand. "And I tell you if that is what you want, I have a backer who will get it for me. No problem at all!" She emphasized this by pointing her finger into the table with a direct look.

"I can wait but not that long, as the party is leaving in a day or so. However, if they do leave I can get the book. It will have to be in an indirect manner. They have a lot of people who will be willing to help protect it, so I will have to be stealthy about my business."

Constance looked at the woman sitting there in that cold room, she smiled as she was close to getting the book, and the people she was dealing with were willing to pay twenty thousand crowns, so she can get the book pay this trash and retire to the country." She smiled at her new friend.

The woman at the table stood up placing the cloaks hood over her head. "I say we meet in a place to be determined to make the transaction. I shall send word to you when I have the book."

Constance smiled at the woman. "Yes we make this final at a day and time to be set." She turned then stopped, thinking. She turned back to the woman. "I do have a question, who is the dog outside up there in the alley. He is not someone I thought you would have as a companion?"

The woman stood there and smiled. "Oh no... he is just a hireling, someone to come with me, I plan to pay him and be done with him. He does, however, know of you from what he says. As a matter of fact, I think he is smitten with you Constance."

Constance looked at the person, she placed her hand to the razor sharp knife in her belt. "Let him be stupid."

The person looked at her smiling, "Do not worry, I plan to have him leave with me, once I pay him, he will not bother you." And at that the woman turned and quietly left the room through the side doorway leaving Constance alone in the cold room. She stood there for a moment and heard their footsteps grow fainter. Excitement built in her chest, her heart pounded with joy. "I never believed in all my days." She said smiling and at that she turned and walked back outside.

She made her way up the steps and the large man who guarded its entrance was nowhere to be seen. She looked around in the falling snow, and bundling up her cloak, she smiled and walked back down the dark alleyway and to her shop.

The next morning dawned with their room cold, the fire in the fireplace went out in the night and inside the fire grate were white and gray ashes smoldering, the slight wisps of smoke floating up into the chimney from the gray ashes. Don walked over to it and placed the remaining two small logs onto the ashes, and they sizzled and soon the wood caught, small licks of fire coming from them.

Speaking to the guys Pat could see his breath steam in the cold air. "Well I am looking forward to being with Lee this eve; here we are inside and its warmer out there than in here!" He was staring into the fire and jerking a thumb towards the frost shrouded window.

Hutch walked over to the window scraping off the frost that covered the cold pane and exclaimed. "Holy cow! Take a look we got dumped on last night!" Everyone walked over to the window and saw that there was a large amount of snow on everything. The whole street was white and there were very few people out and about as it was still very early. They could see grayish blue smoke coming from many chimneys and most of the windows that they could see were still covered with shutters.

"Well, it looks like it just got a little more unpleasant; it will be our luck we will be told we have to go to the next city." James quipped.

Hutch looked at him, "Yeah I gotta agree with James on this one. Traveling in the wagon in this weather would not be pleasant at all." And at that they decided to go down to the warmer common room and wait for Kord and Freya. They gathered their things and Hutch suddenly laughed, he had pulled out his cell phone looking at it, he flipped it open, holding it open he quipped,

"Gee Texton Cell phones are good, look at it still has its charge." And chuckling, he placed it back into his pocket and to that they all went down stairs. However, when they got down there they saw that Kord and Freya were already sitting at one of the tables and that Kord had a bowl of watery porridge in front of him with a pot of ale and Freya had some strange looking brown fruit with tallow spots that she was eating happily.

Kord looked up from his breakfast seeing the group walking down the rickety wooden steps, "Morning my friends! I was wondering if I was going to have to send a banshee upstairs to wake you?" Kord said good naturedly.

The men sat down at the table and Freya proceeded to tell them of the plan. "We are going to take you to a man named Samfor Chamm, he is someone I know well; he is a Mage so do not snub him as he is very old and very easily insulted,"

Don looked at James, "You stay in the back and no talking, ok?" James gave Don a dark look but said nothing about his smart comment.

"He is a very wise man, and he will know what to do; I think also he will know what kind of magic brought you here."

Pat looked at Kord with a relieved expression on his face, "You have no idea as to how grateful we are to you and Freya, we just want to get home."

Kord looked up from his bowl, porridge stuck to his beard dripping onto his tunic, wiping off his face and beard with his sleeved arm, he laughed, "Yeah, you four men are like a pig in a snow storm, you don't know if you are coming or going, but you two," he said pointing a dripping spoon at Don and Pat, "are good to have in a fight, you both showed us that." Smiling Don and Pat gave their thanks to the compliment and after Kord finished eating they got up and walked out of the Inn and into the snowy cold day.

The snow was mid-calf deep, and as they walked out, they saw several men with leg irons on, Freya was standing off to the side looking at them with an expression if pity on her face. The men looked very cold, their feet wrapped in cloth using thin boards to shovel the roads and walks, they looked miserable and barely had rags on, one could tell they were cold and miserable they kept their eyes down while they worked, there was a large man with a wicked ball tipped whip watching over them, along with the large man were two bored looking older soldiers. One of the men stopped rubbing his hands together and the large man yelled at him to get to work then struck the man with the whip on his back causing the man to yell in pain.

"Prisoners." Kord said simply seeing Don's and Hutch's stares and looks of pity.

"The king uses prisoners to do all the menial tasks and work in the city, he is a smart man. Why pay top gold for backs when you can get them for free, plus honest work always makes a dishonest man better in my eyes?"

James gave Kord a hard look but kept silent. They walked past the men in irons and up to Freya, she looked at them and smiled. "More King's justice," was all she said, then with a sigh she turned and walked with the group.

"Freya, you are far too soft, those men deserve their lot in life. They paid for it with lies and misdeeds." Kord said to her as they walked. Freya didn't look at him, and she didn't say anything.

They headed down the street then Kord led them into an alley and then down several more through the lightly falling snow, it seemed they were walking for a very long time passing rundown buildings, they heard ten bells sound, and they continued to walk passing more and more people, some wearing finery and some wearing weary and wore out clothing. Some of them gave them dark looks as they walked by and others shouted obscene comments to Freya as she walked, Freya merely ignored them and once even laughed at one of the comments that was yelled by a young man who was on standing in an upper window. They walked for a bit longer and then entered what only could be described as a warehouse district as the buildings tended to be large and long made of wood, with shuttered windows and stout doors, some had large men with swords standing in front of them looking darkly at passersby.

"You will find a large portion of the wealth if this city behind some of these doors." Kord said to them as they passed one stout door with two men standing outside keeping watch. They walked down a very narrow street, so narrow Don could hold his arms out and touch both brick walls that lined the alley. The alley was clogged with snow and there were few doors and no windows. They stopped in front of a heavy wooden door. The door had no handle or seemingly way to open it and Kord simply walked up to it looked at both ways and tapped the door with his finger lightly.

There was a pause and the door creaked open slightly, a small boy appeared in the opening saw Kord and Freya and wordlessly opened the door and stood aside.

"His greatness is in the lower chamber," he said, and at that Kord and Freya wordlessly walked into a small hall and down a narrow set of wooden steps, as they walked down the steps curved to the right and then the left and Pat estimated they must have walked about two floors down, the stairs terminated into a large room, the ceiling was domed slightly with sturdy wooden buttresses holding it up. Torches lined the walls and all around the room were tables and chairs, work tables with many machines with levers and gears, and beakers with bubbling contents; the room had a sweet strange smell, and Don was shocked when on one wall was a cage with some horrible looking creature in it. He was staring at it as it was manlike about the size of a large chimpanzee but it had no hair and its skin was mottled yellow and tan. The creature had no tail and its head was surmounted with a pair of long pointed ears, it had large black eyes and a large mouth that had many razor sharp yellow teeth. It was hissing and growling looking at the party as they walked in.

"Holy crap, what the hell is that thing?" James exclaimed when he saw it stepping back in fear.

"It's a Vortax[10]" a dusty voice said from the side causing everyone to jump, "It's safe where it is, I have enchantments keeping it in there. Don't get too close as it has a long tongue, and it is razor sharp; they feed off of the blood of the living." Turning, they saw a man, he was wearing a loose light blue robe ornately covered with red and yellow designs, his hair was very long and yellow with age and his beard was short and cropped neatly. He had many gold rings on his fingers each surmounted with a brightly colored gem. He seemed totally at ease.

"Samfor my old friend I am pleased you agreed to see us at such short notice," Kord said bowing slightly to the old man. The old man looked at Freya and smiling broadly he approached Freya embracing her,

"What? And ignore a request from the most pretty adventuress in the Realms" The old man said chuckling. "My girl, it has been far too long, why do you always ignore your Uncle?", she looked a bit embarrassed and warmly hugged him back.

"Uncle, I have been traveling a lot, forgive me for seeming to be inattentive, plus I was here last eve remember?" The old man smiled warmly and then turned to the men, smiling.

"And these are our strange fish, hmmm let me see... and you are?" and at that each one of the group introduced themselves to him. As he was introduced the old man walked to each one taking their hand, as he did he held their hand and closed his eyes for a moment as if concentrating while greeting them. "You are not from here, something there is more about

---

[10] One of the ten abominations that Malphit Doom created. Magical and vilely evil. It knows no pitty.

you, but what I will need to determine," he was looking at
them oddly.

"Uncle, they have the book like we told you of last
night." Freya said aloud and at that the old man perked up a
bit,

"Yes, yes the book... interesting I am anxious to see it.
You," He pointed to Hutch, "you are the one who carries it,
no?" Hutch looked a bit taken back looking at Don then to
James and Pat, then he hesitantly looked back at the old man,

"Yes sir, I am," and at that he took the book out and
handed it to the old man, immediately the old man turned
around his robe swirling behind him, he walked over to a table
and started examining it under a large crystal vessel of water
so it would be magnified. He sat there muttering and
murmuring to himself, meanwhile Don had a chance to look
around a bit.

The work shop was oval shaped and there were all
manner of devices and experiments. He had an extensive
collection of books along the shelves. Don walked up to a book
case and there was a series of black bound books and what
appeared to be human teeth embedded in the spine, there was
a series of twenty books all bound with what appeared to be
some yellow speckled leaf and on the spine were strange letters
and symbols. Looking at one red book, Don reached up and
touched it then pulled it off the shelf, he looked at it and it had
an odd symbol with a series of words in what looked like runes
on it. He opened the page the book making a cracking sound
from the brittle pages,

"DON'T do that! that tome is Elemental Magic, you
might start something you are not prepared to finish." The old
man said without even turning his back or looking up from his

examination of the book Hutch gave him, Don placed the book back quickly and decided to not touch anything else.

After about twenty minutes the man stood up and addressed them, "Tell me of what happened to you and be honest as what you say as it may determine if I can or will help you." He seemed no longer frail and good natured, he seemed serious and stern. He was looking at the men.

Don proceeded to tell him of what happened and with the periodic input of the other men the old man seemed to relax a bit as their story unfolded before him.

"Like I said, you are not from here, your world is far away, and I am afraid you won't see it anytime soon as this book is not normal; it is very Dark Magic and I am sure it is an ancient tome that was thought forever gone. I believe the symbol on the cover is of a large Guild of Dark Magic Users that disappeared in the great purge almost a hundred years ago. It puzzles me why it is here, the incantation on the page that you read," he said pointing a bony finger at Hutch, "is powerful magic and that is what brought you here. I imagine it is a finding spell." He looked over and walked to his book shelf taking down an old dark green large book, sitting it down he thumbed through the pages stopping at one.

"Look here is what it is." Everyone walked over and saw on the page was a drawing of an old man and a tower. The book seemed to tell a story and it didn't look good, as the old man turned the yellowed pages the tower was shown to blow up and at the end it showed the book with an evil looking man seemingly pulled into the book, screaming. Don and the rest were silent and one could sense the tension in the room. The old man looked up from the book seriously then spoke quietly.

"Hmmm... yes much to talk about here, much also to explain and that, you, my strange guests, will do." There was a silence in the room; the sound of the fire cracking in the fireplace, Then James spoke.

"Why can't we you just send us back? You are a magic user, aren't you? And what does this old book have to do with our book?" James said pointing at the open book on the table.

The old man looked at James for a moment then spoke, he was speaking quietly, and it seemed he was worried.

"What you see before you" he said pointing at the book on the table he had seemed he choose his words carefully. "What is open on this table is a legend, a fairy tale that many believed was just a story to amuse the ignorant over there ale pots. However to many it was known that this was indeed not a story as there are only five books like this," he said patting the large green tome hr had sitting in front of him. "This and its four mates tell the true story of what happened and also foretell the dread day that this book," He said this pointing to the small brown leather book on the table, "will come back. You see, I know who you are and I know you come from a faraway place and what you hold. This book is Dark Magic but also it is special as it holds a beacon that will bring back Malphit Doom and that, my friends, is a very bad thing indeed. This book was the book that was made to destroy the very magical weave that controls light magic."

The old man sat down almost in a dejected way placing his head in his hands.

"Uncle, what does this mean? Who is this Dark wizard?" Freya asked stepping forward placing a concerned hand on his shoulder.

Kord stepped forward placing a hand on the old man's other shoulder and with a jolly tone said. "Samfor, my old friend, this Dark wizard may come back but let me stick my long sword in his chest and he will go away for a long time." The old man smiled warmly looking up at Kord.

"Kord, my friend, you do not realize your sword will not have any effect on this Mage, he is one of the original ten that broke away from the Original Order of Light." At that Kord took a deep breath and was visibly shaken.

"How can that be they are all dead, that is impossible!"

Pat looked at Kord and was alarmed as he saw genuine fear in Kord's face, even Freya stepped back with a worried frown.

"Uncle, the Original ten are gone and have been gone for a century as everyone says, have they not?"

The old man leaned back in his chair. "Yes the original Ten are long gone, however there were a group of Dark Mages who broke away centuries ago from the original order of Light, they were led by Malphit Doom, the most vile and evil man to ever wear the black robe. Almost a hundred years ago there was a meeting of the Order of Light, they deemed that Dark Magic was far too evil for the world and decided to destroy it and its followers, what came after that was the great purge, hundreds died and Malphit Doom was rumored to have been killed. It was also rumored a book was created to destroy the very threads of Light Magic however the Dark Mages feared this book would fall into the hands of those coming for them so they sent it away. Some say to another dimension or world. That, my friends, it seems is where you came into this, you happened across something that was better left alone."

Hutch looked at Pat, Don and James with a shocked look, "I'm sorry guys, I had no idea." Don looked at Hutch and smiled a half smile looking at the book sitting there silently on the table.

"Look, it wasn't and isn't your fault; it was a book, how could you have known?" Looking at the old man seriously Hutch leaned on the table taking a drink from a cup of wine that was in front of him,

"So what is the solution then, how do we get home?" The old man looked at Hutch for a moment, the fire in the fireplace cracking and popping startling everyone.

"How do you get home... Well that is the easy part all you have to do is to throw the book into the Stone Gate." Pat looked relieved and James then spoke. "Well where is this Stone Gate at? Heck let's do it and get home!" The old man smiled at James a tolerant smile.

"The hard part is getting to the Stone Gate. That is the hard part indeed." The old man said looking to the book that was lying on the table, silently with a worried expression on his face.

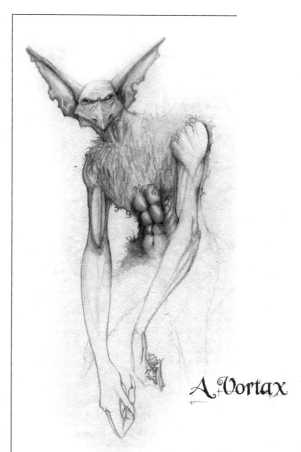

A Vortax

Hard to catch and impossible to tame
their magical properties are prized by
Mages all over the Realms

Trust no man that is not of our lands

...... Hafarian Merchant Proverb

10

UNEXPECTED COMPANY

"The Stone Gate? Where is that, and am I willing to guess it is guarded?" Pat asked the old man with a cynical look on his face. Kord grunted, then spoke up.

"Yes guarded it is indeed, and it is not in a place those that are smart like to tread. Freya looked troubled and looking at her Uncle she stood up and walked over to the fire place with worried look on her face. The fire making her hair look like it was on fire. Turning to everyone she spoke to her Uncle directly.

"Uncle are you sure this is the only way, I mean, why can't we use some form of magic to destroy it, after all, it is just a book?" The old man stood up and walked to one of the shelves picking off a book from the shelf. He opened the old dark maroon book thumbing through the pages slowly, reading intently. He did this for a few minutes then spoke.

"Yes here it is; this book is the chronicles most of the magical lore of the Realms, in its pages is valuable information that if read correctly tells us of that book's creation and how to get rid of it, I will read from it, and you will understand." And to that the old man cleared his throat and started reading aloud.

"And the great conclave of Mages met and their meeting was one of great debate. Upon long discussion, they decided to forever ban the hideous and dangerous magical abomination called Dark Magic. They agreed to hunt down and destroy all those that practiced its ways, as they knew that Dark Magic's only purpose was to harm, warp and instill vile evil onto the world. To this end they started plans, however unknown to them, two Dark Mages be present in their midst and these two mages immediately met with their fellow vile mages upon the meeting's conclusion to set forth a plan to destroy the good and righteous magic before they could be hunted and discovered.

They created a book, vile, dark an abomination upon the Realms, for when this book's magic was unleashed it would attack the very threads that held the light of good magic together, tearing away the good and just magic of the Realms. However, timing and fate were on the side of good, for once completed the book was lost and if ever found would have to be destroyed, however this book could not ever be destroyed, unless it was placed in the Stone gate, a gate that led to the very threads that powered Dark Magic for if the book was ever thrown into this gate its dark energies would backfire and forever destroy the dark magic which itself feeds on.

Everyone stared at the old man for a moment, and then James leaning forward placing his elbows on the table in front of him spoke in an excited tone.

"Why this gate, I mean there is no other way, can't you wave a wand or something?" The old man looked at James for a moment, he seemed to have an amused expression in his face.

"My young friend, it is not that simple, if it were you would already be home in front of your hearths." He then looked at Kord, "My friend, the gate is not in Amaria anymore either." James looked at Kord, then to Don; seeing James was ready to speak, Don interjected.

"What is this Stone Gate and where is it, I mean how far away is it and what do we have to do exactly, we throw this book in it? And then what?"

The old man looked to Don then to the others. "Come upstairs and I will tell you of your task, as if you wish to go home you will do it, then again, Da' Naan is not that horrible of a place. However, enough of dark places and books, it is time for wine and food, rest for a moment. Don't worry, you all are safe here." And at that he got up and led them upstairs. The room he took them to was covered in ornately carved paneling, it had narrow windows along one wall and one could hear the sounds of the street emanating from them.

"So, what is next then and what do we do with you four?" Kord said looking at them intently while sitting down, and grunting in the process.

"We don't expect you to help us anymore; you already have done so much, if you tell us where to go, we will have to manage this on our own." Hutch said to Kord.

Don looked at the old man and saw an amused expression on his face, then he saw Freya look at her feet, staring as if thinking, she then went over to the window looking out of it.

"We will do what we can to help you. However, I have to offer this advice," she turned looking at the men, "Don't go on this road; settle here and make a life best you can. You do not want to go where this path leads." She was serious and for the first time Don saw fear in her face.

"This is not our home, we have to do this. We have people who care for us there." Pat said. James broke in,

"Yeah, my Bri is missing me, and I want to go home, this place stinks and I am sick of being here." At that Freya walked up to James angrily.

"Do you know where you are headed? Do you really know what it means to go to the Stone Gate? You do not! So do not complain, you sound like a Lunite Maid. I know what my Uncle's books say about it, I have read them all as a child, I know where we go!" James shot her a look and was about to speak when Kord spoke.

"We all are tired and weary of this, Freya and I have been on the road for almost 3 months and yes, our patience wears However, we will go with you. The Stone Gate is in a place of danger and one that will take not only courage but a good sword arm to get to, I fear." He looked at Samfor with a smile, "I am right, am I not? It is in a place of danger, is it not?"

Don looked at Kord and then to Freya, and then he looked at the old man, in a dejected manner he spoke. "Please tell us what we need to know, I am sure there are things we will need to do to get started." The old man smiled at Don's comment, and then he leaned back folding his hands into each other and rubbing them.

"Indeed there are Don, there truly are many things to know, and I shall tell you. Sit down all of you," he gestured at the table and suddenly there were six more chairs there that were not there a few moments before, also on the table were glasses and a large decanter of a blue liquid and a platter with bread and cheese.

"Let us drink some wine," the old man said pouring several glasses full of a dark blue liquid, "and I will tell you what you need to do." They sat and drank the dark wine that had an odd flavor, it seemed to burn Don's throat as he drank it and after a few moments, he was warm and light headed. Looking around he saw the rest of the group nodding off. Panic hit him as darkness enveloped him, his heart lurched for he wondered if the old Mage betrayed them. Then deep warmth wrapped around him, and he slept a dreamless sleep.

Standing outside the door was the servant; he had his ear pealed against the door listening to what was being said. He had no self motive by listening other than monetary gain, as what was being said was gibberish to him. He looked down the hall as he heard a creak, seeing no other servant he figured he had heard enough and walked to the back of the house, opening a narrow door that is used to dump kitchen slops, he stepped out into the narrow snow choked alley.

In the shadows, a man in a black cloak stepped out, smiling. "Well my friend, did you hear anything?" The servant looked back into the house then down the alley, paranoia grabbing his gut.

"Yes, yes but I don't understand what they say. I am a simple man and poor at that."

The man in the black cloak smiled doubly as he knew the letch was greedy. Poor and greedy, the perfect combination for his needs. He handed the man five Silvers, a sum more than the man made in a month. Smiling and instantly feeling more brazen, the servant told the strange greasy man of the conversation in the room. Smiling the man in the black cloak gave him another silver.

"I promise you ten more every day for every important bit you give me, you help me, and I can help you. I also know of someone who may hire you up on Lord's way, there you can make a Gold a month. Do these favors for me and I will see it done."

The servant almost leapt for joy; he smiled broadly and promised to get all the information he needed. He smiled and closed the door and the greasy man in the black cloak, smiling, disappeared into the alley.

When Don awoke, he was still sitting in his chair. However, it was evening and the windows were dark; the old man had many glowing lanterns about the room hanging from the wooden beams each one had colored glass in it. The lanterns were casting a warm multi hued glow over the room, the shadows of the beams dancing on the walls. He looked to see if his friends were there, and they were and they were also awakening, also on the table in front of them all was the book that brought them all to this strange world. Kord and Freya were stretching and looking very relaxed.

"Well, do we all feel better now?" Turning Don saw the old man walking in with a servant behind him holding a platter with several steaming bowls on it.

"What the hell happened?" James said as he was looking around confused rubbing his neck, the old man sat down and his servant placed a bowl of the hot soup in front of each person.

"You were all needing rest. I simply gave you a draught of mine; you should now be rested and able to think more clearly." Don sat there and realized that he felt more relaxed and rested than he had felt in a very long time. Even when he was at home. He felt lucid like he could sit there forever.

"Uncle, please don't do that again, let us know OK? We don't like being drugged." Freya said as she was arching her back stretching. The old man looked amused, then sat down at an empty chair at the table, smiling, and spoke.

"Well my friends, do you want to now know how to get home?" There was a general murmur of agreement, and with a serious expression he spoke.

"You must know that what you are about to do is fraught with danger and will not be easy. However, if you are successful then the magic will be reversed and anyone within ten feet of the person placing the book into the Stone Gate will be released to where the book came from, that means one firm rule must be held true. You must be within ten feet of each other when the book is placed in the Gate, those that are not will forever be left here, and where you will be going to you do not want to be left behind if you manage to get to the Gate alive."

Pat looked perplexed, "I am sorry, but you say that when we take the book and throw it into this Gate then the magic that will take us home works only in a ten feet circle?" The old man looked at him for a moment.

"Yes, that is what I said."

Pat shifted in his chair, "Where is this place? Is it on the top of a mountain or some other hard to get to place?" Thinking of the snow capped mountains, Don looked at Pat shaking his head.

The old man spoke quietly as if the words pained him to say them, "No, it is deep, very deep in the Dungeons of Kal-Aldoon, it is in the deepest recess of that awful place,"

Freya took a deep audible breath in causing everyone to look at her, and her face was worried.

"And you know what that place is, don't you Freya?" the old man said looking at her with sadness in his eyes.

Hutch, looking at Freya then at Kord, who also seemed troubled, his hand rubbing his face and scraggly growing beard, "What is this Dungeon? And is it hard to get to?" Hutch asked leaning forward.

"No, it is not hard to get to, in fact, no one wants to get to it. It is a vile and despicable place and one that no one with any brains ever treads to."

Everyone jumped as the person who said it was standing in the doorway. Freya took one sharp look at the woman then jumped up with a huge smile on her face.

"Sister!" Freya ran over to the woman hugging her fiercely, the both of them smiling. The woman was tall and had sandy curly blonde hair, she wore it short cut just above her shoulders and was wearing a dress of peasant design, she had a narrow leather belt and a dagger was at her hip. She was feminine but also had an air of confidence.

"Yes Freya, I am sorry I did not tell you, Tena arrived a short time ago while you all were resting, she wanted to surprise you," the old man said smiling,

"And a wonderful surprise it is indeed." Freya said with a smile still on her face. Both of them sat down with the mysterious woman sitting next to Freya. "Everyone this is Tena, she is my Sister, whom I have not seen in a very long time." Freya said this to everyone smiling at her sister warmly while holding her hand. Everyone exchanged awkward hellos.

Pat got up and offered her his hand, "Hi, I'm Pat, nice to meet you.

The woman awkwardly took his hand, and not sure how to react, she simply laughed.

"Why do you speak of this place so? Freya what does your sister speak of when it comes to this Dungeon, we have adventured in many dungeons together, yes they all are dangerous but the Stone Gate is supposed to be in the temple of Amaria, I have never heard of this Kal-Aldoon, and Amaria is not far away and..." Tena broke in,

"Kord, I know you and I know how brave you are but this place is not an ordinary Dungeon. That place has been over ran by things from the Underhalls. Making it worse is a very old Dark Mage and his enchantments rumor to still occupy it. The Stone gate in the Temple of Amaria is no longer there. It was taken to Kal-Aldoon according to legend, and leads to the strands of Light magic, the other one leads to the strands of Dark Magic. One of Obsidian, one of Marble, each gate is similar in it purpose."

Then the old man spoke, "And as he is a Dark Mage he will want what you have there." Freya's Uncle said pointing to the book on the table with a skinny finger. "And he will not stand by and allow you to simply have access to the Stone Gate and throw that book into it."

Don was confused here, he leaned forward clearing his throat causing Tena and Freya to look at him and the old man to smile.

"I have to understand something here? You both are sisters?" Tena looked at Don smiling.

"What? Is that so hard to believe?, yes we have the same mother but different fathers, we were once very close but time and circumstances have come between us." Freya then turning to Kord spoke,

"Yes my friend I never told you of that place as it was always something that I never would have wanted to adventure to, there is no gold, no jewels, just death as the legend I have heard said it so."

James spoke then. "Are you sure there is no other way to get rid of this book, I mean is there not another one of these gates, it has to be thrown into this dark one? Are you certain of this?" The old man looked at James then to everyone,

"I wish truly there was another way. However, the Stone Gate is the only way I tell you, the only way to be rid of that book and break its enchantment. If there were another way I would say as I do not want my precious niece going to that place." Freya smiled at her Uncle warmly, and then Tena spoke.

"Sorry Uncle there will be two nieces going there, if Freya goes, I go." Tena said sitting up.

Looking at Tena and Freya with sad eyes the old man bowed his head for a moment then got up walking to a book case.

Kord cleared his throat, "So I have two of you to deal with, aye, I hope you are of better mood than your sister in the mornings." He said this lightly and Don could tell he was trying to break the morose mood that infected the room and table.

"Well I take it we will have company then?" Hutch said to Kord looking at him.

Kord looked back then to Freya, "Well, do we send them to their deaths or do we gain more honor and glory for being the ones to beat the Dark Mage at his own games?"

Freya smiled looking at Kord. "You my old friend are a crazy old Northsman."

She laughed playfully smacking Kord in the head.

"I guess we beat a Dark Mage."

At that Kord slammed his hand on the table turning over a bowl and a few glasses, "HAH! There have an agreement; see my new friends, we won't abandon you. Before this adventure is finished we will know what metal you have in you."

Don looked at Hutch and he looked back smiling in an insincere way, this was not what they thought at all. Don started thinking and realized that if he were home right now he would be at home eating dinner. Instead here he was sitting with strangers getting ready to go on an even stranger adventure into what appeared to be a vile and dark dungeon; he would be ticking off some evil Mage and for what? To throw a book into a Gate and all this based on the word of an old man who drugged them. His thoughts went to the lady in the bookstore. He decided he needed a second opinion.

Who were the crazy ones here he thought? He hoped that it would not prove to be him and his friends. Looking around and seeing the looks and stares of his friends he knew they were thinking the same thing.

He was going to live a game.

If I was in a real game I would be kicking butt
and stealing gold.

...... James one evening after a game

Samfors Living Room

Give me a good sword, over a silly stick with an iron tip any day. Any warrior worth his own salt wouldn't be caught dead by an arrow.

...... Kord talking about arrows versus a good sword.

11
BETRAYAL

Across town the man in the Black cloak entered a wooden door. Inside was a woman, she was standing among a lot of old books and looked at him with anticipation. "Well, what news do your lips carry?"

The man took his cloak off shaking it out, flecks of melted snow spattering about. "Well, they meet with the mage Samfor, and they have a book. I paid his servant for information, the book they are told is the one you seek. Further, they have been told to go to something called the Stone Gate. That is all I know at this point, I have promised the servant more tomorrow for any information he can give."

The woman looked perplexed, but she was smiling broadly. "I need to know their plans, are they staying here, are they leaving if they are planning to leave, I have to know when. This Stone Gate I haven't heard of I know someone though who can tell me of it. Watch them, place eyes on Samfor's house. We need to know when they go, where they go and who they meet. We also need that book at ANY cost. And I mean ANY!" And to that she tossed a jingling leather pouch to the greasy looking man. Smiling he placed it in his cloak, he turned to leave then stopped, turning his head to the woman, he asked a question.

"Constance, tell me? If this is the book you told me of, then are you sure we want to sell it to the Dark Mages. I mean would they not use it to do great evil?"

The woman looked at him hard saying nothing, he shrugged deciding to not care as long as the gold flowed and then walked back out into the cold.

Back at Samfor's home they decided to stay at the old man's home for the next week while they got organized and formulated a plan. During that time Kord and Freya made several excursions into the city on their own, to get information and also take care of their own affairs. The four men also made several short trips into the city. Pat asked Tena several times to join him, yet each time she smiled and politely refused. During that time Tena seemed to always be at Don's side, and they also made several trips out into the city together. Tena showed Don many things, and they talked of the world that Don had left behind,

"Does it snow like this in your Michigan?" she asked Don one afternoon while they walked, her arm in his, her shoulder pulled next to his, the snow was falling lightly large flakes sticking on her long eyelashes and in her hair.

"Yeah it does, we have snow storms, but we have no magic in the way you think." She looked at Don with a look that told him she thought he was teasing. "No, seriously we do not have magic, no spells, no magical items we just have technology that to your eyes may be magic like."

Tena looked at him with a confused look, she opened her mouth to speak several times, thinking of her words she then looked at Don.

"Technology? Is that not like magic?" Don looked at her and realized yet again how pretty she was. The snow was falling and sticking to her blonde hair and due to the cold her cheeks and nose were red,

"Well we have things that can fly, we call them airplanes, people climb in them, and they take people to faraway places very fast."

Tena looked shocked then leaned into Don whispering, "Maybe one day you will take me on an airplane?"

Don smiled and it then hit him. He was confused, he liked this strange woman and was taken aback by how she seemed attached to him, how could he so fast feel such an attraction for a woman? He knew her only a few days. He walked on and he smiled thinking of Emily's words to him so many weeks ago, but he knew she wouldn't want to leave her world and her sister. He decided to throw it out of his mind and make the day a good one and at that they walked the afternoon quietly talking arm in arm in the falling snow.

Meanwhile, in another part of the city Hutch and Pat decided to explore its old quarter, they determined early on that this was one place that they didn't want to go at night.

"Reminds me of some of the books I have read, ya know Pat." Hutch said, Pat looking around agreed,

"Yeah, this is not a place I would want to make my home, we need to get going on this fiasco and get back home. Lee has probably moved some guy in by now, and I know Emily is most likely freaking out about you missing."

Hutch looked at Pat, "You know, you need to relax a bit about her, she does love you."

Kicking his feet into the snow he was suddenly agitated.

"Doesn't it do anything but snow. This place is worse than Michigan." Pat stopped and turned to Hutch,

"What's up with James? He has been quiet and standoffish and acting like a jerk. He won't leave that house, instead sits there reading those books the old man lets him read." Hutch looked at Pat and shrugged,

"You know, when we get back, I think I am done with him, I mean he has shown his true colors since coming here, whining little baby." Pat smiled in a knowing way.

"Yeah, let's get home then talk about him, he has always been a whiner but what did it with me was his wanting to steal Kord's and Freya's horses, I mean them two are our friends, I can tell that much."

Pat then turned to Hutch, "Hey, Hutch, do you think Freya's sister and me have a chance? I mean I think she is pretty good looking."

Hutch looked at his friend in the falling snow. "You're married Pat. Lee is back home worried about you, I bet. Plus Tena and Don have been spending a lot of time together."

Pat looked angrily at Hutch, "Lee is probably doing half the block while I am gone..."

Hutch interrupted him, "Man you know that bullshit isn't true, you're pissed but you two need to work things out."

Pat looked at Hutch, "Well, maybe this is the time to move on, find a new woman, that chick Tena I think likes me, I can tell the way she looks at me,"

Hutch gave his friend a hard look and thought about saying more, but he just knew that Pat was hurt over things with Lee, so he decided to drop it for now. They walked the rest of the afternoon. Then as it was getting late and with the sky turning darker in the falling snow they made their way back to the old man's home.

That evening the old man said he had more information for them. He was standing over by the large oak book case.

"I have been researching the Dungeon for you and have two gifts you may find interesting and helpful. The old man came walking back to the table with a pair of scrolls in his hand, and he had a sad look on his face, he sat down rolling out one of the scrolls and Hutch and the rest could see it was a map of what appeared to be a large land mass. There was what one could tell where mountains, forests, hills and sees all neatly drawn out.

"You are here in Dark Home" the old man said placing a finger on the map in the lower left corner of the map. "And you want to go here" he said pointing what appeared to be very far away on the map.

"This is the Southern Jungle, and Gott is where you need to go." The old man said scratching his chin.

Tena spoke, "Great... mosquitoes and Vramak. I really hate Vramak."

Don looked at her with a puzzled look on his face. "What is Vramak?" She smiled at Don warmly and leaning over, she touched his arm,

"They are blood sucking worms that crawl into your feet and eat you from the inside out. They are only found in the area of Gott."

Don heard an "oh great!" to his left and looking, he saw James shaking his head placing it into his hands.

Pat spoke up smiling, "Don't worry Tena, I will make sure you are ok on the road." He said this with an air of confidence that caused even Hutch to almost laugh.

Tena looked at Pat smiling, "Oh, don't worry Pat, I think I will be well protected," She said this laying her hand back on

Don's arm. Pat suddenly got a dark look on his face, he sat back saying nothing. Hutch smiled.

"Well, we know where it is, and we know what lies in it, so all we need is to get our gear and some rations and go to it." Kord said cheerfully.

"Kord, this is different than we both have done before; this place is vile in the worst way and if the legends are even half right then it is by far the most singly dangerous place in the entire of the Realms and one that we should not enter lightly." Freya said this with obvious caution in her voice causing Kord to look at her oddly.

"Yes, it is vile and evil. However, also know that there are far greater dangers than monsters and beasts, one must also be more weary of the enchantments and the traps, for he is not only evil he is also cunning, and even if is he long dust and bones his enchantments and traps will be still present." The old man told them sternly, The Chronicles of Yognar the Brave[11] tell of the place in detail, and also give us a small map. So we know how to get into Kal-Aldoon.

James cleared his voice then spoke with caution in his speech.

"I know I am not from here. However, I have a question? You say there is a chance the crazy evil mage may be dead?" The old man looked at James and smiled,

"Yes a chance there is, and it is most likely so." James had a hopeful look on his face,

"Then, if he is dead, he won't be there looking and guarding the place. Isn't there a back door, maybe a direct way into the area where this well is?" Freya spoke this time she was obviously trying to be calm as she seemed agitated.

[11] Only 2 tomes are known to exist, one in the possession of Samfor Chamm of Dark Home

"James, you do not understand, the book there" she said pointing at the book lying quietly on the table, "has powerful dark magic in it, so powerful every dead dark mage will be turning in their grave as it passes, now that this book is here it will attract the vileness and evil that inhabit the very place that we are going to..." Tena then interjected,

"And do not forget that there are all manner of ways that this book could release that crazy old wizard once we are in that rot hole, and if HE! comes to be then we all are going to wish we were in a vat of Vramak on a hot day." Don looked at her and smiled feeling a little bold,

"Well Tena, then we will just have to make sure that doesn't happen now, wont we." Tena looked at him and laughed,

"You are the optimistic one now, aren't you; we will see how that holds up in the coming days."

Kord looked troubled, "Yognar the Brave, I have heard of his exploits, he made it to this place and gave you a map Samfor?"

The old man looked at Kord, "No, he did not. However, he chronicled his exploits in two books, I have one of them. The other is in the Royal Library in Loc Amar[12]."

The rest of the evening was full of discussion of the dungeon, and of how they would get there and also how they would gain entry. The entrance as Samfor explained was at the base of the central spire in the middle of the ruined city. He further explained that no one would have any trouble finding it, even though James pressed him for how he knew it.

Once ten bells sounded, they all agreed to leave for the Dungeon the day after tomorrow, so they could have the next

[12] Capitol of Amaria, and the Religious center of the kingdom.

day to get ready with supplies and provisions, they agreed to stay at Freya's uncle's house until they left; Pat felt this was a good idea as did Don and Hutch, so they could study the map. However, James felt it was better to get out of the stuffy house himself and do some thinking, he got a leather cloak on and Don looked up at him.

"You're actually going out, want someone to go with ya just in case there is trouble?." James looked at Don with an irritated look on his face. "No I am a big boy I think I can handle going for a walk!" and at that he spun around and stalked out of the room with no further comment. The others looked after him, Hutch made a snorting sound and went back to the map on the table, Pat smiled shaking his head.

"Let the big baby go, he gets locked up by the city guard he is on his own." No one said anything at that comment. Kord excused himself telling them that he was going to go back to the Inn and get the money he stashed in the room. Saying goodbye, he left also and said that he would be back by twelve bells.

Kord walked out into the brisk cold, a rough wind was blowing, and it was snowing heavily. The snowflakes were hissing as they hit the torches and lanterns that were lit here and there on the street. He walked down one narrow alley then another, the snow swirling around him, he passed one door that was cracked. Bawdy laughter and music emanating from it the smell of rotting cabbage and bad ale following the sound. As he walked down and into another alley, he was confronted by two thin men, one leering at him, an empty eye socket and yellow teeth, smiling,

"Well whom do we have here... ah it's you. Palmer is waiting, he is in there." The man pointed to a door that was made of heavy oak and had steel rivets on it; knocking on it twice he was greeted with the door being cracked and a rough voice demanding who was there.

"It's me, open the door Orlin or you will feel my boot in your arse. I am cold and in no mood for your games." The door was opened and revealed a small room with rickety furniture with several smoking tallow candles on the only table, sitting at the old rickety table with a small glass of wine was a hooded individual, he looked up and Kord could see via the flickering candle light the features of a man, he looked frail but there was an air of superiority to him. The man behind to door bowed and asked Kord if he wanted some wine, Kord declined.

"Orlin leave us now!" The hooded man said in an even tone, The man called Orlin backed out of the room through a doorway while groveling apologies.

Kord stood there looking at the man the man sat there seemingly not worried about the man staring at him,

"Well will you sit or stand there?" The man said quietly. Kord sat down then spoke.

"I know where it is that they go, and yes, it is the book as you thought; we plan to leave the morning after tomorrow and I plan to do as I promised at first chance once we enter the Dungeon." The hooded man smiled exposing yellowed teeth,

"Yes thank you, as I said you will be rewarded in ways far greater than simple gold." He said this while tossing a fat leather bag onto the table in front of Kord. Picking up the jingling bag Kord opened it and saw it was full of Gold Crowns.

"Gold is fine Palmer, however it will cost you as I will have to kill not only the four but also Freya's sister, the meddling wench is insisting on coming." The old man looked up and drank from his glass, then spoke.

"Do what you have to do; once I have the book you will have your ten thousand crowns and more. You will be a king among men, and you will have lands and a Keep." Kord smiled at this comment,

"That's all I want, and I will get you that book, my plan is to act when we are in the dungeon as I know there will be chances when we are in there. Also I want one more thing."

The man looked quizzically at Kord. "What is that?"

"I want a Draught of Living Death."

Puzzled the man leaned forward. "Why is that? That draught does not kill, it only makes the person appear as though dead? Why do you want that?"

Kord shifted in his seat. "I want the money, but Freya I won't kill. We have adventured together and I will not kill her. I need to make it appear as though she ate something and she died. Then I will be free to take matters in hand with the others. They trust me and that will be their downfall."

The man smiled at Kord,

"I have waited a long time for that book to return, do as you must when you must. I will provide the draught, but I must have that book no matter the cost. Even if it means the woman's life!"

Kord seemed at that point to have an idea, "If I may borrow your two sneak thieves scum that are prowling the alley outside, I may be able to make my task easier and thus get the book to you sooner. I could use them to thin out the herd in a manner of speaking, maybe by two or three."

The mysterious man smiled a mirthless smile. "So be it, they are yours to command and do as you may need. What of the angry one you told me about? Is he the one that we can use?" The mysterious man looked to his empty glass on the table. He then yelled for his servant.

"Orlin get in here, I need more wine!" The man came in groveling apologies for not giving him more wine, he was scared of the man and while pouring the wine he was whimpering and begging forgiveness. Kord thought for a moment,

"He is a weak man, weak minded also, but I do not think he will betray his friends. I will kill him on the road, he is a liability." Kord stood up, "I am leaving as they will get suspicious if I am gone for too long; I will return within a few weeks or so with your book, just have my money waiting." And at that he stood up, turned and left the room walking back into the cold snowy alley, passing the two men pulling his bear skin cloak tightly about him as the night was far colder and windy then when he first ventured out.

The old man sat at the table smiling, watching Kord walk out the door. He sat there excited as soon the book would be back in his possession, and he could finish what he started, he needed that book. Far too long he has waited, and he was within reach now of getting it. He was in such a good mood he decided that this eve he would spare Orlin of his nightly lashings. He ordered Orlin to get the two men from the alley. The two men a few minutes later came in both nervous about being called in the room by the man.

"Aglar and Terc, I have a job for you." Both men smiled evilly looking at one another. "I want you to go with the large man that just left, he will tell of his needs. Follow his words as if they were mine. Once he is done he will pay you and so will I. Fifty gold sovereigns to each of you if you complete his work as he instructs."

Both men smiled, "Master you have no worries, we will go to the ends of the earth for you," the one eyed man said eagerly. The man sitting at the table took a drink of his wine, smiling to himself, he spoke softly.

"So you may, my friends.. So you may."

James stepped into the outside air and was surprised at how dark it was, and that it was snowing; he pulled the cloak tighter about him looking around he decided to stick to the main road that trailed next to the old man's building. What he did not know was that a man was watching him, he wore a black cloak and his greasy dark hair was matted to his forehead due to being wet. He saw James walk out and start walking down the street. He stepped quietly into the light of the lanterns and followed.

The man followed James for a ways watching James when he decided to take action, looking around to ensure no one was watching, he quietly walked up to James. "Hello." He said causing James to jump a bit. James turned around seeing the man standing close to him, he looked around and saw they were alone on the street.

"Hello back at you, who are you?" James said in a suspicious way, his eyes narrowing as the man did not look like a trustworthy type of person. The man smiled at James.

"I am someone who works for someone who can help you with your problem." James's heart took a skip; he looked at the man then spoke with some excitement in his voice. When he spoke the greasy man smiled to himself in a knowing smile.

"You can help us? Seriously, you can do that how?" The man looked at James still with a smile.

"You are being fooled my friend, that old man you stay with is known all over Dark Home. He is a charlatan, a liar and has scammed so many people he is being watched by the City Watch. We know him well."

James looked at the man, suddenly worried. "You are the Watch, look, I was rude the other night, I..." The man smiled waving a dirty hand at James.

"No no... don't you worry, I am a special magistrate here. I specialize in lost persons and of those that take advantage of those in need. We know you are here lost, and I can help you, but there is one problem."

James looked at him, worried now for another reason. "What's the problem?, the old man says we have to toss it into the Stone Gate, whatever the hell that is."

The man frowned a bit, and then recovered quickly, "My young friend, that's what that crazy old man said. Let's go have a drink, I will buy, and I can tell you of the easy solution, you can be home by twelve bells tomorrow if you like." He was patting James on the shoulder. James smiled, he was so happy, by this time tomorrow he could be home further he could stick the other guys' nose in it, he knew Kord and Freya were no good, and of course they take them to HER Uncle. Home... he couldn't believe it, he smiled agreeing to go get that drink; this was a very nice man he thought to himself as he walked down the street and into a dirty tavern.

Back at the old man's house, Freya was going over the map; further away, the old man unrolled the second scroll he had and that was a partial map of the Dungeon of Kal-Aldoon. The yellow parchment glowed in the light of the three candles that were burning in brass sconces on the table. It was obvious that the Yognar the Brave didn't make it too deep in the place, but the good part was that it did detail on its crackling yellowed page the entrance and also a large part of the first level. "Well, one area is better than no areas mapped out, I suppose." Freya said to herself while looking intently at the map. Meanwhile Hutch was sitting in a chair by the fire and Pat was sitting at a small table reading a book that the Old Man gave him on the history of the Realms. Don and Tena were sitting down on the floor in a bearskin rug by the fire talking, "What is your world like. I mean..." she hesitated thinking of what to say, "I mean you don't have Goblins and Trolls and Vramak?" Tena asked Don looking at him and smiling. Don told her about the various animals, and also of Dinosaurs and how they were no longer. After about an hour Tena seemed amazed.

"I would love to see those things, I never have liked this place," she said looking around. "I mean, it is my home, but I have always felt there was more to be seen." Don looked at her, and he felt oddly attracted to her, she seemed strangely vulnerable in the firelight and was tempted to kiss her but decided better.

"You look at me oddly?" Tena said to Don with a puzzled look on her face.

"What do you mean by that? You are fine Tena, I am really enjoying us talking, I can tell you are a very special woman." Tena looked at Don smiling broadly then Don saw her cheeks turn red. Looking at the two of them talking Hutch couldn't resist a smart comment to them.

"You two going to hug and get it over with?" Hutch said out loud causing Tena to look at him then to get up giggling and walk over to Freya. Don turned to Hutch, who was smiling. "She likes you, I can tell." Hutch told Don, then Pat spoke.

"I don't think so, she is just curious is all about our world. Tomorrow I will tell her some things." Don looked at Pat and Pat looked at Don, he seemed to almost challenge Don to say something. Seeing this, Hutch decided he needed to head off a fight. "Don, be careful, if all goes well we will be going home, we don't want any little Donald's running around here, that may do some mumbo jumbo in the time line or something?" he said smiling. Don looked at them both. However, he spoke to Hutch directly.

"Look... she is pretty and yes I like her, I can tell that already, but I think the chances of little Donald's running around is slim, I want to get home also."

Hutch smiled at Don, "Yeah I am going to bed, eleven bells sounded a while ago, and I think this may be the last night I am going to be able to really rest for awhile." Everyone agreed and settled in for the night in the rooms that the Old Mans servant led them to.

As Don got into bed, and as he lay there he thought of home and of what his friends' wives were doing, he figured by now the Police were called and was wondering how they were going to explain this to the cops and whomever else would be talking to them. He was looking out the window the snowing had stopped and the clouds were scudding across the sky letting bright moonlight occasionally peer in. He was laying there for a bit when he heard a light tap at the door, the door opened slightly and Tena poked her head in.

"Are you up Don?" he sat up suddenly wide awake a little surprised at seeing Tena's head looking around the door,

"Yes I am awake, is everything ok?" Tena walked in, she had a night dress on and was barefooted. She walked over to the bed, her bare feet making padded sounds on the wooden floor, she stood there and Don could see her body outlined on the wispy fabric she smiled sitting on the edge of the bed.

"I don't mean to bother you, but I could not sleep, I have so many things I want to talk to you about. You are so different."

Don looked at her, his heart racing, and he was having a hard time putting a response together... "Tena you are very pretty and I would love to tell you more if you want to hear it." Tena looked happy and smiled then she crawled into the bed, snuggling into the covers surprising Don, she lay next to Don placing her head on his chest draping her arm over him, she breathed in deeply then let it out slowly.

"Tell me of Michigan Don, tell me more about your home and of TV." Smiling at her simple request, Don talked for about a half hour telling her of the many things that his world had in it, he told her of ren fairs and of how people dress like elves, trolls and like Kings and knights. Laughing Tena had trouble grasping the concept.

"Why would people dress so, Don?" Laying there he smiled and suddenly thought how odd it must seem to her, imagine going to a faire where people dressed like lawyers and bankers, Don thought.

"I know, it seems silly but in my world people do not know this world exists and the things you think as normal are unique and fun in mine. Just like riding on an airplane to you is magical, in my world it is normal."

She laughed, her laughter light and warm, when he stopped his talking thinking she was asleep he lay there quietly listening to her steady breathing. Then not knowing why he looked at her face, which was bright silver as it was lit by the bright moonlight peering through coming in from the window and he saw that she was staring at him, her large pretty eyes just looking at him, her breathing quiet and low... they looked at each other for what seemed like minutes then not knowing why Don kissed her, she returned his kiss warmly rolling onto him.

Silvery Moonlight

When an Amarian female gives herself to
another, That bond is forever. Death only breaks
it.

...... Amarian Law

I give myself to you.
For you are my one.
For you are my choice.
I make it freely and of my choosing.

...... Tena in her choice of Don

12
AMARIAN WOMEN

Pat lay in his bed thinking. His wife he knew moved on, and after all he didn't have anything really to look forward to. As he lay there he made his decision, one that he knew his friends wouldn't understand, after all they always were on him to go back to Lee, and that also made him wonder... Why couldn't they be supportive of him, he was their friend supposedly. However, they always were for Lee, she moved on and so would he.

His thoughts then went to Tena, and he decided it was time for him to pay her a visit. He got out of his bed, the floor cold on his feet, slipping on his pants and boots, he opened his door. The hall was lit lightly by a single candle on a small table against the wall. Walking past one door he heard James snoring away, walking to Tena's door he hesitated. He then tapped lightly. Nothing, no hello, no come in. He tapped harder and still nothing.   He decided to open the door a little. He peered in and saw her clothing on a chair and a small fire in her fireplace lighting the room. She was nowhere to be seen, the smell of a light perfume in the air. He stood there for a second then it occurred to him. He peered down the hall to Don's door, anger welling up in him. He walked over to it, placing an ear to the door. He heard talking, low... quiet talking, then he heard Tena's laugh. Pat spun angrily, storming to his room. "This is far from over!" was all he said aloud as he crawled back into bed, his thoughts going to dark tasks and dark deeds. Enough was enough!

The next day was busy; Kord and Freya poured over the map of the Dungeon talking of the best way to get into it safely. They poured over the book that detailed the exploits of Yognar the Brave. The book was ambiguous, it referenced seeing the Stone Gate, and according to the old man the other evening the description matched what the gate should look like. On this day, however, the old man was oddly missing and when James asked one of his servants where he was he was informed that the "Master" was busy in his laboratory working and was not to be bothered. That morning Freya and Tena left with Tena telling Don that she would be back in a bit.

"So, I saw Tena leaving your room this morning, you seem a bit tired buddy, stay up late did ya?" Hutch said to Don smiling. Don looked at Hutch sitting there with a grin and decided to take the high road.

"You know, you see too much, and it's not what you think." He said to Hutch with a grin.

"Yeah right, well lover boy just don't fall too hard most likely in a couple of days you will be back home, and Don no matter if you like her or not she can't follow you." Hutch said.

Pat said seriously then, "Yeah she isn't coming with us, plus you are making a mistake playing with her feelings. She is vulnerable and you are taking advantage of that."

Don looked at Pat with disgust, "Your joking right? Here you are talking to me about her, when your old lady is back home worried and you are acting like a jealous school boy in heat!"

At that Pat jumped up knocking over a glass, Don stood up with Hutch jumping between them. "Enough of this shit both of you, this isn't going to happen. Pat you need to back off and leave it be. Don knows what he is doing." Pat turned grabbing his cloak and stormed out, they heard the door slam below as he went out into the cold morning air.

Hutch placed a hand on Don's shoulder, looking at him seriously he spoke. "You like her... You know she can't come back with us buddy... Right?"

"Yeah I know Hutch and I admit I have become very attached to her. Man I just don't know what to do, this all in some strange screwed up way... It seems so right when I am with her."

"Look I know you like her, she likes you that's obvious as hell but Pats right man, she seems like a great woman but you know she can't come with us back to Michigan." Don looked at Pat and smiled. He started to have an idea and decided to keep it to himself.

Hutch and Don decided to go for a walk to get their minds off of things, so they got their cloaks on and went outside, James also decided to leave as he secretly had another meeting with the man in the Black cloak. Don and Hutch stepped outside and walked down some of the narrow alleys and were out for about an hour when Hutch noticed something.

"Don, we are being followed, two guys about fifty feet back, one has a knife in his hand." Don turned and saw two men, one of them suddenly acted as though he saw something interesting above him, the other bent down as if adjusting his boot.

"Yeah I don't like this, let's get our butts back to the old guy's house." As they tried to lose the two strange men they got turned around and found themselves in a dead end. Turning they saw the two men at its entrance, they both had brown stained dirty cloaks on, their hoods were down exposing greasy hair and evil smiles with yellowish brown teeth, one of them had one eye. It seemed the morning was indeed going to get worse for them.

Pat stormed out the door the cold air hitting him hard, irritated at how something so simple was being made so complicated, he walked down the street and saw that lot of people was out and about already. He walked down towards where there Inn was, and he noticed that the roads were already brown and slushy, with wagon tracks creating muddy slush. There was a dog, thin and starved looking, eating out of a pile of garbage that was just laying on the street. He needed to think, he needed to decide how to handle this. He knew he was tired of home, he was tired of Lee's lies and blaming him for not having any money. He lost his job, so what? He wasn't going home, he knew that much. He just had to figure out a way to not be dragged by his friends into the gate.

This wasn't too bad of a place, he thought to himself looking around, heck he could come back here maybe get a job from Samfor, maybe even ask Samfor to use him as an apprentice. Sudden thoughts of him casting magical spells and brewing positions to control came to mind.

Smiling to himself, he decided it was time for guile and deception. It was time for him to be happy for once.

"Gold! Give it to us now!" One barked out, his breath steaming in the cold air. He was holding a rusty knife low and menacing.

"Yeah gives us yer gold and silver, or we be gutting ya good," the other said harshly. Looking around Don saw there was nowhere to go.

"What gold? We are very poor merchants and only have a little copper." Don lied. The two men looked at each other uncertain.

"You got gold, dontcha we want it now!" The one with one eye said aloud.

The shorter man looked at the taller one eyed man with a puzzled expression. "Don't we just killz zem."

The taller one-eyed man looked at the shorter man angrily. "Shut up! I have this handled."

Hutch looked at the men and decided to try to be bold to maybe scare them off. "We don't have any gold. However, if you want to die then stand fast for we are Wizards, and I am going to curse you." He then started yelling a gibberish of fake words that made Don almost smile; he started jumping around yelling... "I feel the demons of Hacknar coming, I feel them and their evil coming, yes come vile demons, slay these two that threaten us." He then took out his cell phone and opened it, the cell phone lit up from being opened and at this sight both thieves looked around frightened, looking at each other not believing what they were seeing, then bolted.

Don looked at Hutch. "You got to be kidding me, demons... Wait till Pat and James hear this, now let's get the hell out of here and get back to Freya's uncle's house."

Hutch, smiling, agreed and they made their way back looking over their shoulders and around corners as they went. Arriving back at the old man's house they found that everyone was still gone, and the old man was still mysteriously somewhere else doing something secret.

James stepped out into the cold, he thought of the other eve when the man in the Black cloak met with him, he thought of the man's offer, the problem was to get home; today he had to steal the book, he didn't want to leave his friends here. Well maybe Pat as he was a real jerk, but the others he wasn't sure. Home... he could be with Bri this eve. He decided to try to talk to the man, he had to meet him again and the man would be wanting the book. He walked down a narrow alley and then down another, standing there in front of the seedy tavern they had drinks in was the man, who was smiling broadly as James approached.

"Well hello, have you thought of my offer to help you, my young friend?" the steam from his words floating in the ice cold air from his mouth as he talked. James looked at him with a worried expression.

"Yeah I did, but is there any way, I mean... any way I can take at least two with me?" The man looked irritated for a moment, then recovered; he stepped forward and decided to try guile and a lie.

"My friend you need to get me that book and get it soon, the magic is failing in it; I have consulted the Kings own Mage and he has informed me he can get you home, but the magic only works with the person holding it. Look... get home, the others can stay in this world. You have your woman back there, right?"

James looked at him, thinking of Bri and of getting home, he thought of a hot shower and a comfy bed, he thought of all the times the guys made fun of him, how they are always on him since coming here. It was Hutch who did it, why were they so cruel to him?

"I will try to get the book, if I can I will meet you tomorrow at this time. We are planning on leaving in a few days. I will do my best, OK?" The man looked at James with a smile, the idiot was falling into his trap so readily; he agreed and walked off into the falling snow. James looked around making sure the Special Magistrate was gone and headed back to the old man's house.

Across town, in a dark building, the two thugs that Hutch scared off met with their employer. "Well did you complete your task?" the man asked from the deep shadows of a dark room. The one-eyed thief looked frightened at the man,

"No we cornered them and one of them tried to curse us, you didn't tell us one of em was a mage, they had a magical device, they did." Their employer got angry,

"You dolts! They are not mages, you have been fooled by two fish out of water, all you had to do was kill them. That was all." The man yelled angrily stepping forward causing both the thieves to step back in fear.

"Yous didn't tell us that! Yous just said we had to kill em, it wasn't our fault, we didn't know they weren't Wizards." The other pleaded, "They has a magical thing, I saw it glow with fire!"

Their employer thought for a moment. "I still have a need for your services, we are leaving town to go to Gott, follow us to there, once we enter the Dungeon, I want you to follow at a distance. I will meet with you once in order to finalize their deaths, we then head back to town. That is my plan, the next time you see them, you will be able to gut them." Both thieves smiled wickedly at each other, and the strange man turned and walked out after tossing several silver pieces on the floor.

Tena and Freya came back to the house just as twelve bells were striking; Tena walked in walked up to Don and kissed him on the cheek, her nose cold against his cheek.

"Hiya!, we are back" she said in a bouncy cheerful way. Freya smiled at her sister.

"We have a wagon with pretty much everything we are going to need, I got everyone leather armors, so we can still move, and also short swords. We have torches, oil, lanterns, food and other things we will need. Where is Kord?" she finished looking around. No one noticed that he had left.

"Beats me! We didn't see him leave at all." Hutch said. Freya shrugged then turned to Don.

"I need your help unloading the wagon." Don said OK and they went downstairs, but when they got outside Don saw the wagon was empty. Looking at him, she turned to him with a serious expression.

"I know my sister and I know she has decided to give herself to you, she told me about last night. She also told me that she wanted to go with you to your world." Don looked at her and the direct look she was leveling at him, not knowing what to say. "Well, how do you feel about her? Is she a mere entertainment for you till you go home?" Freya said this with an edge to her voice.

Don looked at her in the eye and said, "Freya, your sister is very special to me and in the short time I have known her I have become very attached to her, she is no entertainment. I have wrestled with my feelings for her inside me. I want her happy." Freya turned for a moment as if thinking.

"Don, if she wants to go with you, what will you do? I have heard your friends talking, and they do not agree she should go, they think she should stay here. Time and distance don't matter when two have each other in their hearts."

Don took a deep breath then decided to just say it. "Freya if she truly wants to go with me then I will make sure she does, or if that is not possible I am staying so I can be with her. My friends have no say in this, it is up to Tena to decide, but she has to know if she decided to change her mind once she comes, there is no way back."

Freya smiled at Don,

"Are you aware that Tena would not have given herself to you, unless she decided you were the one? Amarian women make that decision, and once it is made then it is final and forever." She was looking at Don now very serious.

Don looked at Freya solemnly, and placing a hand on her arm, he told her. "I am serious when I say she is going with me if she decides. I will handle my friends when the time comes." And at that Freya hugged him.

"I will miss her but knowing she is happy will bridge the gap; I will leave it to you to handle with your friends." She then turned and walked back into the building leaving Don in the cold with his thoughts.

That evening they met in the old man's living room and there was an air of excitement; it seemed they were finally going to be on the way to getting home. They were sitting there quietly talking when the old man came in carrying a wooden box, as he walked everyone heard a clinking coming from the box. Setting it down on the table everyone peered into it seeing that there were seven bottles inside, the old man reached in and removed them. The bottles were small, about the size of a thick test tube each one had an amber liquid in them that was stopped with a cork.

"My friends, these are potions of healing; when you are severely injured drink the entire bottle and your pain and injuries will go away, it will not, however, make severed parts grow back." The old man seemed serious when saying this.

Hutch looked at Pat and leaned towards him whispering. "Severed parts, I plan on keeping all of mine." The old man went on,

"Be careful also as you must drink the entire contents to get the effect, so use them only when you need it, I hope you won't need more than one each as they are very difficult to make." Kord looked at the old man,

"Samfor, we thank you. I am hoping we will not need to use them all. However, leave it to you to aid us in this adventure in such a gracious way." Freya walked over to her Uncle and kissed him warmly on the cheek. The rest of the evening was spent finalizing the next day's plans. They agreed to leave at first light and Kord attempted to make light of the situation.

"Well my friends, at least where we are going it will be warm" he said chuckling, Freya smacked him in the arm,

"Funny man you are, I will check your sense of humor when you have three Goblins gnawing on your ankle and a Gastar chewing at your neck." Kord smacked his hand again on the table laughing out loud.

"Yes, this will be an interesting adventure for all. For all indeed".. That evening James again ventured outside he went to the meeting spot but the man was not there. He hung around for a bit and when he turned Hutch was standing there looking at him. "Well James, whatcha up to here? Hanging around like you are waiting for someone?"

James looked sheepishly at him then got angry. "What, you my baby sitter now? I can't stand around getting some fresh air? You and Don go for walks all the time, I have to report now? You know what? Screw you all, how's that!" and at that he stormed off with Hutch looking after him with suspicion. He looked one last time around the area not seeing anyone and he walked after James, seeing James going back to the old man's house. Once back Hutch filled Don in what happened.

"Do you think he was meeting with someone?" Don whispered looking at James sulking in a chair reading a yellow bound book. Hutch looked at James.

"I am not sure, he stood there for awhile as if he was waiting for someone. Don, would he screw us over, do ya think?"

Don looked perplexed, he couldn't believe James would stoop that low; James could be at times a real jerk but screw his friends around.. "No, I don't think so Hutch, let's keep an eye on him, maybe he was meeting a woman." Hutch grunted in agreement and the evening progressed normally until Pat walked up to them.

"I need to talk to you both."

Hutch and Don looked at each other, then at Pat, and getting up, they followed him to Pat's room. Pat walked in and turned around.

"Look, I am sorry about the way I have been acting. I know I have been a jerk, it's just a lot of things are on my mind."

Don and Hutch looked at him smiling, Don held out a hand, Pat grasped it. "No problem, this is something we all have been stressing about, and I know you have home things weighing on you also."

Pat smiled at the two others, and they smiled back. Hutch and Don walked out leaving him in the room. After they walked out Pat smiled to himself. He now was convinced he wouldn't have any problems staying here.

The next morning they awoke before dawn, got dressed and Pat and James seemed to be back to normal. Don's headache was back in full swing, seeing him not himself Hutch told the old man about his headaches.

"The old man left the room and came back with a small vial of yellow milky liquid. Walking up to Don, he held it out to him. "Here drink this; it will make you feel better."

Remembering the last time he drank something he politely declined, "Umm, no thanks Samfor, I am used to them."

The old man smiled. "No, take this, you will never have a worry of one again," he pushed it towards Don's hand.

Taking the vial he removed the tight fitting cork sealing it, he smelled it, he pulled his nose away as it smelled like bad chemicals, seeing the old man looking at him intently, he took a deep breath and downed the concoction. Instantly, he felt warm, and his headache literally stopped on the spot. Looking around amazed he smiled.

"Holy shit Samfor, that worked instantly, my headache is gone. THANKS!"

The old man smiled at him, Hutch looked at Don amazed. "Man you have had those headaches as long as I have known ya, and it is gone just like that?"

The old man spoke. "Yes, you will never have one again, what ails you is no longer. My draught took care of it."

Smiling, Don took his word and finished his packing."
Pat walked out of the room and gathered up their packs and
bags.

"Well we will leave in one-hour time, now is the time to
take care of anything you may need to. Once we leave, we will
most likely not be coming back.

The next hour went by without incident and the men
watched Freya and Tena say their good bye to their uncle, who
hugged Tena warmly, "Well my girl, this may be the last I see
of you if by chance your path takes you where you are hoping
to do not forget a tired old man in a faraway place who loves
you and will miss you." Tena looked at her uncle warmly.

"You have been there for me all my life, and you will be
there always until the end of my days. I won't forget you and
what you have done for me." She then walked out the door
and Don and the rest could tell she was crying. Freya said her
goodbyes also and walked out after her.

"Well, Samfor I will take care of them, no need to
worry, my sword is sharp and my arm is strong." The old man
looked at Kord taking his hand,

"You are my friend and will always be, I know they are
safe with you." And at that Kord walked out; Don and Hutch
Pat and James all offered sincere thanks to the old man and
followed Kord outside. Once outside they all got onto the
horses that Samfor gave them, shifting in his saddle Pat
groaned,

"Sheesh! This leather armor is stiff and smells. I hope it
loosens up." Kord looked at Pat,

"Don't worry my friend it will get better. A new armor
is always hard to get used to, however when it protects your
back you will be glad to have it on." Everyone else also seemed
to be having the same problem, Hutch was twisting this way

and that way, and James was looking at his belly trying to adjust the straps on his armor. Kord cleared his throat,

"I need to go back in I forgot my dagger, I will be back in a moment." Hopping off his horse, he walked into the old man's home again.

"You know he would forget his horse if it wasn't under his arse." Freya said smiling, they sat there in the bitter cold waiting for Kord, their horses snorting and stamping their feet in the snow, their snorting breaths steaming in the cold air.

Don leaned over to Hutch whispering to him, "Do you think that fat guy Pat told us about will have men at the front gate? I mean, I don't think he will appreciate us leaving."

Hutch looked at him with a concerned look painting his face, "I don't know bud, I just don't know."

Walking back into the home Kord pulled out a small dagger from inside his breast plate, the servant approached him smiling. "Yes sir, did you forget something?" Kord smiled at him,

"Yes, Yes I forgot my wet stone; one can't sharpen a good blade on a rock." The servant smiled at the comment then turned to lead Kord back to the study where Samfor was. As the servant turned, he felt strong hands around his mouth, stifling a scream as he felt a knife enter the back of his skull darkness coming over him. Kord laid the body on the floor wiping off the blade on the dead man's tunic.

Moving into the study he saw Samfor sitting at the table reading. Looking up the old man smiled. "Ah, Kord why are you back?" Kord smiled at the old man,

"I am sorry my friend, I left my wet stone over there behind you." The old man smiled turning seeing the stone on the table waving a hand behind him, he smiled,

"Well, you have to make sure your knife is sharp, a dull knife won't ever do a proper job."

Kord smiled a knowing smile. "Yes, my old friend, that they don't." Walking around the old man Kord picked up his wet stone that he purposely left on the table.

Samfor was leaning over the book about to ask Kord to tell Freya and Tena to be careful when he felt the blade enter the back of his neck, looking down in shock, he saw the tip of a long blade sticking through his throat, feeling the wet warmth of his blood running down his chest, splashing on the page in front of him, he then felt the blade jerked out of his neck, then strong hands yanking his head. The sound of snapping bones the last thing reaching his ears before darkness enveloped him.

Kord wiped the blade looking at the dead old man. "Well, my old friend, it ends, luck and chance did not smile on you, but do not worry in your death you will soon see both of your nieces." He looked at the old man whom he called friend for a moment laying over the table in a pool of blood, then turned around and moved quickly back out the door, he did not want Freya or Tena coming back in. He walked out and saw everyone sitting there still,

"Are you finally ready? You are worse than an old maid", Freya said laughing. Kord smiled at her getting on his horse,

"Let's move we do not have time to tarry and your uncle says he will see you soon," and to that, they kicked their horses into motion and made their way out of Dark Home towards what everyone was hoping would be a way home.

Samfors Study

Betrayal is a bitter herb that is washed down with Golden Ale.

.... Hafarian Proverb

Clutter to you my friend
Organized chaos to me better still.

...... Samfor Chamm on his messy study

My precious nieces, be careful for you do
not really know who you venture with.
For a man's soul can be corrupted by something
as simple as a coin of gold.

...... Samfor Chamm's warning to his two
nieces years ago when they parted.

13
FEELINGS OF HOPE

They traveled for the remainder of the day without any incident, and they failed to notice the two riders that left the city behind them. Traveling was hard as the men were not used to this pace. Stopping only periodically to rest the horses, as evening approached, they slowed with Kord leading.

Hutch rode next to Kord, "It's getting late and there are two feet of snow on the ground. Where do you think it would be wise to camp?" Kord slowed then stopped shifting in his saddle,

"If memory serves, there is a small cave on that rocky outcropping", he said pointing in the distance about a half a mile ahead of them. Hutch looked, they had been traveling South East for most of the day towards the mountains, then around noon, they shifted course to the South with the large mountains looming to their left. The area that they were riding in was full of low scrub and rock, here and there were large boulders littering the ground.

James noticed them.

"Wow, these rocks are huge. How did they get here?" Freya looked at James,

"They came from that mountain there, the one with no top on it, and about a hundred years ago it blew its guts out and threw rocks in all directions."

James didn't believe her. "How can that be? Those mountains are at least thirty miles away." Tena looked over at James,

"My sister doesn't jest, and what are 'miles'? Those mountains are no more than twenty leagues away." James looked to Pat who was next to them.

"Impossible I say there is no way a volcano popped its cork and threw those rocks like that." Pat looked at James with a scowl, and in a disgusted tone he said to him,

"You don't believe much do you? Bet ya if I said there were real Goblins a week ago you would have called me a liar, also don't you remember reading about Mt St. Helens, and what it did?" James turned his head and didn't respond so Pat shrugged and moved towards the front where Kord and Hutch were.

"We are riding toward a cave a bit ahead, at least it will be dry and we can make a warm fire." Kord said to them then kicked his horse into motion. The others followed suit and followed after him.

They found the cave and it was really no more than a small rocky outcropping open on two sides with a stone cover on it. They spent a cold and uncomfortable evening and early the next morning as they stood around the smoking fire, Pat got irritated. "Where is this place, I mean how long will we be traveling until we get there?"

Freya looked at Pat and Don could tell she understood his agitation. "We will be there within two weeks or so, it is a goodly way off and Gott is difficult to get to no matter how good the weather, plus you will see over the next few days it will become warmer, the area that Gott is in is forests and the air is so thick you can cut it." Kord then spoke.

"Complain about the cold all you wish. However, once we enter the area Gott is in you will all wish you were back here in the cold."

For the next week or so they rode steadily south and traversed into a milder climate. As they got further south they also noticed that daylight hung around longer and also that the snow disappeared. They entered an area where there were a lot of trees. They were low spruce looking types and also some huge large bodied odd looking trees with a green bark that made the area smell like berries. Tena explained to them that the trees were prized for perfume, however, they had an innate defense mechanism. If they were cut in the wrong way they let loose a poisonous gas, "Many a man's bones lie about those trees of those who thought they would become rich in the Hafarian perfume houses."

Kord laughed. "Greed is good but it isn't good when you trust your luck to a tree." When Kord said this he broke laughing hard, Freya joined him. They traveled for a few more days then turned sharply East; they rode this direction for about two days, then one day around late morning they were riding on a muddy road, the weather was becoming warmer and there were thick swarms of flies. It seemed that no matter what they did the flies were there biting them landing everywhere in their mouths, eyes and even the poor horses were being tormented,

"What is with all these damn flies?" James complained.

"We are close to the Bogs of Jamar, and we will have to deal with them most likely for another day, but have heart, they will go away." Tena said swatting her arms in an irritated way.

"Yes, if you want to get rid of them, there is a way to make sure they do not bother you." Kord smiled looking at James.

"What's that", James asked spitting out a fly. Tena giggled causing him to look hard at her.

"You rub horse pee all over yourself." Kord said with a straight face.

James looked at Kord grimacing, "Funny to think I would actually do that, you think I am that gullible?" James said in a tone that indicated he thought Kord was pulling his leg.

"No James, he is telling the truth. That is why the flies stay away from the backsides of the Horses, they are repelled by the releases." Tena said looking at James. He turned looking at his horse's haunches and the others and saw those were the only areas that didn't have the irritating flies. They rode steadily East for two days, the flies finally disappearing and something worried Hutch. Pat was for the past two or three days getting more and more quiet, he seemed to withdraw from everyone, and when someone talked to him, he gave short curt answers. Hutch figured he was thinking of Lee again and letting it get to him. He decided after talking to Don about it to let Pat just deal with it.

They stopped that early evening and were setting up their camp. It was warm and starting to get muggy, the air hazy, and they were all sweating, no one was in a seeming good mood in the oppressive thick humidity and heat.

"I can see what ya meant by wishing there was some snow, Kord." Don said while he was helping Pat take the saddle off his horse.

"It is going to get much worse also." Freya said, she tied her long red hair into a pony tail and was sweating heavily, she had also removed her leather tunic and had instead a flimsy tan colored linen shirt; she was wearing nothing under it and everyone could not help admire what it showed. Hutch looked at Pat, who was staring at her with open admiration.

"You know, I would pull your jaw back into your head or Lee may find it odd that you want her to dye her hair red." Pat looked sharply at Hutch,

"What? Oh... no I can't help it. She is really pretty and that top is not helping with the way it is showing her ta ta's." Pat said morosely, Hutch looked at Freya who now was sitting down talking to Tena, then at Hutch,

"I know but I am not sure how she would take it if she looked up and see us staring at her."

Just then Freya looked at and saw him staring at her. "What, is something wrong?" She said standing up looking down at him. Pat smiled, eyeing her chest,

"No, no nothing at all Freya." Hutch said reassuringly. Tena laughed,

"Sister, I think they are looking at your top as it is practically hanging out." Freya looked annoyed for a second, then smiled. She then flipped up her top showing them her breasts at the two now embarrassed men.

"There you men have never saw a woman's top before?" Hutch and Pat turned embarrassed, Don laughed as did Tena and Kord, who was staring at Freya's chest in admiration.

"Nothing wrong on my end Freya", Kord said laughing. Freya seemed to get a kick out of embarrassing the men and continued talking to Tena. Tena was also sweating and had placed her hair into a set of pig tails. Kord had removed his furs and armor and was standing at this horse bare chested and Don saw for the first time how huge he really was. His chest was the size of a barrel, and he was covered with thick black hair.

They set up camp and settled in for a hot muggy night. After they ate Kord explained that they were within three days of the Ruins of Gott and that the Dungeons of Kal-Aldoon was located in those ruins. The fire was low and no one wanted to be too close to it, the air seemed to cling to them and the air was thick with mosquitoes.

"Well, it looks like we are almost done." James said that evening while he sat there, sweating.

"Yeah, it will be cool to get home, I guess we really don't know how to thank you all for all the help you have given us." Hutch said aloud looking at Freya, Kord and Tena.

"You are helping us in many ways yourself, don't fret it will all be over soon and everyone will have what they want." Kord said.

Don noticed that Tena seemed to be more and more distracted and quiet as the days wore on. He decided take direct action and talk to her. He walked next to her leaning into her, holding his hand to her.

"Here, let's go for a walk." At that she took his hand, and they walked a bit away from the group. Don turned, looking at her. "Tena, you are worried that I am going to leave you behind, aren't you?" Tena looked at him with tears in her eyes.

"Yes and I understand fully," Don looked at her seriously, he looked directly into her eyes.

"Tena, I won't leave you no matter what, either we leave this world together, or I stay with you. No matter what, you have me ok?" Don said this smiling. Tena hugged him .

"You sacrifice so much, do you really feel so for me?" Don held her face in his hands looking into her eyes.

"Yes I feel that much for you. Stop crying, we are not leaving each other, no matter what. Where I go you go and wherever you go, I will follow." Tena smiled wiping her eyes with her shirt.

"What of your friends Don, they do not want me to go. I have heard James talk of leaving me in the dungeon." Don looked sharply at her.

"He has really said this?" She looked at him, sniffling with a doe eyed expression on her face making her suddenly seem very vulnerable.

"Yes. He told Hutch he wanted to leave me in the dungeon but Hutch got angry and told him to shut up. However, I know also Hutch and Pat do not think it is wise for me to go back with you." Don was angry and he looked at her.

"Tena, I swear to you, I will not leave you. I mean that, ok?" She smiled again and hugged Don fiercely.

"Thank you. I will never leave you either." And at that they walked back to the camp holding hands with Don thinking of James and how he was going to handle him.

Later that night Don and Tena were lying on their blanket sleeping; Don was dreaming of home and of his doorbell ringing, when he answered the door several Orc's were standing there selling encyclopedias. His dreams continued like this when he started to have an odd dream, he was in his living room again and heard screaming, lying there thinking how odd, it dawned on him as consciousness flooded back to him that the screaming was real, and waking, he turned seeing Tena grabbing him with Kord and Pat swinging their swords at something large and scaly.

"Don, wake up!" Tena was yelling while dragging out her sword, "Get up, Morgs are attacking!" Kord was yelling at everyone. He had his sword out and was raising it to defend himself,

"What the hell are these things?" James was yelling while swinging his sword widely at one of them. There were three of the creatures, one attacking Kord, one James and the final one was running at Don and Tena. They were taller than Kord, around seven feet tall, and had short stubby tails, doglike faces and had scales. The thing that scared Don to his core were their eyes, they actually glowed red with an insanely evil fire in them, they had an odd yelp to them almost like a hyena, and they had long arms with claws.

Kord swung his sword striking the creature in his arm, a large gash throwing yellowish blood on the ground, the creature screamed and ran back into the jungle yelping loudly,

"They are breaking, the cowards!" Kord yelled, the other Morg had James on the ground swiping at him, with James barely able to fend his claw strikes off with his sword. Freya let loose an arrow with it striking the creature in the back, yelping the creature stood up and followed the other Morg into the jungle. The final Morg ran past Hutch shoving him causing Hutch to fall on the ground striking his head on a rock knocking him unconscious. Tena jumped in front of Don,

"Stand back." She yelled. Don looked at her in amazement, then shoved her to the side knocking her down; by that time the creature was on him jumping into Don and knocking him to the ground in a tackle, clawing him on the face opening a gash. Stinging pain ran over Don, and he felt a warm wetness splash over his face blurring his vision. Pat suddenly was there jumping on the monsters back using a large rock hitting the creature over and over in the head, Tena jumped forward and stabbed the creature through the back causing the monster to collapse on Don.

"Oh, my Gods are you ok, Don? Please don't be dead! It clawed him, the thing clawed him!" Tena cried out loud. Don was laying there in a daze his face hurt so bad, he felt a warmth settling all over his body. Nausea grabbed his gut, he wanted to vomit but didn't. He rolled to one side breathing heavily,

"I'm ok, I'm cut but ok... I feel weird, I hurt bad." Pat was grabbing Don's arm, "Man, you ok? Christ's sakes what the hell were those? Don, you are bleeding man bad!" Don slowly sat up his face stinging, reaching up touching the wound he felt that it wasn't as bad as he thought, Tena reached forward pulling his hand down, Don suddenly dizzy, laid back down, he felt oddly separate, everyone was yelling and talking, yet he didn't really hear them.

Darkness settled over him.

Kord and Freya were leaning over Hutch, who was coming around, he was sitting up holding his head,

"Man, what the heck hit me?" Hutch said while Kord laughed helping him up with an outstretched hand.

"You make a bad battering ram my friend." Freya got up walking over to Tena, James and Don.

"Is his wound bad?" she asked in a concerned way.

"No, he is ok, it's venom sack wasn't in yet so he will heal, he will have a nice scar for a memory, but he will be ok." Tena said looking at Don with a smile. Freya reached a hand to her face feeling her own scar,

Don was coming around, he laid there for a moment feeling still light headed and saw Tena and Freya looking down at him.

Freya smiled at him. "Consider them trophies of survival Don, yours won't be that bad." And she turned walking back to Kord. Kord walked the perimeter then disappeared into the Jungle. About ten minutes later, as Tena was finishing up tending to Don's wound by placing a nasty smelling salve on it and bandaging it, Kord reappeared.

"I followed their blood trail, they seem to be an isolated pack, luckily there are no mature ones or this may have ended much, much worse. They seem to be running away from us."

Freya looked relieved, "They tend to be cave dwellers. Why are they out and attacking a group like us?"

Tena looked up with a frown. "Yes, I do not get it either? They tend to be cowards with three or more attacking maybe two travelers. I do not understand why they are out?" The rest of the night was spent with everyone not getting much sleep. Don laid back down as he was not feeling well, and as he lay there he thought of Tena and how she was willing to defend him against such a horrid monster. Looking over he had to smile. Tena was lying next to him sleeping soundly.

"I wish I could accept this as normal and sleep." Don thought to himself then he also fell into a troubled a fitful slumber.

Pat was laying in his small tent, he was thinking. Was it time? As he lay there he thought of Lee and of home. He thought of the bills, the calls from the electric company. He also thought of not being able to find a job. He leaned onto one elbow and thought of his friends. "I gotta be happy." he said in a low voice to himself. Getting out of his bedroll, he crawled out of his low tent, seeing Kord standing there.

"Hey, Kord, I will take watch, I can't sleep and need something to do, plus you always are on watch, go get some sleep. I will yell if I see anything." Kord looked at him, surprised. "I am plain tired. I will be in my roll. If you see anything odd. Any problems come get me."

Pat agreed smiling, watching Kord crawl into his low tent. He waited for about an hour, and hearing the steady snoring of Kord, he quietly gathered up his things and pulled his horse out. Stopping for a moment looking at the tents his friends were in, he quietly whispered with tears in his eyes.

"I gotta do this, guys; I gotta be happy."

And to that he quietly led his horse away. About a quarter of a mile from the camp he got on his horse and headed back the way they came the best he could. He headed back to Dark Home and to hopefully work with Samfor.

The next morning dawned humid and muggy, Don awoke to a slight commotion, he heard Kord raising his voice, "Yep, he is gone alright, his things, his horse, he left in the middle of the night."

Don laid there thinking that James was going to regret this so much, he rolled out of his roll and out of the tent. Standing up the air was thick and misty with their footsteps creating eddies in the fog that hung low on the ground. The sound of frogs and other swamp loving insects were loud and everywhere.

Hutch was standing there next to James, seeing Don Hutch walked over. "Pat took off, he packed his shit and booked off." His voice was tense and Don could see tears in Hutch's eyes.

"NO WAY!" Don said with total shock and disbelief, Don grimaced and felt something draining down his face, "We gotta go get him, which way could he have gone? He doesn't know his ass from a hole in the ground." Hutch looked at Don with concern.

"Man, you got yellow shit draining bad from your face Don, that shit looks nasty."

Don felt it, pulling away a finger he looked at it. Sure enough it was yellowish green, and sticky. His face felt hot also and tight."

James was pacing, "He couldn't have made it that far, any idea what time he took off?"

"I would guess within two hours after we all went to bed, he relieved me then, and I think a short time later he left." Kord said scratching his beard, and picking the knots out of it.

"Nothing we can do, he could have gone anywhere, and we should reach Gott today if all goes well." Freya said. "We have to press on, he has made his decision and dragging him back here kicking and screaming will not help. We have to move on. We are far too close and there are things around Gott that we do not want to see in the dark!" She said seriously.

Tena, seeing the yellow ooze on Don's face, walked over to him. Taking the bandage off she swore. "This is already badly infected." She looked at Freya, we have to give him one of Uncle's potions,"

Freya walked over with one of the healing potions. "Here drink this and drink it all."

Don grabbed it and started to drink it, he stopped almost vomiting. It tasted like a cross between rotting meat, and rotted onions. He gagged.

"Yep, he doesn't like it," Freya said smiling at Don. He finished drinking the potion, forcing down every hideous drop, once it was down he laid down for a moment. He felt odd and his face suddenly started to itch, Hutch and James walked over and were looking at Don with amazed looks.

"Man, Don your wound is like... It's actually closing right here on the spot... Wow man, this is so cool!" Hutch said in amazement as he yanked out his cell phone, swearing as it was dead. The battery was finally dead, so he wouldn't be able to video the potions effects. Don felt great, he rubbed his face and felt that he did have a nasty scar. However, he had no pain and the wound was closed. Tena placed a nasty smelling salve on it, then bandaged it, telling him the salve would make the scar smaller.

Hutch walked over to him, "Do you think he is ok?" He said with a worried look. Don looked at him with a frown shaking his head.

"You know Hutch, I don't see why he wouldn't be, Pat is pretty smart and maybe this is best. If he got back, he and Lee wouldn't last; I think he gave up on his marriage weeks ago. Who knows.... I guess we are at the point where we need to move on. You have a warm Emily waiting for you."

Hutch smiled, nodding to himself. He turned and started packing his things up.

"We must be careful as we get closer, the Mage may have placed wards and guards to make sure company doesn't arrive uninvited." Kord said aloud as he was oiling his sword.

James looked confused and a bit angry. "I thought you said this Gott place was an abandoned city?" Freya looked at James took a deep breath then spoke with obvious patience in her voice,

"Gott is an abandoned city that according on the legend you heard was abandoned due to disease, monsters invading from the Spine mountains, or a natural disaster. Who knows what is true? However, even though Gott is in ruins there still are inhabitants, and if the Mage is still alive you can be assured that he will not want company." Her look was direct and James seemed to be about to say something more but turned and walked away to his horse. They then packed camp up and mounted their horses.

Don's face was numb at this point. Reaching up touching the bandage Tena had placed on it, she looked at him.

"Don't pick at it. The salve I placed on it will make it smaller, but if you pick at it, it will scar worse." Her tone was oddly direct and Don decided to listen to her.

James looked at Hutch,

"Yep, he is whipped, already being told what to do." James laughed to Hutch. Looking at Don, he laughed.

"Yeah, do as you are told boy." Hutch spoke out loud laughing. Tena looked sheepish and smiled then rode her horse up to Freya where they started to talk.

"You're a funny guy ya know that?" Don said chuckling while Hutch was laughing and James was looking at Hutch shaking his head.

As they rode on they noticed that the muddy road they were following became paved off and on with rocks, and to the edges of the jungle were rocks and boulders that as they looked more closely was actually a small building in ruins. The buildings were made of smooth granite-like stone, some were covered in a thick green moss hanging from open doorways and from roofs that had no rafters, their rafters long ago rotted away in the humidity and heat, their inhabitants long gone for some unknown reason. In addition, here and there along the edge of the road were pointed spires around ten feet tall, some of them were toppled over, some leaned at odd angles covered in the same green moss, but they seemed to be at regular intervals.

"What are those stone columns?" James asked Kord. Kord looked over at one,

"They were markers for the road; the citizens of Gott were very advanced for their time. They used these as a way to mark the distance to Gott for travelers. They would have had writings on them indicating how far from Gott they were. You will find them all over Amaria also." James seemed impressed, which was surprising to everyone as he seemed to come out of his weeks long bad mood.

"Actually, that's a cool idea Kord, mile markers." They continued to ride till around noon when they crested at a jungle-packed hill and saw there was an old archway that at one time was very large and impressive, it was made of fine stone and still had some remnants of writing on it, and as they approached it, they saw that it was collapsed and blocking the road partially, and the writing was odd and very ornate. As they approached the old archway they saw Gott on the other side.

Don was amazed it was in ruins but even when in ruins one could see that it had been, at one time, huge. The ruins of the city were visible through the trees as there was still cleared partially but was also still partially choked with the jungle, the buildings in the entry to the city having large trees growing through their walls and ceilings. There were vines growing over the road twisting and winding through windows. There were ruined remnants of towers, some collapsed, and some still tall there spires still visible reaching through the jungle canopy. And in the center of the city there was a large odd shaped tower of massive dimensions.

The tower looked like a cork screw with several pointed outcropping emanating from it. Don was taking it all in, "Wow!", he said aloud.

"Yes indeed it is something to see, this is the first time I have laid my eyes on it." Kord said and Don could hear awe in his voice. The others seemed amazed also indicated, by the looks on their faces. They decided to take a break before going into the city and finding the entrance to the fabled dungeon. They dismounted and stretched their aching backs; Don and Tena walking a bit around the horses.

"Do you think there is any treasure there?" James asked aloud to Kord. Kord with awe still in his voice spoke quietly to James his voice hushed, one could tell his mind was racing also.

"Yes enough to make you a rich man for a thousand life times my little friend. However, the trick is finding it and getting out with it."

Freya looked at James, "James, you see there is treasure there and a lot of it, however many a skilled adventurer has made the trek here to get it, very few have come out alive let alone with any wealth. Those that have talk of rooms filled with gold, caverns full of jewels, chambers stacked with platinum. However, in reality, you will be stepping over the bones of the hundreds that did not make it out alive."

James looked at Freya, puzzled, "You said at your Uncle's home that there was no treasure in this place, that there was only death?"

Freya looked at him. "I know what I said, however you have to understand that the treasure that I just spoke of is myth and legend, also the men and women that have made it out alive of this cursed place speak of the gold and silver, although their claims never were believed by anyone, but I truly believe that those treasure rooms do exist."

James glanced at Freya licking his lips, then to the city that lay in front of them in ruins. "We could get some of that treasure and bring it back home with us, no sense in going home empty handed?" Hutch looked quickly at him angrily.

"Don't even think it for a second; I am not having you fubar this thing over your greed, I want to get home and get home in one piece." Don chimed in,

"James, look, you want to get back to Bri, so let's worry about that. Plus, think of the stories we will be able to tell." James shot back suddenly back angry,

"See? like it is always, you two ganging up on me, always doing it, well I am my own man, and if I see some gold on the ground I am picking it up, screw you two if you don't like it. A little gold isn't going to change the time warp thingy." Hutch, red faced, looked at Don,

"I told ya he would be his typical ass self!"

Tena spoke to James with a hint of steel in her voice. "You are your own man yes, however, know this. I will not go out of my way to help you if you are in trouble due to your own avarice. This place is not the place to be greedy." And to that they started to make their way down the road towards Gott and the Dungeon and, hopefully, home.

KORD

A full purse on your belt is good..
Your head on your shoulders is better...
Don't let greed overcome your desire to keep
it there.

...... Maldoran lecture to new warriors

14
DUNGEON

They rode through the ruins of the archway carefully guiding their horses through the maze of fallen stones towards the large central spire. "At least we arrive at daylight," Freya commented as she guided her horse away from a large green snake that had red stripes all over it. She looked around seemingly very aware.

"Better daylight then night, I bet; I don't think I would want to be here at night." Hutch said as he also guided his horse away from the odd snake. Kord held his hand up halting them.

"We leave the horses for now on, we walk from here." And at that he got off his mount.

"What? What do we do with them?" Hutch asked. Freya looking at him, commented,

"We don't want to tie them up as the inhabitants would attack and eat them, at least they will have a running chance if we let them run loose." Hutch and Don looked aghast,

"So we are leaving them to fend for themselves? Why not take them with us?" Don said and Tena looked at him gravely.

"Don, where we go, they cannot follow. We will be treading in areas where stealth is needed, and also we will be moving in at times tight confines." James hopped off his horse,

"Heck with em, let them run loose, they will make a tasty meal to something."

When he said this Freya gave him an angry look and Pat snorted in contempt, "Meal aye, if you do not make it to the Gate and have to come back out with us, I will remember that when your arse wants to ride one of them. The one that makes the meal is the one that you would have ridden." And at that she turned sharply slapping her horse on its hind quarters, her pony tail flopping over her shoulder.

"Way to go, Mr. Personality." Hutch popped off to James,

"What did I say? It's not like they are pets, they are horses and what will be will be." Kord glanced at him.

"Yes little man, you are right. What will be, will be." And to that they all shooed their horses and watched the animals running or wandering away. With their equipment in hand or over their shoulders they made their way into the recesses of the fabled City of Gott.

They walked through the archway and into what they best could tell was the entrance to the old ruined city; the first thing Don noticed was that there were all manners of small creatures inhabiting the ruins: snakes, lizards and even some large spiders were here and there. Some were clinging to the old stones that made up the buildings, and some hung from the low trees. The pathway that they followed seemed to have been used before as the stones that were lying among the overgrown grass were still exposed in some places and the jungle that overran everything seemed to take over the place. The large spire loomed above them and they were amazed, the spire was at least two hundred feet high, and it was massive in its diameter. They made their way through the crumbled ruins, and up to the base of the large twisting spire. As they got up to the spire, they also saw remnants of an encampment that seemed to have been abandoned only a few days before. Walking among the two tents that had been ransacked, and the miscellaneous debris Kord walked up to the fire pit that was now nothing more than ashes and burned wood. He looked puzzled.

"This is odd. Look there are tents and also clothing, something happened here and not too long ago at that." Freya, walking around the edges also looked concerned,

"Yes, however, there are no drag marks leading into the jungle nor are there any signs of a fight; I wonder if the makers of this encampment walked, ran, or were taken away?" Tena walked to one of the tents looking in; she reached in and pulled out a small doll made of cloth and wood. "There was a child here!" Kord walked over to her taking the toy from her hands.

"This doll is Maldoran in style, whomever was here came a long way, but why bring a child to what you know is danger and most likely death?" Tena looked upset, so did Freya.

"Yes, a child, why here? Something is not right at all... and look!" Tena reached into the tent pulling out some small rope that was knotted and bound on one end. "These are bindings and small ones at that. Look, this child was bound." Freya quickly walked over.

"Damn whoever did this! It seems a child, and not too long ago, was here against her will." James walked over to them.

"Girl? How do you know it was a girl?"

Kord spoke before Tena could speak as she appeared very upset and angry. "James, the doll's style is Maldoran, the Maldorans are of my lands and man children do not play with dolls, only small girls do." Kord looked around, his eyes peering into the thick leaves and vines that clung to everything, he took a few steps this way and that.

"We need to find this child if we can, an innocent cannot be allowed to perish or worse, whatever scoundrel or scoundrels are responsible will understand what Northsman revenge and anger can be!" Kord said looking around upset.

"Wait, no offense but we are here, we are close to getting this damned book into that Gate thing! Why are we dropping that now to look for a kid?" James said angrily causing Kord to spin on him with his hand on his sword. Don thought he was going to draw it on his friend.

Tena stepped in between them placing a hand on Kord's chest. "Kord, he does not know your laws and ways, he needs to know." She then turned to James.

"Maldoran law is loose in many ways, however, all Maldoran males are bound to an oath that they take at fourteen when they are brought into manhood, that oath binds them to help any Maldoran female that is in distress even children, Kord is not ignoring your plight, he is acting on his oath that defines him as a man."

James angrily flung his arms in the air walking away muttering to himself, Don stepped forward.

"What do you think is happening here, Kord? Where could the girl be?" Kord looking around spoke, and as he spoke, he was looking darkly at James, who was standing about ten feet away.

"If a child was brought here then it was brought for a purpose, I am guessing she was brought as a means for sacrifice. Some heathens and scum think Maldoran females are magical as they all tend to have golden hair and blue eyes, so we need to look around the vicinity. They would not have cut her bonds if they were not close to where they needed to go."

Don, looking at Kord, decided to try to walk the middle of the road. "I agree with Kord; let's look for her, but what if she cannot be found, if she is not around we will have to move on. Honor you are bound but we also cannot risk this book falling into the wrong hands."

"Agreed, we look around and if we do not find her then we will have to move on." Kord said and to that they mounted a search.

They searched around the area of the encampment and the massive base of the spire for about an hour. James and Hutch were searching in the fading light near a slight path that was cut into the jungle; James looked at Hutch, and in a hushed frustrated voice he spoke. "Look Hutch this is bull, we need to get home, this is delaying us and also this kid, how do we know who it is really, also she is probably dead."

"We made an agreement with Kord, and-" but James interrupted him at this point.

"Yeah, that's my point. We are being browbeat into this by that big moron, Mr. Warrior; I know he and Freya are just playing us, I have proof." Hutch looked sharply at James with suspicion in his eyes.

"What do you mean you have proof? How? And don't be pulling anything out of your ass either. They have helped us and I am not leaving them." James, angry now and red faced, raised his voice a little louder to Hutch.

"I met a man in town, he is a magistrate with the Guard. He told me all about that crazy old man and also, do you know there is another way. YES! Another way to get home with that book. Let's take off, go there and get home. Those two idiots are going to get us killed. And Don, with his nose in Tena's butt, he won't listen."

Hutch looked at James anger boiling in him. "Look, you little bug, Don isn't going to screw us if that's what you're getting at, and I trust Kord and Freya, and you are full of bull if you think I am going to believe you were meeting with a magistrate. Nice try, just stay the heck away from me. One word about this to me and I am telling everyone about your crap. Including Kord! To that Hutch stormed away leaving James standing there.

"Ok, I do it myself, heck with you all! You all can stay here, I am getting the hell out first chance I get. It's all about me now!" James said to himself while he watched Hutch walk away. James decided now was time to get home no matter who got left behind.

Dusk was approaching when Hutch found near a cluster of ruins some severely trampled vegetation and also a small shoe that looked like a child's, and a torch. "I found something!" Hutch yelled causing everyone to come to him. Kord looked at the shoe while Freya poked her head into the ruins.

"This is a Maldoran shoe and a girl's at that." Tena was looking at the torch, she smelled it then felt it rubbing her two fingers together looking for a moment like a female Sherlock Holmes.

"This torch is recent, maybe a day as it still has fresh soot on it. They are near", Freya came back out. "They are nearer than we think, there is an old stairway leading down, this is also the entrance to the Dungeons. It seems we are not the only ones with a purpose here."

Looking around the invading darkness James spoke up. "It's getting dark here, what should we do?" Tena answered, "What to do, well we go down, I guess, light or dark it is all the same where we need to go, and we do not want to be in the city area when it is dark." Kord mumbled an agreement,

"I will go get our gear. You,", he said pointing at James, who was standing there with his arms crossed, "come with me, you can help me gather it." James looked sullen but followed him, the rest stood there contemplating what they were about to do. Breathing deeply, Hutch leaned over to Don.

"Well, my friend might want to take a deep breath of fresh air, if it's like any of the books we have read or modules we have played this could be the last fresh air we breathe." Don looked at him, smiled and breathed deeply the humid sticky air, it smelled like a mixture of rotting vegetation and mold,

"Worst part is, this hot nasty air is most likely going to be very fresh compared to where ever we are headed." Don said wistfully, and deep inside he knew that there was a chance that his friend or one of the others may not make it to see home.

James and Kord came back a bit later as the forest started to get dark, the shadows played with everyone's fears as imagined things moved here and there among the rocks and ruins. Strange noises emanated from the ruins around them creaking, sometimes popping and scratching noises. "Let's go inside and get torches lit, I will lead." Kord said stepping into the ruins with everyone else following close behind.

Don and Pat drew their sword. Don was thinking of how silly he must look holding it, "Like I am prepared to deal with this shit..." he thought as he followed Freya in. The room they entered had block walls, the ceiling was partially exposed with huge blocks laying about that everyone surmised was once the roof. Large vines as thick as a man's waist were growing out of the floor and smaller ones were growing through the walls in places pushing the heavy blocks over and apart during the eons that the city was abandoned. In addition, a low mist started to come in as darkness enveloped the ruins. There was a click of steel on flint, a spark, then Freya's face could be seen in an orange glow as her tinder caught, a welcoming flame licked up. Lighting a candle she placed it into a lantern shutting the lid, the lantern gave off a very welcome glow bathing everyone in orange flickering light. Kord laid a torch to the burning tinder lighting the torch. Holding it up the room became clear.

To one side there was a doorway that had collapsed into itself and was obviously impassable, however, to the opposite side there was a small crack in the wall about man sized. The dust around that crack was disturbed with several large foot prints, Freya walked over to the it peering around and in.

"There are little ones foot prints in the dust. They came this way." Everyone moved closer to see and sure enough Hutch and Don and the rest could see that there were at least three large sets of boot prints with a smaller set that looked like they were half walked and half dragged into the crack.

"She went this way indeed, and where she goes, they go also, either way we go where they need to go to get out, they will all meet some foul devil soon." Kord said quietly and ominously, his voice echoing off the walls. His voice gave Hutch goose bumps.

They stood there and Tena spoke.

"Let's get prepared. Once we enter; there is no time for dilly dallying." At that she reached into her pack pulling out a low belt with two curved knives, she placed the belt on then tied her hair into twin pony tails, everyone also started to tighten their leather armor, tightened their sword belts, looking at each other. The three remaining gamers seemed to be looking for reassurance from each other.

"Well, one for all, and all for one as they say", Hutch quipped as he stood there sweating heavily looking so much like a real true warrior that made even James quip a funny comment,

"Yeah, yohoho and a bottle of rum I guess also", James said smiling. And to that they all shook hands and turned towards Freya and Kord who were looking at them oddly.

"As we will not have time to say the proper words, if one of us dies may your God watch over you, as we will not have the time or ability to carry your body with us." Kord said, and to that, they entered the crack in the wall and into what they did not know.

The road leading into Gott

Behave my child, or I shall take you to Gott

- Hafarian Mothers threat to a child
to get them to behave.

Rotting and worthless. The riches of Gott are
no more in reach to any man, then a dragons
whisker. Let the fools mess with the dragon.

> - Maldoran Warning to those thinking
> of making the trip to Gott.

Once a splendid capitol of a great Kingdom. Gott was
wiped out of existence some say due to its leaders
experimenting with Dark Magic. Its riches now are
forever lost to time, errant magic, and vile monsters.

> - Encyclopedia Magika
> Magical Lore. Section III

15
SURPRISE !

As Don stepped into the crack in the wall he saw that Freya's lantern had lit up a small room with a set of stairs that were exposed by a series of large stone blocks that long ago fell out of the wall. There were intricate designs carved into the walls and ceiling, and the room even though small, looked almost ceremonial. There was a small dais on one wall, and Kord and Hutch were looking around. The flickering lantern and torch light were creating creepy shadows on the carvings, and as Don's eyes became adjusted, he saw that the carvings were of men and women being tortured, some with men standing above them, their hearts pulled out, some were of horrible demon-like creatures.

"I don't like this room, I take it that it only gets better the lower we go?" Don asked aloud, his words echoing off the walls.

"This must be the entry chamber, these rocks once hid the secret door to the Dungeon", Kord said pointing at the fallen stone blocks in a hushed tone that told everyone to keep their voices down.

"Well there is more track here going into the stairway, it is dark down there and there is no smoke coming from the stairwell, so I will say that I do not think anyone's down there wherever there is." Tena said, Don walked over to her, and she placed her hand in his looking at his face,

"I guess we are close to making hard decisions." Tena whispered, the comment caught Don by surprise.

"No Tena, there is no hard decision, like I said to you before, where I go, you go." Don said in a hushed voice. He did not know it, but James heard his comment. Looking at his friend out of the corner of his eye James merely smiled to himself.

"What are you so happy about?" Hutch asked James seeing his smile.

"What? Cant I smile? We are getting ready to get home", James lied to Hutch.

About twenty leagues away Pat was riding his horse, his thoughts were on his friends, and he wondered if he had made a mistake. He thought of Lee and whether Hutch had been right, and he indeed had been wrong. He got off his horse, and settled down to make camp; he had been riding all night and all day and he was sore. He tied his horse up and gathered some wood, using his lighter he started a small fire. Sitting down he leaned back; hungry, he ate some bread and cheese, and then fell asleep. His dreams were of his friends and of Lee.

The steps were steep and curved into a semi circle as they went down, there was a thick coating of dust on them, and as they walked the dust was kicked up causing some of the party members to cough and sneeze, also as they went deeper everyone noticed that the temperature cooled down greatly and the air seemed to lighten. They went down for what seemed like a very long time and the stairwell ended in a small room. The room was square and about thirty feet in diameter with stone blocks making up the floor ceilings and walls, there were four doors in the room, all closed. The doors were wooden with steel banding, all of them had a simple pull ring. Also in the room was what appeared to be a hole in the floor in front of one of the doors. Tena walked over with Don to the hole, peering into it, he turned away looking at everyone.

"You gotta see this", he said to them with an odd expression on his face.

"Be weary, we have traps", Tena said to everyone causing the group to stop in their tracks. Walking over Hutch peered into the hole and he saw that it was only about ten feet deep, however, on the bottom of the pit were spikes, large rusty spikes about four feet long, and on those spikes was a man impaled. He looked as though he just died as the blood was still reddish and he had not yet started to decompose. There were rats on him, feeding on his flesh. Turning away feeling a bit sick Don saw that Kord looked into the pit smiling.

"Well, we now know what door they did not go through." And to that he started again his search of the room. They stood there for a bit until he again spoke.

"You can tell this door was opened, there are some fresh scrapes on the floor." Freya walked over kneeling, holding the lantern close to the floor examining the ground carefully.

"Yes indeed there are scrapes on the floor. I say we go this way, what do you all say?"

Don looking around at everyone spoke first among the group,

"I guess that door is as good as any."

Meanwhile above them in the entry way two men were standing looking at the crack in the wall. "Terc you go first," the evil looking one-eyed man said to the shorter one. The shorter one looked at his companion with a grimace.

"Yeah, I bet you wish that, I know this place's reputation Aglar, I don't want to be here to begin with." When he said this, the other man got angry he flashed a hard look at the shorter man causing him to take a step back.

"We have a job to do, and we are losing time to get it done, we need to act quickly, we have to follow so the big lug can give us the plan. Don't worry, I got plans for him. We bring the book back and get the reward." The man with one eye said harshly while running his dirty hand over a curved dagger that hung on his right hip.

The other man licked his lips tasting the sweat on them. "What if we are being betrayed, how do we know the master will pay us, how's do we know he will keep his part of the bargain?" he said in an almost desperate tone. The evil looking man smiled showing is yellow and brown teeth,

"He will pay us as I have coated this." He said patting the blade at his hip, "In Asparian Adder[13] venom. So much as a scratch with this and he will die within moments. No one fails to pay me." He said evilly, the other man laughed a low shrill laugh, flecks of spit flying from his mouth. And to that they decided to wait for a half hour before entering, as their business was almost concluded.

Below, in the entry chamber, Kord and Freya stood at the door, Kord placing a hand on the door, he grasped the pull ring and slowly pulled in the door. The door opened slightly

[13] A small black snake from Hafaria. One drop of its venom can kill 10 men

with only a slight creaking noise, the noise was low but to the rest it seemed like a trumpet going off.

"I take it that it is now too late to go back to your Uncle's house Freya?" Hutch said in an obvious attempt to lighten the mood. Freya looked at him hard for a moment, then, seeing Hutch smiling, she also smiled and turned her attention back to the door. The door was open about a foot and everyone could see that it opened into a narrow hallway wide enough to fit about two men shoulder to shoulder in it, and the walls were made of rough hewn stone, unlike the room they just came from the hallway had about an inch of water in it, and the walls were wet and damp from water that was leaking down over them, there was the sound of water dripping from the ceiling. Kord looked back at everyone. In a whisper, he spoke.

"Well, we made a good choice as the book that Yognar wrote said he ran into a water filled hall before making it out." And to that he opened the door wider and walked in his torch flickering on the walls, and its light shimmered in the hall from the reflections from the water.

When Don stepped into the hall he saw why there was no water in the room from the hall; when he stepped into the hall he actually had to step down, and as he looked ahead, he saw the hall branched to the right and left. They made their way down the hall about twenty feet and at the T Kord took out a small piece of parchment; looking at it, he said.

"We go right" and to that he simply turned that way. As Don turned the corner, he saw this hall ran about twenty feet and into an open room; as they made their way down the hall he noticed the hallway had a slight incline to the hall became dry, shaking the water from his boot, he hoped there would be no more water. They entered the room and Don saw that the room was round and it had two doors. One to the right and one to the left, one was painted red the other blue, there was a scent of mold in the air.

"We should go through the red door I think." Freya said confidently looking at the others. James looked irritated.

"What does that map Kord keeps looking at, then hiding, show, and why are you choosing that door? Does the map show something?" Kord flashed a look at him and Freya smiled.

"No James, I say that door as it is the only one with fresh scrape marks in front of it. Of course, you can go through the other door if you like." James looked at her with a venomous look and turned to Don whispering to him.

"She doesn't like me, I can tell, we may need if the chips are down to do our own thing." Don looked at James with irritation, then whispered.

"Man, you crazy or what? I wouldn't piss her off up there", he said pointing to the ceiling, "Let alone down here. So far, they seem to know what they are doing, let's not pee in our punch bowl here, ok? You are acting really stupid lately. Chill out and shut up man!" And to that James shot him a dark look and walked over to Hutch saying nothing, but he now knew he had to do it, he had to ensure that those idiots didn't screw it up, so he had to stay here.

Kord reached forward and pulled on the door, as the door slowly opened. Suddenly the door flew open, knocking HIM to the ground. A huge spider was in the doorway, the thing that terrified Don and the rest was that this thing was the size of a large pig. Tena screamed "Spider" while yanking her sword from its sheath, and Freya jumped back dropping her Lantern, which hit the ground with a loud echoing "clank". Kord was scrambling on the floor trying to draw his sword and

Don and Hutch yanked theirs free, James bolted, running back into the water filled hall. The spider was maroon with black hair, its dozen beady eyes seemed to be everywhere. Seeing Kord, it ran at him, its eight legs making a clapping sound like keys being struck on a keyboard. With a yell, Freya loosed an arrow at it, striking it in the side; seemingly unaffected the spider jumped on Kord, Tena ran to it striking one of its legs, causing the vile monster to back off and turned its attention to Tena,

"Get out of the way Tena" Hutch yelled as he and Don ran to her. The spider took one of its long legs and smacked Tena knocking her to the ground, it immediately ran jumping on her, its mouth opening showing its two large spike-like teeth. Screaming Tena struck at it, Don ran to the vile monster striking at it with his sword, hitting it over the head; the thing bled quickly a dark black liquid, it seemed easily hurt and jumped off and ran into a corner. Kord by now standing, had his sword drawn, and right by his left ear Hutch heard a whizz, an arrow loosed by Freya struck the Spider in its cluster of eyes causing it to make an odd chirping sound, it then collapsed its legs scrambling and flailing about, another arrow loosed by Freya struck it in its bulbous back area, then Kord ran up to it sinking his sword into its head just above its eye, the Spider flailed a bit more then spun over its legs curling it being obvious dead.

Don's heart was pounding and Hutch was obvious scared to death. "Oh my God, that thing is huge I mean we just got in here and this already." Don looked at Hutch then at the spider laying dead in front of him, he walked over to Tena. She turned then hugged him fiercely, she sunk her face into his shoulder. Kord, by now standing, had his sword drawn, and right by his left ear Hutch heard a whizz, an arrow loosed by

Freya struck the Spider in its cluster of eyes causing it to make an odd chirping sound, it then collapsed its legs scrambling and flailing about, another arrow loosed by Freya struck it in its bulbous back area, then Kord ran up to it sinking his sword into its head just above its eye, the Spider flailed a bit more then spun over its legs curling it being obviously dead.

"I love you" she said to him then squeezed him hard. Holding her, Don looked at Freya who was looking back at him, and then she turned to Kord.

"Are you ok, it didn't bite you did it?" Kord looked at her, "No if it did I would have been dead, the thing is a Giant Fog spider, they are deadly, one bite, and you are done." Hutch looked at Kord.

"I hate spiders, even little ones." Tena turning from Don looked around the room.

"Where is James? He wasn't bitten and dragged off was he?" she said in a concerned voice. Don looked at them then at the open door to the water filled hallway.

"No, when it jumped on Kord I saw him run that way." He said thumbing at the door. Kord looked angry.

"A coward and more, I thought he was just a whiner and complainer now he is a coward and one that leaves his friends to their own ends, I will deal with him." He said this as he drew a dagger and started walking over to the door.

"No!" Don said out loud stepping forward. "He isn't from here, where we are from, there are no monsters, there are no giant spiders, he was bitten by one when he was young and is deathly afraid of them, it isn't his fault. You have to understand we are not from this place." Kord looked at Don with anger in his eyes.

"So be it" he said pointing the dagger at Don shaking it. "He stays away from me and better not ask me for any quarter, as he will get none from me now." And to that he walked away from Don. Looking at the door, Don walked over to it,

"James, it is dead, you can come back now", Don yelled down the hall, hearing a splashing he then saw James walking into the light with fear in his face and eyes. Don looked at him, "You pissed a lot of people off with that stunt, running like that isn't going to cut it in this place James, we have to know you are going to have our backs!" Don said to him seriously,

James looked at him with a look that made Don actually feel sorry for him. It was a mixture of fear and shame, "I'm sorry, really... I don't like spiders let alone ones the size of a small car. Let a damn snake come along and see what Pat would have done. I bet no one would have yelled at him for taking off." And at that James walked off and stood away from everyone.

After they got all the nicks and bruises bandaged up, they went ahead and moved on through the open doorway, the hall towards which it lead was wide and lined with rough hewn stones, there were large sticky webs everywhere, and they proceeded with caution down the hall. They walked down, their torch and lantern lights casting creepy shadows on the walls when suddenly they ran into a section where the hall lead four ways in a great big cross.

"Well, which way now?" Freya said, Kord looked at his map scowling at James out of the corner of his eye.

"According to my "Secret" map, we need to go left then we should go a long way with no problems and then run into a door that is labeled dead end. That's as far as this map takes us." Kord placed the small map into his belt pouch looking to the group and eyeing James angrily.

"Well?" Tena said aloud to no one in particular. "I guess we should look around a bit here, any signs of the child or the ones that took her?" Don spoke up.

"They couldn't have come this way, right? I mean, the spider was here and the door was closed. If they are down here then they couldn't have come this way."

Freya glanced at Don, "I agree. However, what do we do then?" There was a quick discussion on the path to take. Kord voted to go back and take the left turn in the water filled hall. After a short bit of arguing with James being the sole vote for NO, they decided to do that.

They walked back down and through the water filled hall. The hall like it to the right gradually inclined to dryer ground. They looked around a bit and Kord found what appeared to be slight tracks in the dust, and ran into another T in the hall. They went left at that point and the hall winded this way and that, after about a half an hour of walking, they ran into a doorway that entered a large room. As they peered into the room they saw that there was a door on the opposite wall, they could see torch light around the edges of the door, and they could hear talking. They also could hear a child crying.

Kord turned to them. "The vermin is in there, we do not know how many. Freya extinguished the light." They all drew weapons, Kord smiling with Don and Hutch at his side peered into the room.

The room was small, and there were four men in there. They wore animal skins and had a small blonde girl. She was dirty and had a nasty scrape on her arm, hand bound on front of her she was frightened. One of the men held a rope that was tied to her bonds.

The room has an altar in it, they had incense burning and also a large brazier, old and rusty with a large fire going in it. The heat from the room was stifling. There was a large obese man naked in front of the altar, and he had a large knife, he was chanting with the other man kneeling. He was taking the knife and slicing his chest with it as he chanted. Turning, Don saw he was covered in blood; his look was of crazed bliss. He said something roughly to the others and the man with the rope dragged the little girl to him. The language he was speaking was very familiar, Don was positive he heard it, he even recognized some of it, his heart twisted in his chest as he recognized the language.

The fat man grabbed the little girl by her hair causing her to yell in pain. She was kicking him as he threw her on the altar, at this point Kord let out a huge yell. Barging in the door he struck one man before he could do anything. His head rolled to one side of the room. The others caught by surprise drew swords, Don heard a "FBIZZ" and an arrow sailed past his shoulder striking one man in the eye, he screamed grabbing it, then fell. The other man lunged at Kord but he was far too late, his arm fell to the ground, then as he screamed, his blood spattering the floor, Kord's sword ran through him silencing his yells.

The naked obese man held the knife to the girl's throat, holding her in front of him. Freya and Tena entered the room. His eyes darted back and forth as everyone else filled the room. He was yelling at everyone, Hutch looked at Don shocked at what he was hearing.

"Licentia Vel Is Dies Iam" He yelled tightening the dagger to the girl's throat. His look was panicked.

Kord looked at him, "Speak normal DOG!" he raised his voice.

The man looked at Kord, then at Freya, he was sweating and Don was revolted at how he looked, bleeding and sweating, his belly hung in front of him. Freya walked out of the room, Don was surprised at this. Kord and the fat man exchanged more yells, the fat man becoming more desperate. Suddenly there was a "FBIZZZ" and an arrow struck the man in the throat, he stumbled back dropping the sword, and Kord was on him, he threw the small girl back, and as the man fell against the wall, with a fierce yell Kord swung his sword sideways, the blade cut deep into the man's belly, his intestines falling out in a series of purple loops, blood splashing all over the floor. Don grabbed the crying little girl, and turning her from the grotesque show, he carried her into the other room.

Tena came with him, and a moment later the rest of the men was there. Kord walked to the girl looking at her. "Child I am a warrior of Maldoria and I will help you."

The little girl frightened looked at Kord, she didn't say anything. Tena walked over and was soothing her, Freya looked around. "Well the bastards didn't succeed. Kord, what could they have been up to?"

Kord looked into the room and the bloody carnage he created. Shaking his head he seemed perplexed. "I do not know, they were going to sacrifice her, as I said many heathens think Maldoran children are magical. His language was odd, something I never had heard before. Freya, did you recognize it?"

Freya looked at him, then to the child, she seemed puzzled also. "No I never heard anything like that."

Tena looked at the little girls smiling, reaching in her pack, she pulled out an apple. The girl took it and ate it voraciously like she hadn't eaten in days. "She hasn't been fed in awhile, the dogs were also starving her." She looked back at the girl. "Little one," she said sweetly smiling at her. "Tell me, did they ever talk like us, using our words?" The little girl seemingly to relax a little, shook her head no.

Well, we head back where we came from, I will make sure she gets home once we see you all off. There is no help for this now. She must come with us."

Hutch looked at Don. "That sounded like Latin?"

Don thought for a moment thinking back to school, "Hutch your right, I recognized a few words, what the hell. Latin here?"

James was perplexed also. "I agree man, it sounded like Latin to me also. He said *Is Est Veneficus*?"

Tena looked at James, "What do you mean, what is that.

Hutch interrupted. "Tena it is Latin for *She Is Magical.*" He looked seriously at Don.

"What is this Latin you are all going on about!" Kord said irritated.

"Kord, Latin is an old language from OUR world. You would not have it here unless...."

Hutch interrupted Don again. "Unless someone is here that is from our world!"

"How can that be? Uncle said there was only one book made, and that these Dark Wizards are after it. How can someone else be here from your world.?" Freya asked puzzled.

"I don't know Freya, the fat guy also said something else I caught. He said *Nostrum Dominatio Mos Must Fio*, so that tells me he has a boss, and...."

Hutch interrupted again. "Yeah that tells us the boss is from our world, or knows someone from our world."

"Would you quit interrupting me Hutch, damn man..."

"Sorry Don. I am just now really freaked."

---- GAMERS SAGA - DONALD SEMORA ----

"Why do you say that, what does that mean?" Tena asked.

"It means Our Lords Will Must Be Done. It means they have someone who they call their Lord, so they have a boss." Hutch explained.

"We need info from that little girl, someone is here in your world that is from our world. I don't know how, but Latin is a very old language and one that I bet is not native to this place."

Freya was troubled. "The child is to traumatized to talk right now, let's get you to the gate and me and Kord and Tena will worry about this after you are gone home."

"Yes, me and this Latin man will be meeting soon enough, I swear to that." Kord said in a deadly quiet voice.

They made their way back from where they came from, passing the dead spider. The little girl seemed to stay attached to Tena, and held her hand the entire time. They made their way back to the door that was labeled dead end on the map. Kord simply walked to the door and opened it shocking everyone at his brazenness, looking in the room, there was only one other door that was made of polished metal and had runes around it, the room was large and circular with an overturned table in the center and also several rotted tapestries on the walls, some of them lay in cluttered heaps on the floor. There were two skeletons on the floor, their bones scattered apart, their clothing laying about them in rotted tatters and their armor and weapons rusty and worthless laying about the long lifeless and decayed bones.

"Dead end I suppose?" Freya said more to herself than anyone in particular. The metal door had been at one time recently opened, there was a scraping on the floor that it was obviously made when someone tried to open it.

264

"Literally a dead end for these chaps." James said looking at the long dead bodies. Kord walked over to the door and tried to push it, then he ran his hand over its smooth surface. No rust, no marring, nothing?" he said over his shoulder. Then Hutch walked over to it. Standing there puzzled he ran his hand over it also, then noticed something the others hadn't.

"The door is warm, its chilly down here but this door is warm, even hot in some places. I don't get it?" Don and Freya walked over feeling the door and agreed. Walking over to the bodies James kicked at their bones and the decayed clothing.

"They don't look burned or anything, their clothing is rotted, but that's about it." Kord walked over to James, bending down, he went through the bones and searched the skeletons; amidst the bones Kord saw a small copper pin with a strange design curved into one end and a flat part on the other. Looking over he saw the group standing and talking, and he discreetly placed it into his pocket.

"We need to search the room to make sure we don't miss anything." Kord said aloud standing up from where he was kneeling over the bones. They searched the room for a good hour and found nothing else. The group seemed frustrated and it was slowly dawning on them that the map was most likely right.

"I don't get it. The door is possible a one way door, I mean could it open inwards or have a magical word to open it?" Don said aloud to them. Freya seemed also irritated at the door.

"Maybe it doesn't open, maybe it is designed to do exactly what it is doing. To delay and stop adventurers." James looked at her and agreed, and they sat there perplexed at the door that seemed locked but yet had no handle nor hinges. It seemed they indeed were at a dead end.

The Rescued Maldoran Child

There are many forms of revenge.
The best ones result in the betrayers death!

...... Kord's favorite saying

16
ARROWS AND SWORDS

Aglar and Terc walked down the narrow stairway and into the entry chamber, where they stayed for one hour. Then, seeing the door open they went through it. "Terc, light a lantern so we can see; he didn't leave us a torch like he said he would." A few moments later there were some sparks and a lick of flame, and then slowly blowing on it Terc placed the burning tinder into a small oil lamp and held it aloft in the room.

"Yeah, they went this way; see all the scuffs on the floor, we gonna get this done, so we can git back to Dark Home and doin' what we do best!" Terc then dropped his metal rod that he used to strike his flint to make fire causing a loud "CLANK!" Aglar looked at his companion and sharply scolded him.

"You idiot! Are you trying to tell them we are here? I haven't traveled all this way to have a flint rod ruin it. Terc looked sheepishly and apologized picking up the flint rod and placing it back into his pack. Aglar calmed quickly and decided to be nice as he needed the cretin, and smiled a knowing smile. "Yep, we need to do this and get back, I don't like these open places and sure don't like this dark place." At that they went down the hall and made ready to ambush the unknowing group.

Meanwhile, in the dead end room the group was sitting there talking about what to do. "We need to go back and to the entry room." Kord offered to the group.

"I say we take another hall, there were a few that branched off this and that way, maybe there is another way. And what about the child? Did she ever get through the door?" Hutch looked sharply at James, suspicion hit him as he knew James didn't care about the kid one bit. Freya looked at James for a moment,

"I agree with him, maybe there is another way; it is obvious we can't get through the door. Hutch who was at the door examining it turned to the group.

"Look, there is a small hole. I think it is a hole for a key or something." Everyone gathered around the door and sure enough there was a small hole about midway on the door in the middle. It was actually pretty easily noticeable.

"Kord are you turning blind, I am surprised you didn't see that." Freya said to her companion. Looking sheepish Kord seemed uncomfortable with what she said.

"I guess I missed it!" he said to Freya.

"It is a keyhole, maybe the key is in the skeletons there." Hutch said pointing at the bones on the floor.

"We searched them and there was nothing in them." James said jabbing a thumb towards Kord.

"Well, this isn't getting any place, we need to decide." Then from the doorway far off there was a faint clinking sound as if something metal was dropped, looking over at the doorway, they entered Tena made comment.

"Did you hear that noise there?" She said pointing to the door. Looking over at the dark doorway there was not any other sound other than the sound of the wind humming far off. Standing, Kord walked to the door.

"You all stay here I will investigate." Hutch stood up walking towards Kord.

"I will go with ya buddy." Kord looked sharply at him.

"No, I will go alone, I will be fine." Hutch looked over to Freya who also seemed a bit surprised. At that Kord walked through the doorway and into the hall. They all sat there for about two minutes, then looking troubled Tena started to get up.

"Now that's odd isn't it, why is he being so reckless?" Tena said as she stood up.

"I will go with him in case he runs into trouble." As she walked over to the door looking back at the group she smiled, Don got up quickly.

"You are not going alone, I will go with ya, two of us are better than one." They both entered the dark doorway and disappeared.

"Do you think they will be ok?" Hutch asked walking to the dark doorway and peering into it with a look of concern.

Freya handing the small girl some bread, stood up tossling her hair smiling. "They will be ok, noises are common, and Kord is a seasoned adventurer."

Walking down the hall Kord entered the hall where the webs were and saw Terc and Aglar. "You need to be careful, you have been heard. Also, extinguish that oil lamp and stay a distance away." Kord said agitated. Aglar looked at him.

"Master, we are supposed to kill them and be done, that's all. This place isn't good, let's do it and will be finished here!" Kord looked at the toothless man and grimaced.

"You will have your chance, I have a key to the door, but they do not know. I will get them to come back this way, and you can wait in the room there," He said pointing to the room with the dead spider. "Once there I will kill the blonde headed one, the rest will fall readily." Terc looked to Kord and giggled a mirthless giggle.

"We wound the sister; I have plans for her." the shorter man said with a vile tone to his comment. Kord looked at the man darkly.

"They all die so we can get the book, you get your gold, and I am done. However leave the redhead to me. Nothing more nothing else, I didn't kill the old man for nothing, Understand: my plans won't be ruined at the last minute over an oil lamp!" The smaller man looked darkly at him and sheepishly agreed.

"Also wait for my signal I will lead them back here after I give Freya the drink. Once she is out we will come, then when they come in here you strike."

Both assassins smiled a mirthless smile.

Tena and Don for a moment wondered if they made a mistake as the light from the hall was very dim, they slowly they made their way down the hall they heard whispering, and slowed. Don's heart pounded and he worried that maybe Kord met his end and the killers were talking over his body. As they came to the corner of the spider web clogged hall the talking grew louder, and they almost stopped, they peered around the corner. they were surprised to see Kord talking to two evil looking men, Don recognized them as the two men who tried to rob him and Hutch in Dark Home. They also heard what Kord said Don's heart sank at hearing that Kord killed the nice old man. Tena grasped Don's arm, he looked at her and her face was stricken. Don held a finger to his mouth silencing her. He wrapped an arm about her trying to silently comfort her. They listed to their whispered conversation as it echoed lightly off the stone walls and his heart grew cold. He could not believe his ears, fearing he would be found he turned whispering to Tena.

"We have to go now, warn your sister. We cannot take him by ourselves."

They left as quickly and silently as possible making it back to the room, Tena's choked sobs making Don more and more angry at what he witnessed. They made it back to the group.

Tena burst into the room breathless and everyone could see she was panicked. "What's the matter, is Kord hurt?" Freya asked with concern in her voice.

"He is planning on killing us all. He is right now meeting with two ugly men planning it, also he said he killed Uncle back in Dark Home." Her voice was panicked and grief stricken.

"WHAT! He is doing what? He killed Uncle?" Freya said with tears in her eyes.

"I have known Kord for years he is not a traitor!" Freya said with confusion and grief in her eyes.

"He is a traitor, he is talking to two guys one guy has one eye and the other is a smaller one, and they are talking about the book and also of killing you first Freya. We both heard him as clear as we talk now." Don assured her with sympathy.

Tena looked at Freya, who had a look on her face that was a mixture of anger and grief and total disbelief. Hutch looked at Don for a moment then spoke up.

"Wait a second, you said one guy had one eye, and there was a smaller one?"

"Yeah don't say it, they are the two that attacked us in Dark Home. Kord was telling them he would lead us back to the room a with the dead spider and kill everyone immediately and that all of us would then be easy pickings." Tena walked to her sister hugging her,

"Oh, sister what are we going to do? Uncle is dead, and that beast killed him, we can't let this go unpunished you know that." Freya looked to Tena with tears in her eyes, Hutch spoke up,

"What are we going to do now though, he is a trained warrior, and he has now two men to help him?"   Tena looked to Hutch then to Don with grief in her eyes.   "He doesn't know that we know his plans, neither do his dogs. What he does not know will be his downfall. Everyone act normal when he walks in, no one act as if we know. Freya and I will handle this." James then stood up. "We need to move the little girl in case this gets ugly, I will take her across the room and play with her, then once you two make your move I will jump in. I can't do much but I will help all of you. I didn't agree with what the old man was saying, but he was nice and helped us." To that he got up taking the small child's hand, smiling at her he led her to a corner sitting down. He pulled out a dagger and sat it next to him.

"He also said he has the key to that door." Don said pointing to it with his thumb.

"Do not drink anything he offers you sister, he said he was going to give you something to drink, then do his deeds."

"Double reason to get him before he gets us!" Hutch said looking at Tena.

A few minutes later Kord appeared in the doorway. "It was nothing I retraced our steps all the way to the entry room, no one has been back, however, I have thought of what was said, and I think it may be a good idea to back track and go into another doorway, maybe we can find our way past this infernal door." Freya who was standing holding her bow, acted like she relaxed. Smiling and chuckling, she spoke.

"You know my friend, I almost thought you were some Orc coming through the door and put an arrow in your eye." Kord looked at her and smiled.

"Orc I am not and your arrows are best suited for vermin." Freya laughed.

"That you are right my friend, vermin they are for." Don spoke up trying hard to sound like nothing was the matter so Kord didn't get suspicious. He didn't want to fight this man, he had doubts that all of them put together could deal with the trained Warrior.

"So do we go back or try to knock the door down?"

"I say we knock the door down" Hutch chimed in.

"No. No, I tried to push on it and it is stout, I say we go back to the main room and try again another direction it is obvious there is no way to get through and since the key alludes will never get through it." Kord said to them. Agreeing with Kord's plan everyone stood up and started to get their things together; there was a tension in the room among the three friends as they wondered when Freya and Tena were going to act. Turning towards the door Kord spoke lifting his ankle up and rubbing it with a grimace.

"Freya, I frayed my ankle a little in the hallway back there, can you go ahead and scout? I will be right behind you." Tena looked at Freya sharply as did Don and Hutch. Freya looked at Kord with concern on her face.

"Of course I can, let's get ourselves together, and I will lead, are you sure you are ok?" Kord assured her he was ok just a little sore and at that Freya bent down to tighten her laces on her tall leather boots, she then looked over at Tena, who was looking at her with red blood shot eyes,

"Oh, Kord before we go, I say we try to door one last time force it open to see if it will budge? Or is your shoulder frayed also?" She said laughing. Kord looked over at her smiling.

"I have the broadest shoulder in the realms, I will try it one more time then we must be on our way, time is wasting, and we have far to go." Freya smiled at him.

"Shall I help you?" She said batting her eye lashes at him. Breaking out in a loud laugh Kord smacked his thigh.

"You are far too pretty for your own good." Smiling he turned and made his way to the door. Don noticed that he was not limping as he walked.

Standing at the door Kord bent his shoulder to the door. Slamming it hard a few times he stood there panting a bit out of breath, then it happened. There was a Whizzing sound and a dull "Thump" then another and a "Thump" shocked everyone saw Kord turn with shock on his face and two arrows sticking out of his throat, then another Whizzing sound and another "Thump" and a third arrow struck him in mid chest and then a fourth arrow struck his chest again, grabbing the arrow in his chest with trembling hands, he pulled it out. His blood dripping from its iron tip.

Falling to the ground in a splash of his own red sticky blood, he laid there making gurgling sounds. Walking over to him Freya and Tena stood there and looked down. "Your dogs die with you tonight; my Uncle pays his respects." Tena said to him in a bitter tear chocked tone. Freya also with tears in her voice spoke.

"I trusted you, Uncle trusted you, and so I was the first to die. The tables turn and you are the first, your two dogs are the second and third. Whatever plan you have rots with you in this place!" Kord his eyes wide looking at everyone while he laid on the cold stone floor. His heart was racing as he knew death was coming. His thoughts went to his keep and of his lands that he was so close to having. Looking up, he saw the man he despised walk forward. James walked over to him.

"I was the one who heard you, I followed you told them what I saw. I am responsible for destroying your plans. I wanted you to know that. Rot in hell Kord!" and to that James turned away. Tena, dagger in hand knelt down. Kord tried to shy away. She held the knife to his mouth and spoke quietly and slowly.

"How did you kill him? How did you murder our Uncle? Well, scum." Saying that she flicked the dagger on his cheek opening it up, dark blood ran down his cheek past his ear. Grimacing in pain Kord tried to pull away but instead Tena seizing him by the hair grabbed one of the arrows twisting it causing Kord to gurgle in pain. "Well dog, it is over." Tena said letting the arrow go and standing up. Turning away she walked to Don wrapping her arms around him. Standing above him Freya looked down at him, an arrow knocked on her bow.

"Your plans die, we kill your dogs, and throw the book in the Stone Gate. It seems your betrayal is complete. I called you friend Kord. Why do this, Money? Jewels? I do not understand, but then again, I don't betray friends." And to that she released the arrow, the shaft striking Kord in the eye and to that his betrayal ended.

Standing there for a long moment, tears running down her face, Freya wouldn't move it seemed. She stood there looking at her old friend. Hutch walked over to her placing a hand on her shoulder.

"I am sorry." Was all he said and Freya turned looked at him and then crying buried her face in his shoulder hugging him. Hutch looked awkwardly at his friends standing there patting her on the back. After the two women composed themselves Freya recovered first and knelt down going through Kord's things. Finding the copper key she held it up,

"I got it, he did have it."

Tena spoke up then. "What about the two vermin back there. If we don't tend to them, they will dog our heals." James, to Don's surprise, agreed.

"Yes I agree with her, we gotta take care of them or they will just follow us and who knows when they will strike. There are only two of em, we can handle that, right?" Don and Hutch agreed. Looking at Kord's lifeless body Don admitted to himself he had thought Kord would be a foundation of not only protection but support. Looking at his cold body his lifeless eyes staring at the ceiling it seemed they were a whole lot less safe now.

"What about the map." James offered kneeling down searching for it. Finding it he held it up and opened it. Looking at it for a moment he looked back at the body of Kord. "What's the matter?" Don said looking at him.

"I got the wrong one." James said.

"Let me see that." Freya said reaching towards James and taking the piece of parchment from his fingers. Looking at it, she flashed a scowl. James went through Kord's pockets and found another small piece of parchment however he kept this one to himself, slipping it into his pocket while everyone was occupied with Freya and the map piece. He walked to one side saying he had to pee, standing there in the corner acting like he was peeing, he opened the scroll piece, and what he saw alarmed him. He decided to keep it to himself and make his move when the opportunity presented itself. They would pay for treating him like they were.

"We have been doubly deceived. This is a map, we want is of the other parts of this place. Look here." She said laying it flat on Kord's chest and pointing to a spot on it. "This is the other side of that door, to hell with the other map, this is what we want. Now we go and attend to the two vermin that lay in wait for us." And to that she stood up and knocked an arrow, Tena drawing her dagger walked over to Freya, and Don stepped forward.

"Well, let's get this over with so we can for once and for all be done." And to that they made their way through the doorway and towards the two men who waited in the far off room.

Freya Prepares for revenge

I guess arrows are better than swords.
...... Freya in the Dungeon of Gott

Should we cover him up?

...... Hutch to Freya standing over Kord

No. The corpse worms will cover him soon.

...... Freya's answer

17
ASSASSINS' FATE

They made their way down the halls and back to the room with the dead spider moving slowly, being careful not to alarm the two men lying in wait for them. As they approached the room Hutch spoke loudly. "Kord be careful walking in the room, that spider may not be all the way dead." Looking back at Hutch Freya smiled then spoke aloud.

"Kord, make sure you draw your sword, search the room then call to us to let us know it is clear. Throw a torch in the room first to light it up." She looked to Tena and smiled. Tena leaned over to Don whispering.

"They think their employer is coming in alone so they will let their guard down a bit, that's all she needs to do what she needs to do." Don looked at her red tear stained eyes and smiled, for once he was looking forward to helping kill a man, for a moment he thought of what this meant, however in this world justice took different forms. They stood about ten feet from the doorway, Freya looked to Hutch, who had a torch, and she motioned for him to throw the torch into the room, Hutch nodded then did as she had asked.

"The torch is in Kord, go in now and let us know when it is safe." Freya spoke aloud. Hutch grunted a muffled "OK Freya", they then prepared to burst into the room and once and for all take care of the deceit that Kord started.

Aglar stood in the room seeing the torch light coming down the hall and whispered to Terc, "Here they come, the red head with the bow he will take care of, the men die first then we can deal with the pretty one." The smaller man smiled a rotted grin in anticipation.

"Yes I will stick the one who acted like a wizard!" and to that they waited on either side of the doorway. They heard a woman's voice telling Kord to enter the room first, then her telling Kord to throw a torch into the room. Drawing his rust pitted short sword Aglar stood there thinking that once Kord walked in, he would wait a moment then when Kord gave the signal, strike. Death was visiting today he smiled thinking to himself. He saw a torch suddenly land about ten feet into the room, it hit the floor with a clank rolling a bit. It gave off a muted light flickering over the walls and lighting up the room slightly. He heard the woman tell Kord to go in, and then heard Kord's agreement.

Looking to his smaller companion he whispered. "Don't strike yet, he is coming in first let him get in and give us the signal." Terc looked at Aglar and smiled, Aglar's hand loosed on the hilt of his sword his guard edging slightly.

Freya stood a few feet from the doorway, she looked to Tena, who had pulled her dagger. Hutch had his sword in his hand laying his heavy back pack down against the wall preparing for the coming fight. Don had his sword out. James stood in the back with Kord's old large sword, he looked comical as the swords was obviously too heavy for him, he saw Hutch put his pack down. Smiling Don looked at Hutch and James and nodded to them with a knowing grin. Freya looked to them, then whispered,

"I will run in, get one with my arrow the rest attack the opposite side, they are most likely hiding inside the doorways." Everyone nodded and then Freya ran into the room, turned with a yell and released an arrow, the rest running in on each side of the door.

Aglar stood there wondering why Kord hadn't come in, he heard low whispering the words he couldn't make out, looking across to Terc he saw his eyes grow big with alarm, something was the matter. Looking closer to the smaller man he realized he had heard something in the whispering that alarmed him, Terc opened his mouth to speak when suddenly with a startling yell the red headed woman ran in, Aglar tensed angrily he thought he had been betrayed, she turned to him, an arrow already in her bow, he raised his sword taking a step forward to strike at her when he heard the twang of her bow string, realizing far too late he miscalculated, he felt the arrow strike him in the chest. Pain gripped him and he felt his breath leave him in a painful gasp dropping his sword it making a loud clanking noise at his feet. He looked and saw Terc running for the door anger hit him as he realized he was going to die, he leaned over to pick up his sword, and thought he would at least take the red headed wench with him when he felt another arrow enter the top of his head, darkness then enveloped him forever.

Terc stood there in the quiet, when he heard a woman's voice giving instructions on the attack, his heart raced as he now understood that he and Aglar had been betrayed, he looked over to Aglar who was standing there and was about to yell when a red headed yelling woman ran into the room and shot Aglar in the chest, Aglar dropped his sword then with the arrow in his chest, panic gripped him as suddenly behind her were the others, realizing his time was coming, he dropped his sword and bolted for the door to try to get out, he ran through the door and down the water filled hallway, running into the entry room he realized he was being chased and ran up the narrow stairs, jumping through the crack, he realized it was night out. The heat and humidity hit him his lungs ached from running and panic, he didn't care he would go back to Dark Home and do his own thing.

Don ran into the room and saw Freya had shot one man in the chest and was knocking another arrow, another man was running for the door, he recognized the man as one of the men who tried to rob them. Hutch yelled.

"Get him, he is running." Tena ran past his shoulder chasing the smaller man, he ran through the door making splashing sounds with Tena close behind him. Thinking that Tena could be ambushed, he and Hutch ran also after her and the smaller man. Making their way down the wet hall and into the entry room, they saw Tena standing in the room out of breath.

"The scroll worm ran up there." She said panting out of breath, pointing to the narrow stairs that lead up to the city.

"Let him go, we can't be wandering around these ruins, especially at night."

"He is probably half way back to the main trail by now." Hutch said, she looked at him and smiled. They then went back to the room with the dead spider. Walking in they saw Freya and the rest standing over the man with two arrows in him, James was looking at the guy.

"An arrow in the top of the head, yeppers I think that would do it." Freya looked at James and smiled.

"What? The one in the chest wasn't?" Hutch laughed.

Looking over to Don, Hutch and Tena who were walking in, James spoke. "Well? Did you get him?"

Tena looked at him, "No, he was far too fast he made it up to the city." Freya smiled at her sister then hugged her.

"We have honored our dear Uncle today Tena, no matter what happens now they are in hell rotting and screaming." Don looked at the dead man, he was surprised as there was very little blood, he was crumpled over in a ball and looked a little comical with the arrow sticking out of the top of his head.

"You know you lost that arrow Freya, you aren't going to get it out of his skull." Tena said smiling, Freya agreed and turned the man over and yanked out the arrow that was in his chest, the arrow coming out with a sickening sucking sound.

Terc was out of breath, he realized with relief that they were not following him, it was dark out. He looked around with eyes becoming accustomed to the moonlit dark, luck was with him as it was a high moon out, so he could make his way back to the main trail and hopefully get to his horse, he could steal what he needed when on the road, and he felt a lot better as it occurred to him that he wouldn't be having Aglar always bossing him around. This was Aglar's fault, he never wanted to leave Dark Home and come here, he wanted to stay here keep the down payment the big ox gave them and do what they did best, murder and rob drunken nobles and break into ships at the wharf.

"Good riddance, I make my own fortune now." He muttered to himself and actually felt better as now his fortunes would turn for the better he would place this behind him and make his fortunes on his own. He made his way back to the main road and then up to the hill from the base of the spire then crested at the hill. In the silvery moonlight, he could see the strange spiral tower and the tops of the jungle trees behind him. He took a deep breath in the humid air and turned to find his horse when he saw it.

The thing stood in the middle of the road, it was about the size of a large dog black in color it then stood up on its legs, and he realized with fear it was a Cave Creeper. The thing's eyes glowed with a red light and it mouth opened to expose large fangs, spittle dripping from them onto the ground, it made a low snarl flexing its hands that were tipped with three large claws. Terc looked back to the city and thought about running, his heart was racing in his chest as he realized the trap too late.

He heard the brush next to him rustle then he felt something hit him knocking him to the ground with suffocating force, he felt fangs close around his throat, while a soundless scream mixed with blood came from his mouth, striking the thing that ambushed him, he felt the jaws tighten, his eyed clouded as he felt his consciousness being yanked from him. He managed to reach his knife, striking the monster several times it leapt off of him, crying in pain, Terc managed to crawl to a half stance, looking over he saw two of the creatures about ten feet away looking at him snarling. Reaching to his throat, he felt tore flesh, blood was flowing from the wound, he could still breath. Panicking he had to make it back to the city, he turned half crawling to the safety of the buildings far down the road whimpering to himself his muffled tears of fright were muted by his tore throat, when he felt the maws of death clamp over his skull, pain ripped through him as he felt the bones in his skull crack and split, he collapsed crying, screaming, then he heard the crunch of his skull and then nothing.

The two Cave creepers sat in the middle of the road feeding on the lifeless body in the silvery moonlight.

Cave Creeper

The cave Creeper:

No other creature that inhabits the Southern portion of Da'Naan has more drive in its heart to feed and to eat then the Cave Creeper. They come out only at night and only eat living warm blooded creatures.

There is no known non-magical way to kill one of these beasts. They were created many years ago by the Evil Dark Mage Malphit Doom to guard his keep. Once they attack there is no sense in fighting.

You are already Dead.

- Encyclopedia Exotica Creatures.

18
INTO THE FURNACE

Tena stood there, thinking. "let's be rid of this hideous book and be done." James let out an explosive breath.

"About damn time." Freya looked at him for a moment and Don thought she was going to say something, but she didn't. They made their way back to the room with Hutch picking up his back pack as he walked down the hall. They returned to the room with the steel door and Kord's body, Don and James dragged Kord's body off to one corner, so they didn't have to look at it, and they looked again at the map.

Tena was soothing the little girl still talking to her, the little girl was curled up to her. "What is yur name child, you can tell me.. Come on child I am Tena we all are your friends. No one is going to ever let anything bad happen to you."

The child looked at Tena, then in an almost imperceptible voice she spoke. "My name is Donia, do you know my mommy?" Tena looked at her, she smiled,

"Donia I don't know your mommy but I am going to take you to her. OK. But you have to help me ok." The child smiled a woeful smile and said nothing else.

Freya was standing there, she was looking at the small map intently. "According to this the Stone Gate lies on the other side of this door, we will have to go down a hall then another and through a room. Then the room with the gate."

"Can it really be that easy?" Tena spoke up and she seemed worried that there had to be some hitch. He also felt that it could not have been this easy. One spider and a pit trap and that's all? James spoke up sounding cheery.

"Well let's open the door and get the hell back home." Everyone looked at him for a moment then with no reason to disagree, they put the key into the hole in the door.

The key went in easily, and they turned it but nothing happened. No click, pop or metal sound it simply turned in the hole with no result. Hutch, holding the key looked over at Freya, who stood there with a look of anticipation. "I don't know, I turned it but nothing happened."

"It fits all the way doesn't it, maybe you need to jiggle it or something?" James said to Hutch looking over his shoulder, Hutch getting irritated snapped at him.

"Yeah I'm turning the damn thing, it isn't doing anything. I turned it ten times in the hole." As he spoke, he placed more forward pressure on it causing it to make an audible "Pop" then there was a sound as of several locks came undone along the edge of the door. Everyone stood back including Hutch, who looked surprised.

"Well, what do we do now, push on it?" James asked. Freya looked at James with a perplexed look on her face.

"It seems to have unlocked. I am not sure what we need to do I guess we push on it that would be a start." Don and

Hutch pushed on the door and opened easily. When the door opened it opened about a foot and immediately a hot gust of air hit them, the air was wet almost as if a mist. Everyone stepped back for a moment. Hutch opened the door some more, and they could see a hallway shrouded in mist and the mist had a slight red glow to it and they could smell sulfur.

"Man, that stinks, wow!" James said holding his nose. The smell was strong and carried with it a burning smell also that reminded them of fire and heat. The hot mist came from the hall floating on the floor swirling around their feet. They looked down the hallway, and it started to clear, they saw that the walls had a yellow tinge to them. Stepping into the hot steamy hallway Hutch rubbed his nail over the slight yellow coating, smelling it and rubbing his finger together he looked back at the rest.

"Sulfur. Its sulfur everyone, this place may not be too healthy for us. Let's leave that door open." They started down the hallway and saw that there were several large cracks in the floor, one time they actually had to jump over one that was about four feet wide; looking down, they saw nothing but blackness. The steam that hung low on the floor in the hall was pouring into the large crack flowing into it looking like water flowing into a chasm. They proceeded down the hall being careful and weary and came to a T in the hall.

"This isn't supposed to be here." Freya said looking at the map then around, wiping the sweat from her face, by now they all were sweating heavily from the heat and steam in the hall. "The map shows a right hand turn then a hallway and then a left turn then we are supposed to run into stairs that lead to the Stone Gates chamber." Hutch looked around in the steaming heat.

"Look, let's pick a direction and go, we are too far along not to keep moving. Everyone muttered an agreement, except for James.

"Let go back to the room where we killed Kord, let's think before we do this, I think we need to take other steps." Hutch reeled on him.

"What is your damn problem, you little gatt? Always the great idea, well shut the hell up no one wants to hear your ideas, got it?" James stepped back thinking Hutch was going to hit him, Don grabbed Hutch's arm.

"Back off, Hutch he is just being James, let it go." James gave Don a look of venom. Now it was done and James made his decision. They made their way to the right and then the hall veered to the right but what alarmed Don about all of this section of the hall was that it looked like something went horribly wrong here, there were along with the large cracks and crevasses large stone blocks that had fallen from the ceiling, dirt and debris littered the hallway everywhere. He worried that at any turn the walls would collapse, he was so close. They all were so close to dying due to a cave in.

They traveled around a corner and stopped. In front of them were three creatures. They were hunched over and were black in color but the odd thing was that they appeared to have cracks in their skin and these cracks were glowing red. Freya placed a hand up and motioned to go back around the corner. "Lavacks! We have a problem. They are very vicious they don't kill for food, they do it for fun. They are only found usually in volcanoes. Yes, this is a problem." Her face was wet with sweat, and she had genuine worry in her eyes. Hutch had an idea; he stood there wondering if he should say it, after all it sounded silly. At least it did to him.

"Why don't we throw water on them, won't it hurt them? If they like fire, doesn't fire hate water?" Freya stared at him for a moment, looking at him sweating, she looked to Tena, who nodded in agreement.

"Freya, is this the only way, does the map show any other way?" Don asked looking to the others and seeing them nod. Freya thought for a moment.

"The problem is that once they see us, they will attack, and once they start they won't stop unless we kill them, and I honestly do not know how to do that. I don't think swords hurt them."

"Look, is there another way around or not!" James asked with worry on his face. He was not taking the heat well at all, and it showed, he seemed more stressed and Don worried that he was going to snap at any time. Freya looked at James for a second looking at the map, she turned it this way and that.

"No there is not, I wished there was, how much water do we have to.."

"Let's turn back and wait until they leave ok, this is stupid. Have any of you took a look at those things!" James interrupted the frustration in his voice evident to everyone. Suddenly, the area shook and there was a rumbling, a large block fell from the ceiling to the floor, along with a lot of dirt. Everyone tensed as they thought the ceiling was going to collapse in on them.

"This is BS, we gotta go and do this, or we will end up entombed here." Hutch said looking at the ceiling.

"We have to go and take our chances, there is no other way." Freya chimed in, and at that she took out her water skins, she had two of them, the rest followed suit and between them all they had about ten of them, they put their weapons up and Hutch looked at Don leaning over.

"Do you feel woefully inadequate at this point or is it just me?" He smiled when he said it but Don knew he was dead serious. Don merely looked at him shaking his head in disgust at this whole situation. Freya looked around the corner and at this point there were only two of them, Freya stepped out and to Dons amazement stood there and merely said.

"Hey stupid, come here." The two monsters wheeled around and Don saw their faces or what normally would be a face, instead there was just a black stone like roughness. No eyes, nose or mouth, however, he did see their hands that were dripping molten lava from three short appendages. They looked at her if that's what you could call it and started to shamble towards her, when they were about ten feet away Freya took her water skin and squeezed it at them, the water hit them with a hiss causing both to make a strange sound, almost like two rocks being rubbed together and clacked together, they then simply melted jumped into the crevasse that was along the hall's edge.

"There is no way it was that easy, no way." Hutch said, even Freya was looking surprised at this and had an incredulous look on her face.

"I agree. However, let's get going, let's not tally at all I want to be out of this place." Hutch turned around and exclaimed.

"Where's James at?" They all turned and sure enough James was gone, they thought he might have been dragged off, but they could find no sign of him.

"My god, was he dragged off and we didn't hear him in all this rumbling?" Tena asked them all looking around confused. Everyone started yelling for him hoping he was ok, he would not have run off, not this close to being at the Stone Gate. They walked around the area and did not find him. Finally, Hutch walked over to the large crevasse that was along the wall, looking in it was dark except for far below where one could see lava moving along like a fiery river far, far below.

"You don't think he slipped and fell in here do you?" Tena held a hand to her face. Don walked over, fear and even grief hitting his gut.

"I don't know, he would have come back already if he ran from the lava things. So I don't know where else could he have gone to." Freya looked around, she walked over to Hutch.

"We have to go Hutch, we can't wait here, this hall could cave in anytime." And to that there was another rumble and the hall shook slightly causing more rocks to fall from the ceiling.

"We have to go NOW!" Freya said to them in a frantic tone. "We are close according to this map, around the corner is a set of stairs, we go down and enter the chamber with the Stone Gate. Don and Hutch did a small huddle there in the hall, the discussion was bleak, they wanted to look for James; the women wanted to move on as they felt James fell into the hole. They weighed it and decided to move on, James would have come back by now if he was alive.

Don's heart was so heavy for his friend. Yes, James was a prat at times, but he was still in the end a good friend. What he would tell Bri he wasn't sure.

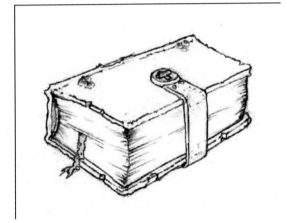

19
LAMENT

James stood in the hallway listening to everyone make the decision to fight the Lava men, they left him out again, and again they are making a decision to jeopardize his life. Plus the map piece he found on Kord shows the gate was gone, moved. He would have told them, but they wouldn't have believed him. He stole the book from Hutch's back pack when they all attacked the two assassins and Hutch was as usual so preoccupied with himself, he didn't notice.

This was it, they were all standing there watching Freya; he knew that she was his friend back in the city, told him all about her and yet again she has the idea to fight, to go the hard way. He was done, he had no friends, all they did was make fun of him, well it was time to do his own thing. He was leaving and getting a horse and going back to the city. The nice magistrate was going to help him, and if they had to be stuck down here, oh well! he didn't care anymore. As they all checked their water skins James quietly stepped back farther and farther and turning, he ran back the way he came and

made it to the room that had the steel door, he made it all he
had to do was to take a second, what the heck was he doing..?

Oh well, he thought. "I am tired of everyone, kill this,
James you're an idiot, James you're a moron, James this, James
that - I AM SICK OF IT!" He yelled to himself. "Yes it's time,
heck with em all, they can stay here; Don and Hutch all can rot
here they would do the same to me, yeah that's it." He said
aloud. He stood there looking at three rats who were on Kord's
chest having a gruesome feast.

James's mind went deeper and darker in that room, and
he made his final decision. He was on his own and would get
home on his own. They were his enemies now, and he knew
they would try to get the book back. He smiled to himself.

Back far down in the hall Don and the rest made their
way down the hall and sure enough there were steps, they
were narrow and at places, there were steps missing, the stone
work was rough and slick from all the humidity. They slowly
made their way down, Hutch slipped once sliding into Tena
knocking them both down a few steps. Cussing, Hutch gained
control but he seemed to have frayed his ankle. He sat there for
a moment grimacing in pain, Don kneeled down.

"You ok, need some help?"

"No I am OK, I just twisted it a bit, still can jump into a
gate no problem." He said with a smile, Don offered him his
hand pulling him up with a groan.

"Man, you need to lay off the frozen pizzas." Freya
looked at them, she had an odd expression.

"What are Frozen Pizzas?" Don looked at her and
Hutch laughed. He told her they were a type of food. Freya of
course did not get the joke. They made their way down for
what seemed an eternity, occasionally there would be a rumble

then more debris would fall from the ceiling. They made their way down and came to a door that was stout wood. It was wet and slimy from all the moisture, and it had what appeared to be a huge built in lock on it. There was a large symbol carved into the face of the wood. It was a circle that looked mechanical almost, Hutch took out his cell phone turning it on. He saw Don's hard look.

"What they have goblins, lava men, and worms that eat you from inside. I think a cell won't be a huge yank."

Don looked at Hutch, Tena looked at Don then to Hutch. "What is he doing?" Don smiled at her,

"He is taking a picture, it will paint the image in a way so he can look at it later on."

Tena seemed amazed, Hutch then took a pic of Freya and Tena. "Sorry ladies but if we are going home I want to be able to remember you both. Freya you are a good woman, and Tena you are one also. We will miss you both.

Tena grasped Don's arm. Don whispered in her ear. "Remember what I told you, where I go you go. I made you a promise." Tena let go and seemed to relax a little.

"Well Hutch you are a good man to have in a fight. I will remember you both fondly," Freya said a little awkwardly. She pressed on the door then, grunting.

"Great, let me guess: it is locked." Hutch said in frustration, "What's next, a red dragon in the room guarding the gate?" Tena looked at him with a worried frown.

"I don't like dragons, they are not nice at all." Freya and Hutch pushed on the door and to everyone's surprise the large door opened easily. Everyone held their breath. It was time. This was it? They would be going home very soon, Don suddenly wondered how the others would react when he said Tena was going back with him, would he have a fight on his hands, his stomach churned. Hutch stood there as the door opened about a foot, what did he have to do, what if the gate had to be turned on, or was it just a swirling bunch of magical energy. Hutch stood there excitement in his chest, he was minutes maybe from seeing Emily. Man, he was done gaming it was time to move to something safe like golf, he thought to himself as he stood there.

Tena looked at Don, he was standing there looking at the door, she wondered what would he do, would he keep his promise or would he betray her and leave her here? Her heart was so heavy with worry, she felt sick and out of sorts, in moments she would know. She took a deep breath.

"Well, do we go in and do this or do we sit out here with our thoughts." Tena said to everyone, they turned to her and her sister looked at her and from her look Tena knew Freya was thinking the same thing she was. Freya merely gave her a comforting smile.

They opened the door more, and as it opened it made remarkably no sound. Peering in the room it was time.

James was suddenly afraid. Did he go too far, he wondered. What if Don and Hutch die? What if those lava things are killing them now. He hated how they treat him, Pat took off, and he thought they would get closer, but they still pick on him. "What do I do... What do I do?" he wondered out loud. He decided to wait, see if they come back, stand at the door talk reason to them, maybe work this out. If not he would close the door and leave them.

He waited...

The room was small, there were several torches along the wall and a four tiered dais around twenty feet wide on the far wall. On the base of the Dais was rough stone, on the walls were painted pictures of a square picture frame like a thing the size of a small car, it was glowing with thread like things in it, a man was knelt before it looking like he was praying. In other paintings the gate as they figured it was sucking what looked like the life force of wizards, or was it giving them power?

They walked around and didn't see a gate, puzzled Freya looked to the map. "It should be here, it is the right shape like on the map and the paintings and murals, the altar. What is happening here?" She said this with extreme frustration in her voice. Hutch was at his wits end.

"THIS is bull, a huge pile of crap! Dammit! All this way and to see it gone, what the hell could have happened to the thing, someone just hauled it away or what?" When Hutch said this Tena gave out a gasp. Don and Pat looked sharply at her.

"What?" Don asked her as he could see she realized something. Tena paced with her hands to her head.

"When I was younger I lived with my Mother, she was an Amarian Scribe. I read a book when I was a young girl, maybe ten, and it told a story a powerful gate, and it being moved to keep it safe, I don't know if it is this one it is talking about. The book is in my Uncle's library and it told the entire story.

"We have to go back to Uncle's house and get that book then right, maybe between the book Hutch has and your Uncles huge library, we can find something that will tell us right." Tena said, Don looked at them, then spoke.

"We need to get the other book from your Uncle's house, he may be dead, but he may still be able to help us even in death."

"OH, FREAKING GREAT!" Hutch said aloud suddenly very angry, he was pacing he walked up on the dais and one could tell that whatever was there was chipped away and removed and whatever it was, was large. "What now? What about that damned book you got Hutch." Don said pointing at him. Hutch turned.

"Yeah, maybe something is in the book showing where it was moved, I never really went through it fully. Do you think they left a map to where it is?" Hutch said taking his pack off and opening it.

"It's worth a chance, never know." Don said a little hope rising in his chest. Hutch opened his leather pack rummaged through it and took out a piece of parchment, reading it, he suddenly went into a rage tossing his pack against the wall.

"That little backstabbing bastard, he screwed us, he fricking screwed us!" Hutch was raging so much Don never saw him like this, Don ran up to him, grabbing him.

"What the hell are you talking about?" Freya also approached him. Hutch holding the piece of parchment in his hands held it up then threw it at Don. Don looked at it and bowed his head sitting down totally dejected.

"He is right, James betrayed us." Freya took the parchment looking at it, she turned it over then made a hissing sound, Tena walked over. On one side of the parchment was a note with a drawing of the Stone gate saying.

LET THE GATE BE MOVED TO WHERE OUR ENEMIES WILL NOT FIND IT.

FOR THE USURPERS MAY SEARCH, THEY SHALL NOT FIND AS THE DAUGHTERS OF THOR NOW HOLD THAT WHICH IS PRECIOUS.

On the other side written in pen was something that told them all the sum of James's duplicity.

IM SORRY I HAVE TO DO THIS, YOU ALL ARE NOT THINKING RIGHT. I GOTTA GO HOME.
JAMES

Don stared at it in total disbelief, he reread it maybe ten times, Hutch was still raging, Tena was talking to Freya frantically, and the little girl was just sitting there, her head in her hands. Don walked over to Freya and Tena. "Daughters of Thor?" Freya was perplexed, she looked at Tena.

"I don't know?" Freya said then she said "We find him kill him and get the book! Then we will figure this out. But we have to get the book first or you all will be staying here." Freya said. Hutch stopped for a moment looked at her and smiled.

Don looked at everyone, "We have to find him that's the important thing, the longer we sit here the farther he gets, let's get our asses moving and catch up to him, there is only one place he can go.." Hutch suddenly broke in interrupting him.

"He mentioned a magistrate in Dark Home, he was talking to, he said the man said Freya and her uncle were con artists, and that he could get James home if he got the book." Freya looked sharply at Hutch and so did Tena.

"What do you mean a magistrate? There are no magistrates in Dark Home only the Justice Council, James is doubly a fool. That man could have been anyone, he even could have been a Dark Mage. James is headed back to Dark

Home, and he will deliver that book to the people we do not want to have it, if he is successful he will die and you all will be stuck here."

They all immediately got themselves together and went back out the door, they traced their steps through the heat and steam, there were a few quakes in the process onetime a huge rock fell almost hitting Hutch in the head. "Yeah put me out of my misery" was all he said aloud when he dodged it.

James stood in the room. He was having a bout of second thoughts, what if the parchment he stashed in Hutch's backpack was wrong, what if the gate was there? He paced the room for about an hour when down the hall he heard voices and saw torch light. Peering through the door he saw Hutch come around a corner. Hutch stopped seeing James, he yelled.

"There he is, kill him!" and started to run down the hall. Panicked, James looked around, he couldn't outrun them, he looked to the steel door, grabbing it, he pulled it shut. As hit closed it made a loud series of "CLICKS", James panic licking at his chest ran back towards the way out hoping he would find a horse, he was right they did want to kill him. He was on his own now, and he now HAD to leave them here.

Hutch ran and was about ten feet from the door when James pulled it close, smacking at the door with both hands open he yelled in frustration. "You're mine James... one day you are going to get it." The rest came up behind him, the door was perfectly smooth and there was no hold to grasp.

"Well we know he isn't out yet." Don offered up, Freya screamed in frustration. "What can be next, I ask." Causing everyone to jump including her sister. Freya looked around angry. "This has to not be the only way, let us think. He no matter will not be that far away, and we have his eyes, as we know where he is going." They all looked around they were in a seeming dead end, until Hutch pulled out a small pry bar.

"I got this in the town square." Freya looked at him walked up to him and kissed him soundly on the lips.

"You are lucky you have your Emily." She smiled patted him on the cheek, and they pressed the pry bar against the corner of the door trying to pry it open.

James made his way back through the crack; the air felt mercifully cool from where he was, the sun was about half way high, so he guessed it around noon, he was glad it wasn't dark. He walked around then up to the path to the top of the hill, he smelled something and to one side, he saw the remains of a man, the man was tore apart, bloated and covered in flies. James turned and threw up from the site and smell and continued to walk. He wandered around for about thirty minutes, and he found one of the horses eating vegetation, he approached it and got on it, remembering that they came from the North West he headed off, he would find Dark Home if it was the last thing he did. He stopped for a moment thinking of his ex friends.

"Screw em, I am on my own now." He said and he wheeled his horse around heading towards the North West and Home he was hoping.

Down below Hutch pried the door with no result, "Its locked I think." He said sweat coming off him, Tena ran her hands over the door then the edges of the wall.

"Here I found a catch, she pressed it and the door popped open, Don practically ripped the door open running into the room he saw via the lantern light no one was in there. He looked to the others and no one needed to say anything they ran down the hallway into the spider room then down the wet hallway and up to the stairs, and through the crack. They searched for James for about an hour.

"What time is it do you think." Tena asked squinting into the he sky and the bright sun.

"I am not sure maybe past noon a bit, maybe a tad later, but no matter we need to not be here when darkness arrives. Look for our horses they may still be about." Freya suggested. To that they all started looking, in the end after an hour, they had found four of the horses.

"Well, we're short one, Tena can ride on mine with me." Don said and to that they got on them. Freya turned to them all seriously.

"He doesn't know the Realms, so he will take time to get to Dark Home. I know the way we can still arrive before him. We will be there when he arrives, and we will get the book."

Everyone agreed and to that, they set off for Dark Home and hopefully getting the book and then hopefully a way to get home.

The race was on now. They had to not only get to Dark Home first, but they had to intercept James before he turned the book over to the strange man Hutch mentioned.

"I thought this whole thing was too easy, Samfor mentioned death and magic in this place and we almost walked in." Don said in total frustration.

"I was thinking that when we walked up to the door down there, too easy." Hutch agreed.

"Well don't worry now. The milk is spilled and we need to find that book, or you both might just as well find some land here and make babies!" Freya said seriously, and to that they clicked at their horses and started after James.

The symbol carved into the Stone gates door

I think I might have made a huge mistake here.

...... James as he headed out of Gott

20

DESPERATE MEASURES

James rode hard for the next day and into the next night, he was afraid for his life. He heard hutch actually say "Kill Him" and that hurt him more than everything they had done to him combined. He knew now his decision was the right one. The only problem was how in the hell was he going to get to Dark Home. He knew they went down this road, but what if they got out, he was sure that Freya knew the way back. He had to find an alternate route.

He settled in that evening, making a small fire and eating some rations that he had left. He looked at what he had in the way of food and water. Two water skins full, a chunk of cheese and some dried meat. He also had some dried fruit that the crazy old man gave to them all. God he hated how all of his friends were so gullible. That huge lug Kord tricked them all, and the Magistrate was right. He tried to tell Hutch, he tried to talk sense into him, and as usual he didn't listen. "Well what did it get em... Nothing." He smiled as he popped a piece of fruit into his mouth smiling.

The next morning James rode most of the day; as he was heading West on a dusty trail, he saw a small caravan winding its way due West about a mile ahead of him. He saw that it was made up of wagons, camels, and also many porters on foot. He decided to take a ride to them to see if they knew an alternate way to Dark Home. As he approached, he saw three riders leave the caravan and riding towards him. They stopped about one hundred feet in front of him as if waiting for him. He approached slowly and cautiously.

"Hello!" James hailed them as he approached. One of the riders rose a hand in what appeared to be friendship.

"Halt rider! Why do you approach the caravan of Padash Akeem, Salah?" The man spoke English but his accent was very thick and hard to understand.

James sat up in his saddle, clearing his throat, "I am no enemy, I am merely a traveler trying to make his way to Dark Home. If you know the way I would appreciate you telling me. Or perchance can I follow your caravan?"

The man looked to his friends, and talked in a language James could not understand. The lead rider then spoke. "No, the Padash does not allow stragglers, we carry goods worth protecting and ask you do not approach the caravan again!" He turned with his friends then stopped and turned, he looked at James. "If you wish to go to Dark Home go another twenty leagues ahead, you will see a small village with a brook, take the north road out of it. From there will run into the City in about four or five days time, Ensa-Halam[14]." He nodded and turned and rode off, the dust from his horse flowing behind him.

"Well that wasn't too bad I guess?" James said to himself, he decided to wait for an hour or so as the caravan was riding due to west; he sat there on his horse looking around, thinking of home. He looked to the North West at the huge

[14] Ensa-Halam is a Hafarian saying meaning "Fortune be with you"

mountains, already it was cooling off. He looked behind him seeing the jungle breaking far behind him. He didn't see his old friends thank god. BUT! He smiled... He knows how to get to Dark Home, and Dark Home leads to Home.

Pat was riding quietly, he finally for the first time in months felt right. He felt totally at ease now with his decision and knew he did the right thing. He made his way along a craggy rocky outcropping, his horse's hooves making clacking sounds on the rocks. The ground sloped down slightly, and he regretted going up here. He thought he would be able to see better from up here, but instead all he saw was grass, mountains in the distance, and also a small village, with nightfall coming on quick he thought of the old man's words who was on the horse so many weeks ago, and what he said about "monsters" in the hills. He looked around and decided to make a quick run for the plain areas at the base of the hills he was in. Far off about ten miles away he saw the forest that he left this morning, he saw a winding group of horses and wagons, moving slowly its dust slowly rising in the sunny cool morning air. He was reminded of a game module he played many years ago called the Caravan of the Doomed. He thought that he was willing to bet the living dead were not getting ready to attack that. Chuckling, he looked around, and taking a deep breath he smiled. He was home.

He decided to get off his horse arching his back as it was sore. He thought of how a four wheeler would come in handy about now. He stood there and in the distance he saw a lone rider keeping pace with the caravan, but the rider kept back about a mile. He wondered if it was a sentry keeping watch. He thought of his friends and he wondered if right now they were home explaining to everyone what happened. "I would like to see how they will explain all this?" he chuckled getting back on his horse and making his way down the slope. The sky was turning red and blue with the coming of evening. Moving unhurriedly, its dust slowly rising in the sunny cool morning air, he was reminded of a game module he played many years ago called the Caravan of the Doomed. He thought that he was willing to bet the living dead were not getting ready to attack that. Chuckling, he looked around, and taking a deep breath he smiled. He was home.

"That little worm is dead, if I have to stick him myself, he is getting it!" Hutch raged while on his horse following Freya. Don was angry also, he could not believe that James would take the book and then dump them.

"I agree Hutch, but I think instead let's leave him here. THAT! would be a fitting bit of justice."

Hutch looked at Don with a grimace, "I say no, he dies. If we leave him here then the ladies will have to put up with him."

Tena broke in, "Oh no, don't worry Hutch, I personally am going to see him in a vat of Vramak."

"I agree," Freya said aloud over her shoulder. For the past day and a half Freya had been riding hard, her pace was relentless, and they only stopped periodically to rest on the horses or for Nature calls. They had cleared the high forest that the jungle gave way to, and were headed. North by North West when they broke into a large plain. Mountains loomed to their left as they rode and the air was cooler, and they could see snow in the mountains.

"Wonderful, soon we will be back ass deep in snow," Hutch quipped. Don was worried about Hutch, he had never seen him so mad, and violence was very unlike his friend.

Dusk was approaching, its pink tendrils in the sky reaching out mixing with the blue sky, they could see the two moons faintly, finally Tena spoke.

"Freya, we have to rest and sleep. So does he and he will have not taken on the pace as we have. Let's get a good night's sleep and go back to the hunt in the morning. He cannot be far."

Freya looked at her sister, stretching in her seat, she looked at the other two men. "What do you think, it is your hides on the line?"

"I say we rest and start back at it in the morning." Don said with a stretching sigh. Hutch agreed also,

"Yeah, then when we get the little snake we'll have a heart to heart; we'll do what is needed then get serious about getting home?" Don looked at Hutch then to Freya.

"Let's make camp then, I guess we can start back first light tomorrow." And to that they got off their horses and set up a very simple camp.

After setting up camp Don and Hutch sat at the fire, it was late and the air was chill. "Don those men were speaking Latin, how can that be?"

"Hutch, the only thing I can think of is that either they are from our world, or they follow someone from our world?" Hutch shifted holding his hands out to the fire.

"But how Don? I mean how can that be. We found the book the book came here with us when I spoke the spell, how is it that someone else is here. The book would be with them. Wouldn't it?"

"Hutch what worries me is just that. Why isn't the book here with them. Could it be that this Stone Gate takes the book back, but leaves the holders of it? I mean what if this is all a waste of time and we are stuck here?"

"I hope you are wrong Don,... I hope you are wrong... Don.... what do you think drove James to do this?"

The question caught Don off guard, Hutch's tone was almost dejected. "I don't know.... I know he was stressed, he has never taken stress well..."

"Do you think we are at fault. I mean we have been on the guy pretty hard at times."

"I don't know Hutch... I find myself hoping he will be one day like tomorrow riding towards us apologizing for leaving us."

"Not me Don. Not me especially now." At that Hutch quietly got up and crawled into his bed roll, leaving Don in the chill air in front of the fire with his thoughts.

James was riding and as it was getting dark, he stopped looking behind him. He couldn't see his pursuers, so he looked to his left and saw low scrub hills breaking into a mountainous area; He decided to camp there; he could make a camp fire and get warm as the weather was getting cold. He made his way there and found a suitable spot. He tied his horse up and gathered some scrub wood. Using his lighter he got a nice little fire going. He lay there relaxing, wondering how far away from Dark Home he was and drifted off into sleep. He was in his living room and Bri was in the kitchen making him some burgers, he felt so happy, and then he felt something? Like someone was pushing him, opening his eyes dazed, he saw several shapes above him. Jerking awake he reached for his sword.

"Oh no, not that my friend, we got your sticker. Now you tell us where your silver is and maybe we won't kill you.

James's eyes adjusted to the firelight, he had two men standing over him, one had a sword at his chest, there were two others about ten feet away going through his things, tossing the things they deemed worthless on the ground. The men were dirty and unkempt and were wearing rags.

James felt afraid, he was so close and he didn't want to blow it now. "I don't have any gold, I was in the Dungeon far back there, and I have nothing." He looked around, and then was roughly dragged to his feet by the two men. As they dragged him up he smelled their breath, and it was rancid.

"Dungeon aye? I say you like, now where is the silver at, then again, you mentioned gold? So I bet you have gold hidden. Give it up or I'm gonna stab you." He emphasized the point by poking James with his sword, opening a small gash in his arm. Grabbing the bleeding wound James panicked, and bolted into the darkness.

"Get him, he's running!" he heard behind him, James ran as fast as he could, he heard the men running after him, he was scared as he didn't want to die. Not like this so far from Bri. He felt his lungs exploding from running, he ran through the velvety darkness, the darkness feeling like a wall impeding his escape. As he ran, he felt something fly by his head, a whizzing sound and realized someone was shooting arrows at him, he dodged right for a bit, he didn't hear his pursuers anymore. Slowing his breath exploding in gasps out of his painful lungs, he stopped and adjusted to the dark. He saw them about a hundred feet away, the firelight from the camp silhouetting them. Then he felt it, the arrow hit him in the right side of his chest, he felt the rusty iron tip pierce his skin and go deep. His lung exploded in pain, he whirled around falling grasping the arrow. He grabbed it instinctively moving it a fraction of an inch, pain seared into his chest. He felt a warm stickiness running down his side.

"Did ya get em?" The small man asked the other with the old worn bow.

"I don't know?" He said peering into the darkness, he looked back at the fire and to the horse and the things laying all over. He looked to the other men in the group.

"Naw, I bet ya missed him, you never hit anything with that old bow Morkor, you can't even hit a stupid rock with that thing." He laughed a horrid laugh, his yellow broken teeth showing.

"The rat is running, is probably half way to the coast," the leader of the small group said in frustration. "Let's go back to his camp and see what we can take." They walked back to the camp and rummaged through the meager possessions. They gathered up what they could find and took the horse. They then slithered back into the darkness where they came from.

James couldn't breathe; fear struck him as he wondered where his pursuers were. He fell over oddly detached from himself. He thought of Bri and of Don and Hutch. They would probably never get home and neither would he. He lay there with tears running down his cheeks as he thought of his Bri and how stupid he was to betray his buddies.

He lay there looking up in the cool air at the stars and the scudding clouds that obscured the two moons. He was trying to get his bearings, but try as he might he could not. The arrow in his chest was painful and with every breath he felt excruciating pain. He knew he was dying and a strange calm over took him. He lay there his breath coming in shorter and shorter bursts, the pain slowly left him as he closed his eyes.

And now book one ends.
What will happen in Book II?

With James now dead and the book possibly in the hands of
sneak thieves, what will Don and Hutch do to get home?
How can they get the book now? And even if they get the
book, with Samfor dead and the gate gone, how are they
going to get home?

They may be forced to make the Alterverse their home
forever.

All hope seems lost.

<u>About the author</u>

Donald Semora owns a small Graphic Design Business in Southern Michigan, and has designed games and done some short story writing. However, the Alterverse Chronicles is his first attempt at mainstream Fantasy. He loves to read Fantasy himself and also English History, namely books on Henry the VIII and England during the 17 and 1800's

Sherlock Holmes is one of his favorite book characters

He lives quietly in Southern Michigan with his two cats, Loki and Freya, where he reads, writes and makes some of the best curries this side of Bombay

You can find him on the internet at
www.donsemora.com
also
www.myspace.com/donsemora
or at
www.facebook.com/donsemora

GLOSSARY OF TERMS AND PLACES

AGLAR
A hired thug that was used by Kord in his failed attempt to gain the book.

ALTERVERSE
A name for the magical world that the players were transported to against their will.

AMARIA
One of the three founder kingdoms of the Alterverse, and the religious and Military center of the Alterverse.

AMARIAN PICKLE BREAD
A bread / food that is famous throughout the Alterverse.

ASPARIAN ADDER
A small black snake around 3 inches long. Its venom is singly the most naturally toxic compound in the Alterverse. One single drop is so poisonous it will kill ten men.

BOGS OF JAMAR
Swampy area in the jungles of Gott, they are known to attract and harbor many foul and nasty things and are the home of Vramak, that are small worms.

BRI
James wife and a fellow gamer of the men.

CAVE CREEPER
A magical monster that is one of the famous ten abominations created by Malphit Doom. They are not killable by normal means. They can only be killed by magic, and only come out at night. Thankfully they do not roam far from their nests.

CITY WATCH
The guards of Dark Home, a wandering police force. They enforce the will of the King and their Magistrates without question.

CONSTANCE QUINLIN
A woman of questionable motives, she is the owner of Ottos Books and Scrolls and plans against the players to attain the book.

CRACKED FLAGON
An Inn in the Central district of Dark Home. Acclaimed for its clean rooms and rat free Ale.

CRIT
A roll on a D20 in Role Playing Games means a "Critical" roll. Usually will spell double damage, or some other critical effect.

D20
In gaming this is short for a 20 sided dice.

DA'NAAN
The formal name of the Alterverse world, also known as the Realms.

DARK HOME
Second largest city in Amaria, only outsized by Loc Amar itself. It is also a main port that acts as a central shipping artery to Hafaria and beyond.

DARK HOME MAGISTRATE
The judges and punishers of Dark Home. These men and women tend to carry out and execute the justice of the king. Not always fair they tend to be highly corrupted.

DARK MAGIC
A form of magic that was created by those who wish to control and inflict pain and suffering. It is also known as the Revenge magic.

DON
One of the four gamers transported to the Alterverse. He is the only single one of the group, and falls in love with Tena.

DONIA
The lost Maldoran child that the players find in the dungeon of Kal-Aldoon in Gott about to be sacrificed by strange men.

DOREEN
Serving wench in the Cracked Flagon that takes a liking to Kord.

DRAKMAR
Small city in the Eastern coastal area of Amaria. It is a traders hub with a large merchant fair held every summer.

EMILY
Hutch's wife back in Michigan. She is a school teacher by trade.

FREYA
Red haired and fierce tempered, she is the female archer who helps the players. She is also the sister of Tena.

GOBLIN
Short yellow skinned monsters that inhabit various portions of the Alterverse. They tend to be cowards and attack only small groups when they are in large groups themselves.

GOTT
Ruined city once a mighty trade city. Abandoned eons ago, or some say cursed eons ago. It is the location of the Spire of Kal-Aldoon, which now is a dark vile dungeon. It is where the players go as they are told the Stone Gate is there.

HAFARIA
One of the three founder Kingdoms in the Alterverse. It sits in the Eastern portion of Da'Naan and its people are very distrustful of all outsiders. They tend to be a merchanting and spying race, and what they do with the information they gather is a mystery.

HUTCH
One of the four gamers stranded on the Alterverse. Husband to Emily, and he is the one who tends to be more of a thinker.

JAMES
One of the four gamers stranded on the Alterverse. He tends to be a complainer and does not feel he is appreciated enough. He is married to Bri

KAIN
The mysterious spy that Constance Quinlin uses to gain information . He provides other services for a fee.

KAL-ALDOON
Also known as the tower of Kal-Aldoon, it is located in the city of Gott at its center. It used to be the city's main meeting place where the Justice of Gott and the Magical Conclaves met.

KING MALRICK
Also known as the usurper king. He is known for his hard unbending will, and his ability to be bought. This king is why most of the thieves guilds in the Alterverse tend to settle in Amaria, and mainly in Dark Home.

KORD
Warrior who helps the players, however becomes corrupted with the promises of gold and lands. He is a long time friend of Freya.

KRALGAR
Officer of the Watch, he is a commander of several small units within the City guard in Dark Home. He is known for his self administered justice he deals out in dark alley ways.

LEE
Wife of pat one of the four gamers, she is a devoted wife and falsely accused of being unfaithful.

LIGHT MAGIC
The polar opposite of Dark Magic. This form of magic tends to be neutral in its innate form, used for good and meant to battle the magic of the dark.

LOC AMAR
Capitol city of Amaria, it is located on the Western coast of Amaria, and is at the entrance of a great river. A center for learning, is also is the religious and military center of Amaria. Loc-Amar is where the king sits most of the time.

LORDS WAY
A large hill in the center of Dark Home, where the rich and wealthy tend to have their homes and mansions. It is highly patrolled by the City Watch, and rumors abound about who really rules. The king or the merchant barons that live here.

LUNITE MAID
An Amarian insult, similar to being called a big baby, or sissy.

MALDORIA
One of the three founder kingdoms. Located in the far north, its people tend to be hardy outdoorsman, and strong warriors. There race is based on combat and most problems are settled by a test of arms.

MALPHIT DOOM
The evilest of all Dark Mages. He was the discover of the threads of the Dark, that power Dark Magic. Rumored to be dead, however most think he lives.

MOORDEEP
A large city in Hafaria that is the only location in the kingdom where foreigners are allowed to make port to sell and deal. The city is essentially a police state within the kingdom, and all foreigners have to register, as anyone found on the streets without proper papers are executed immediately after they are of course interrogated.

MORG
A large creature that when mature has poisonous claws with venom filled sacks connected to them. They are vicious and like to attack, claw then fall back and wait till their prey dies. They only feed on things dead.

OAKEN SEA
Large body of water off the Western coast of Amaria, also called the endless sea. It is rumored that the sea ends at another land mass populated by a strange people of endless life.

OFFICER OF THE WATCH
A man or woman who is in charge of a small detachment of City Watch guards. They tend to carry out the orders and will of their Captains and also Magistrates.

ORC
Large pink skinned creature that is covered in a hard bristly fur, they tend to have tusks and are opportunists, they attack in large groups, and only attack small groups of people. They tend to live close to mountains where they live in small hives.

PAT
One of the four gamers, he is the husband of Lee and is the most head strong of the group. He tends to be short tempered.

SAMFOR CHAMM
Freya and Tena's Uncle. He is a wizard who specializes in Lore and Alchemy, he helps the players and is murdered by Kord.

SPIKEY PEAKS
Series of mountains known for their high spiked appearance. Home of one of the largest clans of Goblins in the Alterverse.

STONE GATE
There are two gates, each one directly leads to the very threads of its controlling magic. One dark and one light. The Stone gate is rumored to be in the Dungeons of Kal-Aldoon however when they gamers arrive there they find it has been moved.

TENA
Sister of Freya, and the woman who falls in love with the Gamer Don. She pledges herself to him thus sealing her fate ultimately.

TERC
One of the assassins that is hired by Kord, he is the leader of Aglar and bullies him all of the time.

---- GAMERS SAGA - DONALD SEMORA ----

THE REALMS
Slang for Da'Naan or also the Alterverse. It is a common referenced name for the world the players find themselves in.

VORTAX
Magical beast that is rare and vicious, Samfor Chamm has one in his study.

VRAMAK
Small yellow worms found only in the area around the Jungle of Gott. They enter through a person's feet and then multiply and feed on the insides of its host, eventually becoming so many they eat the entire victim from the inside out.